To Tracy —
Thanks so much for yor
Kind words about my br
Wishing you all the best
        J Calvin Harwood
              19 OCT 18

WATERING
WEEDS

J.
CALVIN
HARWOOD

WATERING
WEEDS

RAVEN WATCH PRESS LLC

This is a work of fiction. Names, characters, organizations, places, events, and incidents are either products of the author's imagination or are used fictitiously.

Published by Raven Watch Press, Kirksville, MO
www.ravenwatchpress.com

Edited and Designed by Girl Friday Productions
www.girlfridayproductions.com

Editorial: Clete Smith, Amanda Gibson, Marcus Trower
Interior Design: Rachel Marek
Cover Design: Emily Weigel
Image Credits: © Shutterstock/mimagephotography;
© Unsplash/Cole Keister

ISBN (Paperback): 9781732143906
e-ISBN: 9781732143913

First Edition

Printed in the United States of America

CHAPTER 1

Nervy was in a fog—shell shock. She needed to fight through it, but a part of her didn't want to. Accumulated trauma, sorrow, and sleep deprivation had clogged her mental processes to the point that she was pausing noticeably when anyone spoke to her. The trees and people and headstones surrounding her seemed more like some hazy vision than her actual reality.

A priest was directly approaching her. Nervy didn't initiate a response or fully grasp his intent until after he had come to a stop and waited beside her. Eventually she made herself turn toward him and look directly at his face. The priest waited an extra moment, seeming to understand her need for time to process his presence. He then took her right hand with both of his and gently, simultaneously, shook and patted it. His grasp drew her back into the moment and partially restored her clarity. The way he took her hand felt like well-practiced professional benevolence. She was sure it was what he did with all widowed spouses at the funerals he performed. But surprisingly it didn't feel inauthentic, in fact quite the opposite. It really did comfort her.

It also dawned on Nervy that the handshake was a signal to her that the funeral was officially over and she needed to regroup and move on to the next task. The last five hours had funneled Nervy through a progression of scheduled funeral activities, each one sucking her a little deeper into the emotional numbness insulating her from the pain and reality of what she was actually letting go of. At 10:00 a.m. the visitation had begun the day's ceremonies. Intentionally scheduled just before the memorial service and in the same room, it had to be finished before 11:00 for the memorial to begin on time. The rushed schedule had compelled Nervy to be direct and to the point in her acceptance of the sympathies of the attendees. With so little time available for sharing reminiscences, they had been kept brief no matter how poignant they were. Nervy had willingly greeted each one in attendance because she assumed that they all sincerely cared about Walter and his passing, even if they didn't all care that much for her.

The day had then progressed to the memorial service, which had also been mercifully short. The Episcopal priest had presented a mortality-focused liturgy followed by a brief funeral homily that hadn't tried to save the souls of the mourners in the manner of the country church funerals she had attended as a child. After that was the limo ride to the cemetery, where a graveside service was conducted with the requisite recitation of the Lord's Prayer and a cappella rendition of "Amazing Grace" by the mourners. Eventually the crowd had diminished, along with her mental clarity and emotional responsiveness.

Following the reorienting handshake from the priest, Nervy realized that almost all of the funeral attendees had already left and that the funeral director was now standing attentively by the open limo door, waiting for her.

"Thank you, I couldn't have made it through all this without your help. Griffin and I are going to walk home and use the time to do some remembering and planning for what's next. You don't need to wait. We won't be needing the limo."

Nervy turned from the director and began petting Griff. She didn't want to burden the man with her explanation that being in the back of that claustrophobic limousine with just her terrier again would overwhelm her remaining sanity. He solemnly closed the door and remained in position with his hands folded until after she set her dog on the ground and had walked at least ten feet away.

Before heading home, she approached the open grave one last time. This was the moment she had consciously avoided imagining throughout her marriage but had worried she would probably confront. After all, he was seventeen years older than her . . . *had been* seventeen years older than her. She would have to orient herself to the reality that everything about Walter was now "past tense."

Nervy had never thought that he would pass *this* early though. Her marriage to Walter had been the best chapter of her life. He had given her more love and respect than any other man ever had. Together, they had created an "us" that was the priority of both their lives, and she had always thought that they both emotionally thrived upon the benefits that their "us" provided. But nothing good had ever lasted in Nervy's life. Her story wasn't meant to have good chapters, at least not "forever after" ones. She was facing the future alone again. Walter was gone; he would never again be at the office with her or sit at the kitchen table while she made breakfast; he would never again laugh along with her. Instead he had hanged himself with a log chain from a sycamore tree down by the river. When he jumped off the hood of his cherished vintage pickup, he had ripped that "us" out of her life forever. She assumed he had experienced a brief struggle dangling from the chain, but the main picture that was stuck in her mind was his limp, passive body quietly swinging back and forth, a corpse pendulum mocking the second-by-second agonizing loneliness she was unable to escape.

Now, with the funeral concluded, she was going to have to walk away and leave him lying there in his selfish, cowardly, suicidal peace. Clasping her hands tightly together around her dog's leash, she summoned the resolve to look into the freshly dug hole with the maroon casket at the bottom. The glossy finish of the casket had already been violated with an initial smattering of dirt and grass when the funeral home workers had begun removing the tent and equipment used at the grave-side service.

Nervy paused to absorb this moment—what she saw, what she thought, what she felt—hoping that anchoring it permanently in her memory would help summon the strength she knew would be needed to live without the "us." She also intended to use this memory as a reference point and future reminder to never again look beyond herself for shelter or comfort in this world. Her source of security for the past fifteen years had abandoned her, and she had only herself to blame for having invested her affections in another person so much that she could be hurt like this.

After several moments she decided that she didn't need to linger any longer; she had either gathered what she needed or she hadn't, but further time at Walter's grave was unnecessary. Lifting her head and fixing her gaze on the street beyond the cemetery fence, she spoke to her terrier without looking at him, "Well, boy, it's just you and me now."

She crossed the cemetery with her one-eared Jack Russell trotting resolutely beside her. Nervy anticipated the walk home would take about an hour and the time spent with Griffin on this early-September Saturday afternoon would be the closest thing to a calming experience that she could ask for. Having lived in Clay Center continuously for the past fifteen years and worked as her psychiatrist husband's secretary, she'd had ample time to gain a comfortable familiarity with the streets, the people, and the secrets of the community.

With her walk home begun, Nervy focused on the magnitude of what she was facing. However bad she felt today, she understood this was just the beginning, the first step on a slippery-slope, one-way, soul-crushing journey of loneliness that would last longer than she wanted to imagine. How could he have done that . . . to her . . . to *us?* As her anger at Walter grew, Nervy was surprised by how right it felt. The pure self-righteousness of her anger at him quickened her pulse and her step, leaving Griffin trotting at maximum speed to keep pace. Even though she found her anger at him uncomfortable, she reasoned that any suppression of that anger would be a betrayal of her emotions and worth as a person who had already been harmed by his choice. On the other hand, she worried that letting her anger run amok would risk destroying the remaining value of all the years she'd invested in the most beautiful relationship she'd ever had.

Nervy ignored the progression of Clay Center neighborhoods through which she passed. Her mind was preoccupied with exploring the endless implications of her unexpected widowhood: unemployment leading to financial problems leading to housing problems, each set of problems giving birth to more. This inventory of fears and vulnerabilities had so distracted her that she was surprised when she realized the distance she had covered. Now on Fourth Street, she was walking along broken, uneven sidewalks with weeds sprouting from the cracks. Instead of driveways, the cars here were parked in yards of bare dirt with clumps of struggling grass or islands of flourishing weeds. Many houses had threadbare indoor furniture sitting on their porches or in the yard. This wasn't her favorite part of Clay Center, but it didn't particularly frighten her; in earlier chapters of her life she had lived in these very circumstances, both here and elsewhere. She *was* awakened to the possibility of danger, though, when Griffin barked and strained at his leash so suddenly and vigorously that she almost lost her grip on it. Looking down, Nervy saw that Griffin was focused on the yard in front of the house across the street with aluminum foil covering the windows. She studied the scene carefully, failing to see what was demanding Griff's belligerence until a muscular pit bull slowly, unflinchingly emerged from a tangle of overgrown bushes. With an unblinking stare, the big steel-gray pit bull advanced in full domination mode.

"*Griff!* Listen here." Nervy jerked his leash to let him know she was still the authority, even in this situation. Griff looked back at her and grumbled the low, brief growl that he always used to express his disagreement.

"*Hey ya, dog, get back. Beat it!*" Hollering at the pit bull, she tried to discourage his approach, but to no avail. His presence was unmistakable proof of illegal drug activity nearby; pit bulls were Missouri's meth mascots. They were the preferred canine for people involved in the drug trade, which around Clay Center meant methamphetamine. With a reputation for savagery and the tenacity to endure almost any counterattack from man, beast, or weapon, pit bulls sent an intimidating message that the guarded property would be protected with absolutely no regard for the life or limbs of anyone foolish enough to interfere.

Nervy recognized that both she and her dog were limited in their respective movements because of the leash that connected them. Neither of them could afford that disadvantage. Quickly analyzing her options, she reasoned she could wield Griff's leash as a weapon. A heavy bronze spring-loaded snap swung at the end of the leash would be a formidable weapon, but perhaps not enough to discourage a pit bull's attack. She decided to take her chances with it and took Griff off the leash, leaving him to fend for himself. If his previous actions served as a predictor, Griff would heedlessly charge the aggressor, to his certain doom. Keeping Griff on his leash would leave her struggling to control and shield him, as well as compromise her own attempts to protect herself from the fifty-pound canine attacker. The dilemma enraged and terrified Nervy, as she realized that she could be deprived of her beloved terrier and husband within five days of each other. She stooped over and unleashed her canine companion, whispering a desperate plea. "Please, Griff, just this once don't be stupid. This guy will eat you."

With the gray predator closing the last fifteen feet between them, Nervy crouched slightly and leaned forward, securing one end of the leash in one hand while the other swung the free end with the bronze snap back and forth menacingly. Completely surprising her, Griffin stayed near but stepped two feet closer to the attacker, planting himself directly between his friend and his foe. Now free and with his full attention focused on his advancing adversary, Griff growled a lethal threat to the pit bull. Nervy shook her head at the amount of fight that could be crammed into eighteen pounds of Jack Russell terrier, but unfortunately it was not equal in any way to the amount of fight that was in fifty pounds of pit bull.

Engaging the approaching attack dog with an unflinching glare and fully embracing the reality that she and her pet were inescapably trapped in perilous combat, Nervy steeled herself for the battle, slowly and clearly announcing to herself and the pit bull, "Okay, cocksucker, bring it on."

CHAPTER 2

"Smack! *Smack!*"

The pit bull, Griffin, and Nervy each unflinchingly held their ground, ready for combat, as they cautiously looked across the street for the source of the call. Walking toward them from behind the house with the aluminum foil–covered windows, dragging fifteen feet of heavy chain, was a scraggly young man in dirty blue jeans and an unbuttoned plaid flannel shirt with the sleeves ripped off. He had a skinny neck and bony arms and shoulders.

"Smack, get over here, ya bastard. Lady, I'm real sorry 'bout my dog. He's all bark and no bite, gentle as a lamb with my girlfriend's kids. He got away from me this morning on a walk and run off." Skinny-bones was completely unconvincing. Talking too much and too fast, he was clearly a tweaker. Having seen and classified the source of the noise, Nervy and the pit both turned and refocused their hostility toward one another, ignoring him.

"Your dog's loose, no collar, stalking us. He's a killer," Nervy said loudly.

"Look, I'm really sorry 'bout Smack scaring you and your little toy dog but nobody got hurt. I'll just grab him and take him back home." He bent down to place the chain around the pit's neck. Smack reluctantly submitted to the chain and turned away from his intended prey. "You're a bad dog," the bony owner scolded. "Let's get ya home."

"What kind of cricker names their dog Smack?" Nervy commented abrasively under the influence of adrenaline.

The skinny dog owner stood up, tilted his head, narrowed his gaze, and stepped unpleasantly close to Nervy. He looked down on her and growled, "Me, and my name is Jared Grant."

"You're 'Cooker' Grant, and I know who you are and what you are. Why don't you just call your dog 'Meth' or 'Dope'?"

Jared, a.k.a. Cooker, drew a deep breath and addressed her slowly and deliberately. "I know who you are too. The widow of that shrink who offed himself. You're actin' awful high and mighty for somebody wrapped up with that loser. Maybe you shoulda kept your doctor fella on a chain, and then Cindy wouldn'ta died from all his dope."

Nervy sharpened her glare. "Smack isn't the only son of a bitch off his chain today. Does Fatty know you're fucking with me? We both know he doesn't like *his* animals making trouble unless he sets them loose. He and I have been at peace for a long time, and I don't think he would take too kindly to you stirring up any new squabbles between us. I've seen him kill men better than you for messing with me, and I helped him feed what was left of 'em to the hogs." Nervy broke away from their mutual glare and bent over, connecting Griffin's leash back to his collar. Straightening up, she turned her back on Cooker. "Since when did tweakers like you begin caring about other people dying from dope?"

With that said, Nervy resumed her walk home. She never turned to see what Cooker was doing. She didn't need to, because she knew his type and had been around them almost as long as she could remember. The life she had been born into was a hard one and she was proud of how early she had learned and applied the survival skills it required. As a child, she had promised herself that she wouldn't surrender to any abuse she received or any fear she felt, no matter how cruel people were or how frightened she was. Unfortunately, she hadn't always been able to keep that promise. She had endured a childhood filled with physical, emotional, and sexual abuse, followed by a late adolescence and early adulthood spent dealing drugs and enforcing discipline on other dealers until she went to prison at twenty years old. A couple of years after she was released, Nervy met and eventually married Walter. For the first time in her life she had stopped feeling alone and vulnerable, because she had found a partner who stood beside her no matter what she feared or faced. But now, once again she was reminded that her real life, her original life, had never surrendered its claims on her. It was back to retake possession of her. Life with Walter was a memory now, and the tweaker and his pit bull were a wake-up call warning her to freshen up her criminal survival skills and resume trusting no one but herself.

Nervy continued her walk home as her thoughts wandered deeper into considerations of her earlier life. Her nickname was thought of as eccentric by the people she had come to know in Walter's world, but in the hard world she had come from it gave people a straight-up warning to be careful how they treated her. Her real name was Minerva, which was too ostentatious for the only child of an illiterate sharecropper family. Her daddy had heard of the name before she was born and thought it sounded real "elegant." Her momma said that it sounded a little out of character for their family, but her husband made it clear to her that he was insistent on the name. She went to the library while she was in town one day and asked the librarian to look up its meaning. Minerva's momma decided that a "goddess of war and wisdom" might be a welcome addition to a family whose lives and fortunes for generations had been defined by defeat and bewilderment, and so her name was decided. Minerva's transition to Nervy happened because of a singular episode early in her life.

When she was old enough to start her country school, she was noticeably shorter and more slightly built than the other kids, and she expected that she would remain lesser than the others throughout her life. She understood, even at five years old, that neither her size nor her social standing would justify people using a three-syllable name to address her, so she expected to be given a nickname. She wasn't surprised that her miniature stature opened the door for her to be called "Mini." But that nickname only lasted for the first month of kindergarten, because something Mini did completely surprised everyone.

Fatty had been the biggest of the Smith boys, even if not the oldest. He was in the first grade, a perpetual playground tyrant ruthlessly dominating anyone smaller. It was only natural that he stole Mini's lunch on a Monday morning. Mini had tolerated the theft calmly to all outward appearances, but looking back, she recalled a deep feeling of vulnerability that nearly overwhelmed her. She remembered worrying that she and her lunch were going to fall prey to Fatty every day. When she got home after school, she sobbingly told her mother about having her lunch taken by Fatty. Nervy's dad was in the other room and, after overhearing the story, sternly called for "Minerva" to come to him. He usually called her "girl" and only used her name when he was angry. Confused as to why she would be in any kind of trouble, she stood stock-still in front of her father's silent stare for a full minute. He had her tell him the full story again. When she finished, he told her to go outside and bring back a green switch off the willow tree in their backyard that was as long as her arm and as thick as her thumb. She looked imploringly at her mother, who in turn opened her mouth to speak.

Cutting off any intervention from her mother, Nervy's dad reinforced his command with an enraged scream at Mini: "Do it!"

Despite the nausea and dizzying fear, Nervy managed to bring a qualifying switch back to her father as commanded. Back in the house again, he commanded her to take off all her clothes because he didn't want to ruin them. When she was obediently naked, he explained that because she let somebody at school take her lunch and had put up no fight, she had to be taught that the pain of any school yard fight would be nothing compared to the pain she'd face when she came home to her father's house a coward. He sentenced her to twenty lashes. She was instructed to announce the number of each lash she received aloud until she had successively pronounced all twenty, and if one wasn't loud or clear enough for her father to understand it, then that lash would be repeated until she counted it aloud to his satisfaction. He informed her that the whipping would proceed from top to bottom or bottom to top, involving her front and back from ankles to shoulders. Minerva was told to choose the beginning location for herself. Her mother stepped between them and pleadingly protested but was viciously shoved to the floor and kicked at until she scrambled back a safe distance from the punishment.

"Feet first," Nervy cried quickly, realizing there would be no reprieve. Her father commenced immediately. The shock of the pain around her ankles prevented her from initiating the first count.

"Number!" he demanded loudly as he struck her again.

Her introduction to hell lasted about two minutes by the clock but remained unforgotten for her entire lifetime. In retrospect, she realized his concern for her clothing had not been misplaced. Her body had borne the reminders of what might have happened to her clothes for the rest of her life. Only her hands, neck, and face were spared the scarring. Out of necessity, long sleeves and slacks had been her trademark attire ever since. Her mother kept her home from school on Tuesday, but Nervy's education wasn't compromised, because she had learned a lifetime's worth of lessons on Monday. Thinking back, Nervy smiled, savoring the irony that it had been her father himself who first taught her that she must mercilessly destroy her tormentors to survive.

On Wednesday, Nervy showed up at school in jeans and a long-sleeved sweater. Just like two days before, she brought her sack lunch, and just like two days before, Fatty forcefully tore it from her grasp. Engrossed in opening Nervy's fried egg and biscuit sandwich, which had been lovingly wrapped in wax paper by her mother, he failed to notice that Nervy had calmly removed her right shoe. The heel of that shoe crashed into Fatty's nose at the end of a 180-degree swing. The girl they called Mini hit Fatty in the middle of his face so hard that she pushed his head backward, shifting his entire center of gravity. The combined shock and backward momentum of the blow sent the king-sized bully toppling over like an oak tree felled by an expert logger. He landed with a thud at her feet and lay temporarily stunned. She completed her assault with a swift barefoot stomp to his soft, supine hillock of a belly, then deftly replaced her right shoe and scooped up the sack lunch Fatty had dropped. The kids on the playground incredulously watched her walk away, until their attention was redirected by Fatty's sudden rhythmic retching and bloody facial contortions.

Within a few days Fatty resumed his predator-prey relationship with most of the kids on the playground, but Mini was exempted. The students started referring to her by a new nickname, "Nervy," which was also adopted by the adults throughout their country community as the story of the playground events spread. Nervy was the name that she had accepted for over forty years, but she did so with full memory of the fact that her attack on Fatty had not happened because she was so "nervy"; it had been just the opposite. After the beating from her father, Nervy had no choice but to attack Fatty in order to survive at home. Vulnerability to others was something that Nervy learned was too costly for her to tolerate.

CHAPTER 3

As her walk home progressed, Nervy was somewhat surprised that her jacked-up adrenaline from the confrontation with Smack and Cooker had not subsided more. Instead it fueled an assertive attitude that offered a brief but welcome relief to the sorrow she had been mired in the past few days. It had also improved her walking speed and endurance. The sudden sight of her empty house just up the block reeled her attention back to her loss and loneliness, which were now reinforced by the lingering vision of the casket in the open grave. The waiting void of her home provoked a repulsion, which Nervy would have surrendered to if Griffin hadn't been at her side, encouraging her with his eagerness.

"Okay, boy, in we go." Using her key, she opened the door and exposed herself to an overwhelming emotional vacuum that took much more courage to face than any meth cooker or attack dog. Immediately her remaining adrenaline evaporated. Once inside, she willed herself through the steps of turning the lights on and walking through the living room, the dining room, and then the kitchen. She sat at the kitchen table emotionally depleted, resting her head on her hands with elbows planted on the table. She stared straight ahead at the nothing that was left of her life. Having remained motionless until almost bedtime, Nervy was finally stirred back to life when Griffin came to her and grumble-growled that she was neglecting his need to go outside. "Oh, okay. I guess we have to get back to some sort of normal and it might as well be your bedtime potty schedule."

With Griff back in the house, and because she knew the clock indicated that it was bedtime, Nervy reluctantly negotiated her way down the hall to the most intimidating emptiness in the house, the bedroom. Tonight she was committed to finally doing whatever it took to put on her pajamas and crawl into bed, under the covers, by herself. She had repeatedly failed that simple, routine task since Walter's death. She began preparing herself to overcome her dread of the empty bed by mentally tallying the events she had survived since last Wednesday night.

Her recollections started with Wednesday supper time and the two-hour wait for Walter to show up. She had finally placed a call to the police, who called her back around bedtime to let her know that Walter's body had been found down by the river. She never went to bed that night. The police came to her home and questioned her into the early hours of Thursday, asking permission to search Walter's possessions to put together a clear picture of his last days and hours. She tried her best to focus on their questions, but her answers were fragmented and jumbled.

Thursday was mostly a blur—she had gone to the first of a couple of meetings with the funeral home director. The police returned to the house that afternoon with a few more questions, a brief statement about Walter's having hanged himself with a chain, and an assurance that the policy of the county coroner was to order autopsies for every suicide. As Thursday afternoon darkened into evening, her sense of aloneness made "their" bed the last location in the house in which she could have gone to sleep. She absentmindedly petted Griffin and eventually fell into an exhausted, intermittent unconsciousness on the living room couch, repeatedly awakening to reclarify what had been a bad dream and what was the nightmare of her new reality.

Friday morning she went to the office to deal with the most pressing issues there, like calling all the pharmacies in a forty-mile radius to tell them that Dr. Corvus had died and clarify that the office wouldn't be able to phone in or provide medication refills anymore. She suggested they tell his patients to contact their family doctors for their psychiatric medicine refills until they found a replacement psychiatrist. The pharmacies that the office did the most business with knew that Dr. Corvus and Nervy were a mom-and-pop operation and understood that Nervy was both Dr. Corvus's wife and his secretary, so as condolences were offered to her she accepted them graciously. She decided not to read the accumulation of faxes from the past day or two, but she did put more paper into the machine so that messages could still be received. Perhaps she would read them later. There was no need to answer the phone, since no more appointments were going to be made or rescheduled anyway.

These beginning hassles of shutting the practice down reminded her of the hassles of clearing Walter's schedule so he could attend his malpractice trial. Now he wasn't even there . . . but then again, neither was she. She'd heard the trial had been proceeding merrily along without either of them. To her, the case had seemed like it was in the bag for the Adair family from the very beginning. Since Walter's suicide, she had left all the court stuff to Raleigh. Even though Walter and Nervy figured the malpractice case was lost from the outset, they hired Raleigh Baggs because they saw him as bringing a respected, honest, local face to their cause. The fact that the court was in such a rush to try a man they knew had just killed himself confirmed her contemptuous opinion of the judge and the entire proceedings. She didn't expect Raleigh to pull a rabbit out of his hat or reverse the direction the trial was headed, but she trusted that he would faithfully be in court, maintaining a reputable voice on Walter's behalf in the continuing judicial masquerade.

Friday night Nervy came home and, for the first time since her widowhood, she cooked herself a meal, set the kitchen table, and ate sitting alone. After supper, she went on an expedition of sorts through the house looking for insurance papers, deeds, registrations, and other documents in the various places such items might be hiding. Nervy was bleary-eyed by midnight, and her foggy mind was unable to make any sense of the documents. Reaching the bedroom, she realized it was the bed itself that triggered her searing awareness of separateness from Walter. Finally compromising with her resistance, she lay down on the bed but never changed out of her clothes or got under the covers.

Saturday had been consumed with the visitation, memorial service, and walk home. So now she was confronting the next hurdle, beginning a new normal "alone" bedtime routine of sleeping in pajamas under the covers. While taking off her clothes, an awkward feeling of shame overtook her. Ever since she was a small child, any time Nervy had to take off her clothes when she felt anxious or vulnerable she would experience a deep sense of shame. The nakedness, vulnerability, and shame triad had recurred early enough and often enough in her life that by the time she was fourteen, she had mastered the skill of not becoming paralyzed by her discomfort. Things had been expected of her while she was naked—one way or another by one person or another. So there she stood, partially undressed, experiencing an emotional storm.

Refocusing herself on the here and now of Saturday night, she proceeded to deliberately take off the rest of her clothes and began assuming the familiar erotic poses and required sexual positions desired by the many men she had entertained over the years. In the midst of her ghosts' escalating sexual entertainment, she abruptly stopped her gyrations and calmly picked up her pj's. Nervy's ability to discontinue her performance at that moment, in the face of all her uncertainty and vulnerability, had reinforced to her own satisfaction that being submissive or not was now fully her choice. No one else controlled her. She proceeded to pull on her long-sleeved silk shirt and full-length silk pajama pants. With the inner satisfaction of having reaffirmed her autonomy in the middle of her present emotional turmoil, she pulled the covers back, crawled into what she still saw as her side of the bed, and threw the covers back on top of herself.

CHAPTER 4

Being alone at night was the problem in Nervy's life that led to her meeting Walter in the first place. She had been released from prison at twenty-four years old. She served three and a half years on a five-year sentence for possession of methamphetamine precursors and was granted early release and probation for good conduct. She had nowhere to go except back to her childhood home. Her mother had died while she was in prison. Without her there, it was just Nervy and her daddy and the unhealed resentment of the incident that had freed her from his grip the first time. When she was seventeen, Daddy had brought Boss Smith, the local salvage yard owner, to the house for Nervy to sexually entertain. Seeing her scarred, naked body for the first time, Boss complained that she was too ugly to provide him any pleasure and demanded his money back. Her daddy refused, and in the resulting fight he beat Boss bloody and kicked him out of the house. Within the hour Boss's son Fatty showed up, kicked the door in, destroyed the front room's furnishings with a tire iron, and reduced her father to a broken, twitching, unconscious mass on the floor. As Nervy and Fatty surveyed the aftermath, he explained that his rampage hadn't been because of his affections for his father, but rather his policy that no one went unpunished for messing with his family. He invited her to leave her life with her daddy behind and live with him. Nervy left home that day and didn't return until she was released from prison.

Initially, post-prison life with Daddy was every bit as oppressive as prison. She was isolated twenty miles out in the country. All her criminal acquaintances shunned her, which reduced the likelihood of returning to her criminal life but left her all the lonelier. To satisfy her probation requirements for involvement in employment or education, she enrolled in an online class for medical transcription and finished it about the same time her probation was completed. Exactly one month later the house caught fire and burned to the ground, incinerating all its contents, including her daddy. Despite local rumors of Nervy's involvement, the fire marshal's final report indicated that he apparently had been working on the gas stove and triggered a fiery explosion. With her daddy's untimely passing, Nervy had to move into town, find a place, and find a job to pay for it.

Neither living in town nor having a legitimate job worried Nervy to the degree that staying safe at night did. Her immutable night safety plan required a dependable guardian or warning system; this boiled down to involving a trusted person or, perhaps even better, a trusted dog. Renting an apartment left her with no resources for acquiring a dog, and she trusted no one she knew, so she began searching for a night job that would allow her to be among gainfully employed people in illuminated locations during the night hours. Nervy's search chanced upon a suitable job advertised in the local paper, so she dropped off an application.

The Andrews Psychiatric Hospital wanted a night-shift technician on its adult psychiatry ward. The human resources lady who interviewed Nervy told her that rather than education or experience, the job demanded dependable attendance, dependable wakefulness, and dependable respect for the patients and other staff she would be working with. Her responsibility was to assist patients with any of their requests or needs during the 11:00 p.m. to 7:00 a.m. shift. If the request was beyond her expertise or raised her suspicions, she was to seek the assistance of the RN that would be working on the unit with her.

In closing, the interviewer asked, "Would working with mentally ill people frighten you?"

"Staff or patients?" Nervy asked. For the first time during the entire interview, the personnel worker made prolonged eye contact. Seemingly reevaluating Nervy with a scrutinizing up-and-down gaze, she smiled approvingly. "I believe you will handle both quite well."

Both of them agreed that she would begin that night.

Nervy never had reservations about working with disturbed people—they had populated her family, her drug dealings, and her prison life. Experiences had taught her that people's strengths and weaknesses could be recognized quickly if you were an astute observer. She also found that once she knew what to expect from people, she could find a way to work with them, unless they were exploiting her.

After a few days on the job, Nervy began sensing a commonality between herself and her patients. She was there seeking safety, and so was every one of them. Although they had different backgrounds, they were all in the same boat, sharing passage on their Noah's Ark to safer destinations for their lives. She had no us-and-them mentality regarding the patients.

Settling into her hospital job of monitoring people and activities throughout the night shift, Nervy discovered a completely unexpected inhabitant in the Ark for a few hours most nights. He was the only one of his species she sighted during her watch: a physician. The rest of the doctors who worked in the hospital had always gone home long before Nervy arrived. Dr. Corvus was the exception to this pattern of daylight physician migration. He was usually on the unit when Nervy got there a few minutes before 11:00 p.m. and frequently didn't leave until 1:00 a.m. or later, spending his time casually talking with staff or distractedly reviewing charts. Though he was at least fifteen years older than Nervy, he was never condescending and always addressed her with professional dignity. This had surprised Nervy because she assumed all doctors felt themselves superior to other staff and displayed it in their conduct. After several nights of watching this doctor, Nervy sought an explanation for his presence from the RN. "He's avoiding going home to a marriage that is falling apart" was her answer. Eventually Nervy and Dr. Corvus began greeting one another every evening. After another couple of weeks, they began having daily conversations. The frequency and intimacy of their conversations increased over time to the point that Nervy shared with him her view of the psych unit as a Noah's Ark of sorts.

One particular night Nervy arrived at work and noticed a store-bought white frosted cake in an unopened box on the break room table. An hour into her usual rounds, Dr. Corvus popped up in the hall outside the patient's room where she had just taken an extra blanket, appearing brighter somehow than she had seen him before. He walked beside her on the trip back to the nursing station.

"I'm celebrating my divorce. It was finalized today and there's cake in the break room."

"Congrats. I guess you won't have to hang around the Ark at night to avoid her now."

"Quite the contrary! The Ark is my favorite place. I'm quite fond of a particular passenger."

Frustrated with herself for feeling caught off guard by his remark, she abruptly demanded, "What are you talking about?"

Pausing in the middle of the hallway, he looked directly into her eyes and said, "You."

She stood paralyzed. The best man she had ever known had just told her she was worthy of his affection. Nervy had had stirrings of desire for Walter but never believed they would be reciprocated. With his announcement, she knowingly turned her heart loose and didn't try to talk herself out of believing that her life could have a chapter that didn't involve abuse and criminality.

With his desire for her clear, their conversations began occurring over dinners in local restaurants, then at his place during evenings of pizza and TV. They talked of their shared respect for one another's professionalism. She found his lack of self-centeredness surprising in a man, making her appreciate him all the more. His love for her was awakening a love in her for herself that she had never realized was possible. More and more he opened his life to her—his outpatient office practice, his enjoyment of taking walks on the path that wandered among the big sycamores down by the river, his restored 1951 Chevy pickup.

After six months Walter proposed to Nervy among the trees by the river. Before answering, she started telling him the secrets of her childhood and her years as a criminal. He stopped her and told her that he was comfortable with his decision to marry her and that she could decide later whether sharing these details would be necessary as their life together unfolded. She accepted his terms and accepted his love for the next fifteen years of their marriage.

CHAPTER 5

Remembering her and Walter's romance, Nervy drifted into the sleep that had evaded her for days. She dreamt of an enjoyable stroll along the familiar path by the river. Even though she was alone among the giant sycamores, she felt no fear or despair and blissfully anticipated the return of the partner she had begun her walk with. The partner had lingered away from the path longer than expected but was sure to return and resume their walk together. Emerging from sleep, she awakened to the unhappiness of her real life and felt surprised that it hadn't infected her dream. The emotional replenishment of the sleep and the brief respite from her despair created a sense of gratitude which Nervy recognized and welcomed with a smile. It was her first smile in four days. Several urgent tasks, like finding the will, finding the insurance policies, and cutting off the credit cards, were waiting to claim Nervy's Sunday, but as she savored her dream and feeling of gratitude she decided to spend the day in affirming her life as more important than merely managing tragic circumstances.

During her life with Walter, they had not gone to church much, but she figured that if she was ever going to go, it should be now. She and God had a lot of business to settle. First, she needed to say thank you for the years she had with Walter despite the fact they were so few. Why did Walter die and not her? Was God going to protect her physically and financially? Would He please let her talk to her mom for an hour? She hoped He would respond to her in some way that would provide comfort.

It had probably been over twenty years since she had been to the Greenbriar Assembly, but that was where she was headed today. While Nervy was growing up, her mother had been a faithful member, making the five-mile, gravel-road trip to worship every week year-round regardless of the weather. Nervy's father had never once darkened the door of the church. As a kid she had joined her mother every Sunday morning. It was the only demand that her mother ever imposed and successfully maintained against Nervy's dad's opposition. Although she had always been welcomed sincerely and accepted by the church members, she had never let herself feel at home there, because she lived in two worlds. Greenbriar Assembly was the world her mother belonged to. The other world was the one she was regularly taken to by her father, where her mother was never present. He involved Nervy in the worship of his gods—demons actually—as fervently and frequently as Nervy's mother did. Both of her parents were devout worshippers, but their gods couldn't have been more different. What she learned from her mother on the one hand and from her father on the other gave Nervy a breadth of education and training that stretched across the entire moral spectrum.

Greenbriar wasn't the only church Nervy had ever attended. Walter had been Episcopalian before they were married. On the few occasions they went to church, she had agreed to attend the calmer and more organized Episcopal church because she knew that it would be easier for her to sit through the sedate Episcopalian service than it would have been for Walter to endure the exuberance of Greenbriar. Due to Walter's preferences, she had requested the Episcopal priest to perform Walter's funeral. Now, no longer having to accommodate Walter's sensitivities, Nervy decided that she was going back to the church of her childhood.

When Nervy had gone to Greenbriar, the ladies never wore slacks and they all had head coverings, whether scarves or hats. She tucked a scarf in her purse in case she would need it to get in the door. Nervy got off on time, planning for a forty-five-minute drive in order to arrive a little before 11:00 a.m. She headed south out of town on a two-lane blacktop highway draped over the ups and downs of hilly pastureland intermittently dotted with grazing cattle. Turning off the pavement after seventeen miles, she drove the remaining ten miles through the hills on gravel roads that created a continuous roar inside the car and a quarter-mile-long dust cloud behind it. Once off the highway, she passed farmhouses only every few miles, and traffic was so infrequent that if people were outside they would pause and watch the passersby and wave. Finally, within view of the church, she saw that the building was still standing but was underneath a new red corrugated metal roof.

There were at least two dozen pickups and two or three cars parked irregularly around the building. She parked so as to avoid blocking anybody else's vehicle in and exited the car to the sound of a hymn being sung by untrained voices accompanied by drums and an electric guitar. Waiting until the end of the song before she opened the door, she hoped her entrance would be less disruptive to the worshippers, but it was to no avail. Someone was just finishing praying as she stepped in the door. With the communal "amen" having been pronounced, the congregants were all raising their heads to resume worship when the bump of the door shutting behind Nervy echoed through the room. Most everyone turned around in their pews to see who had come in the door. The pastor offered Nervy his greeting from the pulpit and announced that they had a woman visitor. Nervy stood still for a moment and glanced around the sparsely appointed sanctuary, recognizing no one until she saw a lady sitting notably alone next to the center aisle in the very back pew. Even from behind, the woman's bearing and posture exuded authority, as if she were the judge of all that unfolded in front of her. She was older, quite fat, and wearing a decidedly unstylish turquoise straw hat. She held a brightly colored folding fan in her right hand and was slowly, ceremoniously fanning it back and forth to assure anyone who glanced toward her that she remained watchful and on duty. Nervy smiled and thought to herself, "Who else but Bertha would still be here after all these years?"

Without turning to take a look at the visitor, the fat old lady called out authoritatively to the whole church with a matriarch's manner, "And what is our woman visitor's name?"

"Nervy is my name," the visitor replied just as loudly.

There was a pregnant pause as the congregation could hear Sister Bertha draw a deep breath in response to Nervy's announcement. When sufficiently inflated, Bertha loudly called out, "Pastor Sam," and with the practiced speak-pause-speak cadence of a prophecy's pronouncement she addressed those gathered. "This day is an answer to PRAYERS! . . . This is a day of MIRACLES! . . . God has come among us today and returned a lost lamb I thought I would NEVER see again. . . . This is Sadie Goins's daughter. . . . HEAVEN AND HELL never fought for a child's soul like they did for this girl forty years ago RIGHT HERE in this church." By this time all the eyes of the congregation were focused on Bertha as she resumed. "Nervy, you're here today for only one reason—you're beset again by the DEVIL!"

At this point, Pastor Sam intervened, regaining the congregation's attention from Bertha. He again welcomed Nervy, this time by name. He called for another song from the congregation and followed it up with another prayer. He began the sermon portion of the service but only completed a couple of sentences before he paused and assumed a posture of contemplation with a pensive downward gaze. Looking back up at the congregation, he gravely addressed the worship service. "Sister Bertha has shown herself a faithful servant and prophetess of God for over fifty years in this church. We would do well today to honor her witness. Bertha, does God have more for you to testify?"

Bertha responded, "Nervy is here today because she is SCARED. . . . Anybody here ever been scared?"

Ten voices said, "Yes."

"She's scared of who she has BEEN. . . . Anybody here ever been scared of who they has been?"

Twenty voices proclaimed, "Yes."

"She's scared of what she has to DO. . . . Anybody here ever been scared of what they has to do?"

The whole church boldly shouted out, "Yes!"

"She's scared of where she has to GO. . . . Anybody here ever been scared of where they has to go?"

The whole church hollered wildly, "YES!!"

Pastor Sam took over. "Does GOD still love us when we're scared? Does a loving FATHER refuse to love a frightened child?"

The congregation screamed, "NOOO!" and right then any vestige of structured worship fell apart. Some of the congregation were silently praying to God with eyes closed and lips barely moving, others were loudly crying out the feelings of their hearts, some stood lifting their hands, some knelt, some fell on their faces. Tears were flowing, praises were flying.

One last time Pastor Sam called out loudly over the mayhem of the crowd, "If anybody here thinks they've been through bad spells of FEAR AND DOUBT then go . . . GO give comfort to this woman in the midst of her fear and doubt." The congregation quickly converged on Nervy and pressed around her with assurances both whispered and shouted extolling God's love and faithfulness. Nervy was emotionally overcome and had to sit down in the pew beside Bertha. She cried, leaning on the old woman's beefy shoulder. After ten minutes most of the congregation had expressed support to Nervy and were withdrawing into smaller groups, socializing and departing the church. Nervy stood up and was collecting herself emotionally when Bertha unexpectedly reached for her forearm and squeezed it tightly, pulling her down in the pew beside her.

"Child, whatever you're facing, don't you shrink back a bit. I know you and I know your people, both sides, good and bad. You come from strong good people and strong bad people. You grew up bein' brought to the light every Sunday and being thrown to the darkness every week, just as regular. God made you and put you on a zigzag path as a child and you're stuck on it as a woman. Now you gonna have to walk your zigzag path as long as you live, but you know God prepared an ending to your path the day He put you on it. That ending is as sure and as beautiful as He is. You got to do what it takes to keep going."

Nervy could feel Bertha's pity for her plight, but it wasn't providing any comfort. It actually seemed to amplify how desperate her life had always been.

"TODAY God is showing me that your path is not the problem. The problem is how YOU are gonna walk it. Which one of you is gonna walk that path—the you that your *daddy* raised or the you that your *momma* raised? God used your momma to put a whole load of love into you, and Satan used your daddy to put a whole load of deceiving into you. You better decide pretty quick which one you aim to be when you meet God at the end of your path!" With a final squeeze to her arm, Bertha finished and permitted Nervy to leave.

On the drive home, her heart was stirred and her childhood church memories reawakened. She felt strongly that God had spoken to her, but being told to always do the right thing felt too vague to be significantly instructive or comforting. Processing the experience, she found herself wishing she could have met her mother's other friends, Vera or Nola, rather than Bertha. Bertha had a bossy personality and had always talked down to people. It annoyed Nervy.

CHAPTER 6

Nervy woke up knowing this was a particularly decisive Monday, in terms of both the decision the court would reach and the decisions she would make in response. Nervy mentally braced herself as she sat on the edge of the bed, determined to not let the events of the day break her. Once in the kitchen, she made herself drink some black coffee and eat a piece of plain white toast, despite the absence of any hunger, reasoning that her stress would destroy an empty stomach with acid or evacuate an overly full stomach. She sipped the coffee, telling herself that it had the flavor of strength, unambiguously bitter and nearly scalding. Her toast was dry and crisp: no butter, no jelly, no indulgence. Breakfast reflected exactly who she intended to be as she went into the courtroom. This was judgment day and she was going to face it head-on all by herself.

It was a malpractice case. The courts classified the suit as civil rather than criminal, but there had been nothing civil about it. Walter had been the defendant but killed himself last Wednesday evening after listening to multiple witnesses testify that he was an incompetent quack and a menace to the community he had served for over twenty years. In Judge

Justin Tucker's court, the mere suicide of a defendant would not stop the wheels of justice in their race to a decision in a civil suit. Even with the defendant dead, his estate or his insurance company could still be made to pay and, after all, money was the object of the malpractice suit. At no point during the trial had the judge ever displayed any reasonable consideration of the requests of Walter's lawyer. Nervy wondered if the judge's hostility was because of her felony conviction in his father's courtroom twenty years ago, which the young judge no doubt recalled. There was also the possibility that he was embarrassed by the fact that his now retired, alcoholic father, Jules, had become a frequent flier in Dr. Corvus's office. Every four weeks, Jules dependably arrived at the office to pick up his Valium prescription for the month. Walter only provided him thirty pills a month to be used as needed for sleep or panic attacks.

Never content to have them phoned in, Jules always picked up his prescriptions in person. He would linger too long at Nervy's desk, making shallow conversation. Occasionally he smelled of alcohol and, on those days, he often made thinly disguised suggestive comments about her prudish long sleeves and high necklines, hinting at his fantasies. On one day Jules had even gone so far as to remember aloud Nervy's father's horrific fiery death and the suspicious rumors that had been whispered around town about Nervy having possibly caused it. Conversely, there were days he indulged in self-pity, complaining about the contempt he felt his son, the young judge, had for him because of his use of those "psych meds." Walter had wanted to quit providing prescriptions to Jules, but Nervy had countered that maybe the thirty Valium pills were the only thing that made Jules's life bearable. As in most disagreements, Walter conceded to Nervy's wish that the scripts be continued.

Judge Tucker had ruled that the legal proceedings against Dr. Corvus should continue undelayed by his suicide, giving the verdict precedence over mere loss of life and mourning. He opined from the bench that taking time off to show respect, sorrow, or consideration for the defendant's desperate actions would contaminate the emotions of the jury and give undue advantage to the defendant's case. The day after Walter's suicide, Lanny Peltor, the plaintiff's attorney, had commented conversationally to his clients that a guilty conscience could drive a soul to unthinkable extremes. He had said it loudly enough to be heard by the jury.

Walter's entire estate was at risk of being awarded to the plaintiffs. The estate was not enormous, but Nervy's problem was that it was jointly hers and represented ninety percent or more of all her earthly possessions. She had also inherited forty acres from her father and mother. Fortunately, early in their marriage Walter had refused her invitation to make the acreage their joint property. He said he saw it as part of a chapter in her life that he had no involvement in and wished her to manage that chapter and land as she wished. They held everything else jointly; their finances, their possessions, the psychiatric practice, and their hopes and dreams were all held in the grasp of the us of their relationship. Neither the he nor the she of their fifteen-year marriage had ever claimed sole ownership of any part of their lives—that is until he took his own life and left her behind.

The court was now in control of her material and financial security. The only thing she could control was whether she would show up in court today and whether she would face the court's decision with a stone-cold unblinking glare. Nervy had a reputation for unflinchingly facing problems, but she was still reeling from the blow Walter had dealt her. She couldn't understand his choice—it wasn't justified. Yes, this was his third malpractice case, but neither of the first two plaintiffs had received significant awards. Yes, his professional association malpractice insurance had refused to take the first two cases to court and had settled out of court against Walter's wishes, but the settlements were paid for by the insurance company and had cost him and Nervy nothing.

Despite the minimal damage done to his finances, Walter's pride had been crushed and his resentment additionally enflamed by multiple conversations he'd had with Mr. Shemp, the lawyer for the malpractice insurer. It was Shemp who had decided to settle the first suit out of court and deny Walter any chance to defend himself. During the second malpractice suit, Walter repeatedly begged Mr. Shemp for a chance to address the court and counter those accusations of wrongdoing. Shemp dismissed Walter's pleas, accusing him of keeping sloppy medical records with inadequate psychiatric and social histories, making his diagnoses and treatments seem arbitrary. Shemp ridiculed Walter for expecting the insurer to risk its money trying to defend his skimpy records in court. It was cheaper to pay the plaintiffs and hope they went away.

Despite Nervy's advice, Walter's indignation over Mr. Shemp's decisions motivated him to withhold a scheduled quarterly payment for his malpractice insurance in an act of impotent self-righteous posturing. The insurer reacted quickly with predictably uncaring absolutism, despite the past twenty years of Walter's dependable payments. It cancelled his policy and suggested he buy a "tail policy" to continue insurance protection for the preceding twenty years the cancelled policy had been in effect. It would cost the equivalent of four years' malpractice premiums, but without it he had no insurance protection against any lawsuit from any of the patients he had cared for during the past two decades. The company also offered him the opportunity to purchase an entirely new malpractice insurance policy, but the new policy's premium would be two and a half times higher than before because he had proven to be a high-risk physician.

Confronting more liability than he could tolerate, Walter succumbed to the insurance company's pressure and mailed it the money for both the tail policy and the new policy. For its final insult it left him uninsured for three weeks between the old and new policies and provided Walter a carbon copy of the letter that it had sent to the Clay Center hospital CEO and chief of staff informing them that Walter had experienced a twenty-one-day lapse in his malpractice coverage. Walter's bruised pride had created a legal and financial abyss that he soon fell into, dragging Nervy down with him.

In contrast, the local lawyer Lanny Peltor had a winning streak going. He had brought and won two malpractice suits against Walter in the past six years. He had maneuvered the doctor's malpractice insurance company to settle both cases out of court, preventing the doctor from testifying or defending himself before a jury. For him the *third* case could be the big payoff, especially if it had the ingredients that would stir a jury's compassion and sense of indignation. Such a case, with an accompanying lucrative malpractice payoff, would score Lanny the kind of acclaim that would raise him from merely a regional north Missouri lawyer to a multistate personal injury lawyer. His fortunes would naturally follow his reputation. Lanny had intensively canvassed the entire community with phone calls and advertisements looking for just the right case. After thirteen months of hunting, his endeavors were rewarded.

Cindy Adair had been a nondescript sixteen-year-old high school junior, noted by her teachers and peers to frequently complain about poor grades, acne, and a series of degrading boyfriends. Cindy posted her despair on social media when her last boyfriend's sister sent her a message dumping her on behalf of her brother, who couldn't message her because he was in juvenile detention. Cindy's despondent postings were brought to her parents' attention by other concerned parents, whose children had shown them her posts. They took her to see Dr. Corvus during the twenty-one-day period he was without malpractice insurance. He had recommended that she receive counseling and start a trial of antidepressant medications. Her parents agreed and expressed their consent to his treatment suggestions. Two weeks later, on the day before her first follow-up appointment with Dr. Corvus, she overdosed on the antidepressants as well as all the other contents of the family's medicine cabinet. Rushed by her family to the Clay Center hospital ER, she presented completely unresponsive but had stable vital signs. The ER doctor arranged ambulance transport to the university hospital two hours away, where she could be observed in a treatment setting with more lifesaving technology than the Clay Center hospital had.

In transit and resting unresponsively on her gurney in the air-conditioned ambulance, she displayed an unanticipated shiver and moan, followed by struggles against the restraints securing her as she began emerging from unconsciousness. Disquieted by the "agitation" of his worrisome psych patient, the young EMT sought and obtained permission to administer an IV injection of a sedative medicine to calm her. The sedation severely reduced her respiratory rate, with noticeable downturns in her oxygen readings on the monitor above her gurney. The EMT then attempted to increase his patient's oxygen with a manual resuscitation device that he rhythmically squeezed, pushing air into Cindy's nose and mouth through a face mask. His vigorous squeezing repeatedly overfilled her lungs, causing some pulmonary injury and, more harmfully, filling her stomach with air that made her vomit. She aspirated a significant amount of the vomit into her lungs, initiating an aspiration pneumonitis.

Cindy arrived at the university hospital alive but with low blood oxygen, vomitus in both lungs, and dropping blood pressure. She expired two days later in the hospital ICU due to a variety of complications from a variety of treatment misadventures. The two hospital days of Cindy's deterioration involved multiple heroic and increasingly drastic medical interventions, each one's failed promise gnawing deeper into the dwindling hopes the Adair parents desperately clung to. The eventual bitterness Mr. and Mrs. Adair experienced following Cindy's agonizing multistep death began unconsciously serving as a vehicle by which to reunite emotionally with their only other child, Cindy's older sister Candy. She had been emotionally estranged from the family as she had drifted ever deeper into the wrong crowd, eventually shacking up with a druggie and having a couple of children. Candy and her parents hadn't even seen or spoken to one another for the better part of two years when she joined them at the hospital on the day Cindy died.

Through the local gossip grapevine Nervy heard that Lanny landed the Adair family's malpractice suit following a "consultation" with them in his luxuriously appointed office. She was told he presented the lawsuit as a big-dollar, slam-dunk winner of a case that would vindicate their deceased daughter and suitably punish every doctor and hospital and anybody else involved in her tragic death. There were many deep pockets to be picked by a good attorney: two hospitals, a psychiatrist, two ER docs, an ambulance company, and a group of five intensivist doctors who oversaw the ICU where Cindy ultimately passed away. Lanny's rich inventory of villains was reported to have been the final factor convincing the Adairs to sign on.

Nervy calculated that it must have been about two weeks after landing the case that Lanny realized Walter's malpractice insurance was not in effect during his one and only appointment with Cindy. The likely look on his face amused Nervy as she imagined him mentally translating the absence of an insurance company into the absence of any deep pockets to raid. Now the only treasure to seek from the psychiatrist was his personal property and savings. Dr. Corvus and Nervy were not wealthy and had never given the appearance of such, and she hoped that also distressed the lawyer. Lanny eventually filed the suit against Walter separately from the other defendants. It appeared that he had decided the case against Walter wasn't strong and didn't want it to weaken the larger case, in which all of the other various defendants and their respective insurance companies had been lumped together, creating a massive treasure chest.

Unfortunately, from Nervy's point of view Lanny caught a lucky break in Walter's case when the judge tossed out Walter's lawyer's motion for a change of venue so the case wouldn't be tried in Clay Center. The judge decided the case would be tried locally, guaranteeing that images of the dead schoolgirl would be shown and recognized in the local paper and TV news, eliminating any possibility of a neutral jury pool. The rumored friendship of Lanny Peltor the lawyer and Justin Tucker the judge now seemed undeniably confirmed. From that point on, Nervy and Walter's hope in the fairness of the trial had been extinguished.

CHAPTER 7

Nervy finished getting ready for Monday morning court. She attired herself in her characteristic long-sleeved, high-neck blouse, choosing a striking red one. Black slacks and red shoes completed the ensemble. She didn't expect the day in court to be very long, but she took Griff to doggy daycare because she didn't want him alone in the car in the courthouse parking lot while this case was in session.

As the two of them walked into Dog Day Spa, Susie looked up from her desk; she greeted the woman with a smile and the terrier with a wary glare. Griff's reputation for antagonizing her other guests had been established two years ago when he tried to settle a dispute with an English mastiff through a chain-link fence. Griff's ear was ultimately the only part that he succeeded in getting through the fence, but it proved to be no match for the entire mastiff waiting on the other side. Rather than banishing him from the spa, Susie instituted a policy of keeping an empty kennel on each side of him. Griff grumbled as Nervy handed Susie his leash.

At the courthouse, she parked neatly between the lines in a space inconveniently distant from the entrance, intending to avoid any potential closeness to someone walking into or out of the courthouse. She remembered the first day's jury selection. She and Walter had been shocked to watch two women summoned for jury duty—one current patient and one former—attempt to squirm out of it. The judge's snide comments in court repeatedly reminded all those gathered of his disdain for the defendant and psychiatric treatment generally. During the jury selection both ladies raised their hands when the jury pool was asked which of them felt they could not be impartial because of prior court rulings against Dr. Corvus. Walter and Nervy had glanced at each other with raised eyebrows, knowing that each of the ladies had accepted and returned for repeat appointments despite knowing of his previous malpractice settlements, one of them for years and the other for months. The older of the two had even referred family members to Walter.

Nervy had returned her gaze to the two patients, who never even glanced in her direction. Throughout that day Walter's face reflected his growing discouragement. At home that night he began discussing the possibility of quitting his practice after this trial. Every subsequent day of court had deepened his demoralization. By the third day a sort of ritual had developed: at the end of each day, the jury members would make empathetic eye contact with the Adair family, nonverbally communicating their sympathy for the family's case. Walter had left court each day looking like a cancer patient whose metastases were multiplying, but Nervy had never believed he would kill himself until they found his body swinging from the tree down by the river.

Once in the courthouse, Nervy went upstairs to the courtroom and took her seat in the gallery in the front row right behind the defense table, where Raleigh sat next to the empty chair signifying Walter's absence. Judge Tucker had permitted the presence of the empty chair despite Lanny's objections. On the other side of the courtroom, Mr. and Mrs. Adair sat at the plaintiff's table, with Candy sitting in the first row of the gallery behind them. As Nervy assumed her usual position, she felt Candy's routine hateful glare directed her way. The glare was only diverted when the court was called to order and its proceedings began.

Judge Tucker entered and summoned the jury. The courtroom was a fine example of late-1800s architecture, with wood floors, plaster walls, and high ceilings. The circumstances were perfect for echoing sound, and Nervy's senses were hyperaware this morning. The sounds of the shuffling feet and scooting chairs seemed deafening as the jury entered the jury box and took their seats. Throughout the trial her modus operandi for managing nervousness had been to sit rigidly upright and anchor herself emotionally by staring intensely at the presidential portraits behind Judge Tucker's bench.

"Has the jury reached a verdict?" the judge initiated.

A big-bellied car salesman serving as jury foreman stood and faced the judge. His plaid sport coat from twenty years ago was noticeable for its now unstylishly bright colors and its awkward inability to even remotely reach around his girth. Looking at him, Nervy envisioned a circus at which a clown entertained the crowd by trying to hijack the ringmaster's responsibilities. The only thing missing was a red ping-pong-ball nose.

"We have, Your Honor," the foreman sternly and ceremoniously responded. The bailiff then took the written verdict from him and delivered it to the judge.

"In regard to the charge of wrongful death, what is the jury's verdict?"

"Guilty."

"The jury will now begin deliberations to determine the damages to be awarded to the plaintiffs."

"We already have, Your Honor," said the ostentatious foreman, who remained standing and facing the judge.

"The court does not *accept* your conclusions in matters it has not yet delegated or instructed you about," the judge corrected.

"I'm sorry, Your Honor. We all . . . I mean, the jury directed me to ask the bailiff if he would bring us the statutes to review about sentencing."

"Be seated!" By now Judge Tucker's facial expression seemed equal parts annoyance and exasperation. He proceeded with a fifteen-minute lecture informing the jury of their responsibilities and options for sentencing.

"Do you understand these instructions?" the judge concluded.

"Yes, Your Honor," replied the large plaid-jacketed man, seeming unfazed, "but we have reached a unanimous decision in keeping with your instructions."

"And that is?" asked the judge.

"The maximum award permitted by law," answered the foreman.

"Seven hundred thousand dollars?" the judge questioned.

"Exactly," replied the car salesman, sealing the deal.

The judge thanked the jury for their valuable civic service and dismissed them. Upon their departure from the jury box, the gavel came down. Nervy glanced down from the face of President Washington to her watch. It was 10:23 a.m. and she had a lot left to do today.

CHAPTER 8

Raleigh and Nervy stood as the judge exited the courtroom and then simultaneously turned and looked each other in the eyes.

The lawyer raised his eyebrows and shook his head. "I wish I could say that this was a complete surprise."

"Me too," she answered, walking up to the table the lawyer had been seated at. "I guess the next step is to file for bankruptcy," she continued.

"There are several next steps." He took a breath for his next sentence but hesitated as Lanny approached them from the plaintiff's table, briefcase in hand.

"Come to gloat?" Raleigh inquired disdainfully.

"No, to offer my condolences for the way this worked out."

"And *I'm* sorry you won't be able to continue building your career by savaging my dead husband. Guess you will have to find a new host to suck blood from," Nervy sneered, tilting her head to the side.

"I had second thoughts about speaking to the two of you at this time, but I thought it was the right thing to do."

Nervy put her hands on her hips and took an exaggerated breath as she glared at him hatefully.

"It isn't personal!" Lanny protested calmly. "It's the law. When someone is injured, they receive compensation. When someone does something wrong, they must pay for it."

"What you have done is wrong—completely unfair to Walter and to me," she shot back.

Lanny lifted his briefcase from the table, indicating his imminent departure.

Intending to conclude the conversation, he said, "This is a court of law—it is not a court of justice. We all have to live and accept our circumstances within the rules, limitations, and authority of laws." He turned and proceeded toward the side entrance of the courtroom.

Nervy rebuked him to his back. "The 'law' is a gutter! It is the lowest, dirtiest common denominator people use on each other. What's legal is a shitty compass for life. I feel sorry for you if you really believe the crap you just spewed out. I swear to God—I *pray* to God that somebody you love gets stuck having to suffer through something that's fucking 'legal'!" Depleted, Nervy sat in the chair that had been empty since Walter died.

"Wow, did you ever think of becoming a lawyer?" Raleigh asked.

"Fuck you!" she retorted, still fired up and not bothering to look at him.

"I deserved that," he responded, shrugging his shoulders. He gathered his papers off the table and placed them in his briefcase. "Coffee?" he asked.

They left the courthouse together and walked across the street to the coffee shop. Sipping coffee, they talked priorities and strategies for Nervy to consider as she faced the court's acquisition of her and Walter's joint property. He wasn't telling her anything she hadn't already realized. Although she appreciated his support, the discussion was depressing, and she was anxious to prepare and implement her own private plans for the loss of her husband and her property, which had been pre-occupying her thoughts and stirring her creativity.

"Thanks for all your help; it couldn't have been easy for you to be involved in this either."

"It was my privilege," the lawyer said. "Walter was a good man and he deserved to be treated better by this community. The coffee is on me. Call if you need anything."

Nervy headed straight to Dog Days from the coffee shop because Griff's was the only company she wished today. With her terrier retrieved, she went to the office. Her plans for surviving the next few months included taking care of some paperwork she had often thought of doing but had never gotten around to. Along with their house, the office was one of the two worlds where Nervy and Walter had lived ninety percent of their lives together. Almost half of their waking hours had been spent at the office working as a two-person team with clear divisions of labor. His were the activities generating the charges that put the money in the bank. Hers were the tasks that kept patients, information, and money flowing through the practice smoothly.

Bankruptcy loomed unavoidably, so using her current resources intentionally was critical. She was going to need the office space and utilities.

"I'm sure glad Walter and I decided to pay a year's worth of rent before he died," she muttered sarcastically, writing a rent check for a year with the previous Monday's date on it. Next, Nervy wrote a check paying for the remainder of this year's malpractice insurance.

"Even a dead doctor can be sued. You never know who might try that sort of thing," she mused, licking that envelope.

Surveying her desk for her other priorities, she glanced over to the cubbyhole where she kept the prescriptions that had been written for patients early last week and hadn't been picked up yet. Walter provided Nervy twenty or so pre-signed blank prescriptions at the beginning of every week with which she could write refills for familiar long-term patients who had remained stable on well-established doses of medicines. Walter and Nervy had a good understanding of which patients she needed to check with him about before renewing their prescriptions. Knowing that he was going to be unavailable to the office while he was in court, Walter had signed several extra blank prescriptions for Nervy to use. She looked for the signed blanks in the back part of the drawer, where she kept them out of sight. Finding them, she held the papers in her hand, fanning them like playing cards so she could count how many there were. Smiling to herself, she had to admit that she would make a lousy poker player. She couldn't suppress her smile when she was holding thirty aces. She put them back in the drawer and, before leaving, dialed up Jules Tucker to tell him that she had some signed prescriptions for Valium at the office available for him to pick up. He didn't answer, so she left a message.

CHAPTER 9

With those tasks concluded at work, the next step in her plans required her to go home and begin sorting untraceable valuables, collectibles, weapons, or other items that she and Walter had accumulated. Nervy organized them into categories: 1) useful possessions she needed to keep nearby and available; 2) items to be liquidated for their cash value; 3) items to be hidden securely so that no one would take them.

The storage container holding the high-value items she feared losing was hidden in the back of the closet behind stacked shoeboxes. The pillowcase full of objects she was intending to liquidate tomorrow at a pawnshop was placed in the trunk of her Avalon underneath the spare tire, with the jack and toolbox positioned to hide them. For her final housekeeping tasks, Nervy found Walter's .38 Special revolver and examined the cylinder methodically, rotating it clockwise click by click to assure herself that there were unfired bullets in all six chambers. Satisfied, she went to the garage and placed the pistol in the car in a readily reachable position on the floor between the driver's door and seat. She made sure she could sit in the driver's seat legally seat belted and still easily access the gun and raise it to a usable position with her left hand and then with her right. She went back in the house and retrieved Walter's other firearm, his .22 revolver. This time she had to assess eight rounds of ammo instead of six; then she placed the gun in plain sight on the nightstand by her side of the bed.

Her early life had taught her that to run short of money was to open the door to exploitation. She was going to do everything she could to avoid both dangers. Tomorrow would be her first foray back into the fringe of the underworld. Exchanging jewelry for cash was usually an unfamiliar and uncomfortable process for people that lived their lives within the confines of the law. Businesses that convert personal valuables into impersonal cash represented the frontier where the lawless and the lawful collide. People that survived and prospered on this frontier were uncaring and self-interested, more concerned about things than people. Theirs was a world of unmasked predation. To ignore that was as perilous as walking across a busy street blindfolded. Nervy didn't relish the idea of returning to this frontier, but she had survived in that world for years, and she trusted that she still retained those skills. Like riding a bike, she thought, faintly smiling.

With various aspects of her various plans begun, she was feeling much less vulnerable at the end of this day than she had since Walter died. Undressing for bed, she found her sense of accomplishment and self-confidence made her long for Walter in an unanticipated way. She wished he were with her so she could share herself and celebrate the ways she had been powerful and strong today. Initiation of sex in the relationship with Walter had always been left to her. He was different than any other man she had known. From the time she was thirteen years old, when her father began abusing her and then bringing "visitors" home to the house, every man had been demeaning, insistent, and impatient, always demanding more. It was all about her being a surrendered slave or subjugated captive, acting out variations of the same basic fantasy every one of them was addicted to. They imagined themselves invulnerable and immune to the shame and fear they inflicted on her. Her body, her openings, her scars, her postures were all distracting entertainment they used to avoid their own sense of vulnerability. When she was younger, her tears had just heightened her abusers' pleasures and fueled their degrading demands. Later she learned that a cold, unflinching stare lessened her sense of vulnerability in the moment and lessened the sense of power her exploiters were seeking.

Walter sought nothing but expressions of affection. His reluctance to initiate confused her, but she never once knew him to decline her advances. Tonight she readied herself for bed by leaving her pajama shirt unbuttoned and her pajama bottoms in the drawer. She lay down alone on top of the thrown-back covers, leaning against her and his stacked pillows. She turned off the bedside light, allowing herself a deeper immersion into her vivid recollections and sensations celebrating her and Walter's love, before drifting into an exhausted and fully relaxed sleep.

Tuesday morning was overcast and cooler, confirming that summer was losing its strength. After Nervy awoke, she began reviewing and rehearsing for the pawnshop, excited to pull off the performance planned for today. She savored the prospect of the drive to Middleton too. A two-hour road trip, a chance to view the passing fields and rolling hills of north Missouri's farmland through her windshield while the radio played a soundtrack of country music for her. It was the perfect preparation for arriving relaxed and refreshed. She planned to get there, get her money, and get back in plenty of time to have supper at home.

Middleton was a much larger city than Clay Center. It had a private liberal arts college, a dental school, and a medical school, each with their own campuses. There was also a college football stadium and basketball arena. It was a regional shopping destination for central Missouri. With the college student population, the college dropout population, and the usual number of people struggling to get by, Middleton also had a nice selection of pawnshops. Charles Darwin could have used Middleton pawnshops as an illustration of species selection based upon adaptation. Each of the pawnshops had evolved a particular identity based on the unique expertise it had developed for specific items. Some shops specialized in antiques, some in firearms, some in jewelry and coins, some in musical instruments. Nervy intended to visit a seedy-looking shop in a semi-industrial part of town that dealt mainly in jewelry and precious metals. She figured being two hours south of Clay Center should put her at enough of a distance from home that she could conduct her business unrecognized and unremembered. She wore nondescript blue jeans, sunglasses, a ball cap, and a long-sleeved gold-and-blue sweatshirt with the college's mascot emblazoned across the front. She would look like just another mom with a kid or two enrolled in the college, showing typical middle-class university allegiance—except with five thousand dollars' worth of assorted jewelry that she would transport in a Walmart bag and offer to sell for twenty-five hundred dollars cash.

Nervy left her cell phone turned off on the kitchen counter but took her blue tooth earbud. She didn't need a trail of cell phone towers tracking her travels. She had met at least two inmates in prison who had made that mistake. Having grabbed a diet Mountain Dew and one of Walter's old ball caps off the coat hook, she was in the car and out of the driveway by 8:15 a.m. She and Griff hadn't been on the road ten minutes before the Dew was being sipped and a tear was pooling in her eye from the country song she was enjoying. Walter had repeatedly joked with her that country music, with its sad themes of hard times, hard hearts, and hard liquor, was the best marketing a psychiatrist could ask for—even though he wouldn't let her play it in the office waiting room.

An hour and a half later, as she approached Middleton, Nervy channeled her thoughts back to today's mission. This was probably going to be the toughest of her moneymaking days. First off, she was going to be doing business with a less-than-top-tier pawnshop. If it was on the up and up, it would want solid, believable identification for this quality of jewelry and would document it for its records. But she wasn't going to provide any ID, because she wasn't going to let this jewelry or the money she got for it be documented and liable to any court settlement. She hoped that the shop she was going to today would be a little loose with the ID requirements, especially if she allowed it some extra profit on her transaction.

CHAPTER 10

Nervy drove around the block a couple of times, planning her best egress following her transaction with the Smithson Pawnshop. It looked a little shadier than she had expected. She selected a parking lot that was two businesses away and behind a discount furniture and carpet store that was advertising a going-out-of-business sale. It was a quarter to eleven and the bargain furniture hunters had barely begun using the lot. Parking in the shade near a dumpster, she made sure that she was completely out of the pawnshop security camera's view. She stuck a fresh piece of gum in her mouth, put in her blue tooth earbud for appearances, tucked her hair under the ball cap, and put the .38 Special in a convenience store bag. After popping the trunk open, she pushed the spare and the jack over to the side, pulled out the stashed jewelry, and transferred it from the pillowcase to a Walmart bag she had in the trunk. Nervy left the windows cracked for Griff and assured him she would be back in a while, despite his growled dissatisfaction.

Walking away from the car, she initiated a very animated and impassioned conversation through her earbud with her frustrating imaginary son Curtis, who was in deep trouble with a local girl's parents and was needing mom's help to withdraw from school and leave town as quickly as possible. She continued to talk much too loudly and gesture too emphatically as she turned the corner of the building next to the pawnshop and entered the view of the security cameras. She walked through the front door and into the shop, still gesturing and talking loudly.

"Curtis, I'm just now going into the pawn place, so I'm gonna be a few more minutes. Keep on packing. I'll be back when I'm done!"

Now well inside the door, she paused and made eye contact with the man behind the counter, then shrugged, demonstrating her exasperation with her phone conversation.

"Put a sock in it! Goodbye!" She rolled her eyes and walked the rest of the way to the counter and put her two sacks on it. The counter guy had stringy hair and was about twenty-five. His overall appearance screamed video games, Cheetos, weed, and Mom's basement. He'd been working here long enough, though, that he had picked up the required contemptuous facial expression with which to greet customers and prepare them to expect nothing from him but apathy and exploitation. Sitting on a folding chair at the end of the counter was a fat lump of a man who reminded Nervy of an iceberg. He was clearly on display as an imposing sign of security, but she thought he would probably move too slowly to catch anyone and only really represented danger if anyone were to crash into him.

"Do you all buy jewelry?" Nervy asked, trying a simple-ignorant approach.

"You got some?" the kid muttered, giving her an expressionless dull glance.

She dumped the Walmart bag upside down, creating a pile of bejeweled rings, necklaces, and bracelets on the dingy countertop. Basement boy looked down and never looked up.

"Mr. Brown," he hollered.

Mr. Brown quickly emerged from behind the blanket that served as a door to the back office. He was well over six feet tall, with a white Kangol cap atop his shaved head and a Gold's Gym T-shirt accenting his muscular shoulders and upper arms. Unlike the other two employees, he gave the appearance of intelligence, shrewdness, and danger.

He came to the counter, looked at Nervy, glanced at the pile of gold and gems, and then brought his gaze back to her, trying to fake disinterest.

"How may I help you?"

She took a breath to respond but then abruptly and repeatedly waved her hand and motioned to her earbud, signaling she had to deal with a call.

"Curtis, shut up." Looking right through Mr. Brown, she angrily and slowly continued, "There you go thinking like your dad again and you *know* how that worked out for him. Don't call me right now. I'll call you as soon as I'm done in the pawnshop." She focused her angry glare on Mr. Brown. Pausing and taking one more deliberate breath, she softened her glare and explained, "I'm managing an urgent problem for my kid today and I need to get as much money as I can really quick. I don't want my ex or my boyfriend to know about this. These beautiful items have belonged to me for many years, but I need to get my son out of Middleton today . . . I mean *today*, Mr. Brown."

"It will require some time to properly assess the actual value of these items," he mused aloud, looking pensively at the jewelry. Nervy figured he was trying to determine if he was facing an opportunity to exploit someone or if he was being exploited.

"Time is money," interjected Nervy impatiently. "Twenty-five hundred will give you plenty of room to profit from my distress. I *urgently* need to get me and Curtis and his brother rolling on back down to Dallas. Pick that stuff up and see for yourself—I'm offering you a good deal."

"Can you show proof of ownership?"

Nervy picked up two of the rings and placed them comfortably on her finger, showing that they fit her hand perfectly.

"I don't have receipts because they were gifts."

He pointed to the unique gold ring with the serpent's head and ruby eyes. It had been her daddy's and obviously wouldn't fit her finger. He formed an unmistakable question mark with his facial expressions.

"My daddy's, and he died unexpectedly last year. He don't need it no more!" She then exaggeratedly shook her head and with a disgusted look on her face resumed her phone conversation. "Dammit, Curtis, it is going to take at least another minute or two to finish up with Mr. Brown!"

Mr. Brown displayed a puzzled look as Nervy leaned across the counter and said, "Time's up! Twenty-five hundred, going once . . . going twice . . . ?" Brown began nodding his head but then surprised Nervy by telling his two associates to go get him breakfast and lock the door behind them because he was going to be busy with this transaction. As Brown reached under the counter, Nervy quickly put her hand in the convenience store bag and grabbed the .38 Special. She kept it in the bag and banged it down hard on the counter twice in quick succession, like a judge demanding order in the court, and immediately gained the attention of everyone involved. Mr. Brown slowly produced a moneybag and spiral notebook from under the counter and laid them both carefully next to the jewelry. Nervy spoke with intentionally heightened clarity to Mr. Iceberg and Basement Boy, "Mr. Brown just lost his appetite so breakfast is cancelled."

She then cocked her head, responding to another call from Curtis. "Shit!" she screamed, "What don't you understand, Curtis? Get your stuff in the suitcase and quit screwing around—no, you tell Cletus to stay right there 'cause I'll be there in five minutes and I don't want to go looking for him." Nervy then resumed eye contact with Brown and asked, "We about done?" Brown asked for ID as he counted out twenty-five hundred-dollar bills. "No ID!" she firmly countered.

"Name, home address?" he queried again.

"Ida Noe," she said sternly.

He squinted and stared at her.

"I-D-A-N-O-E!" she growled slowly, giving him time and hoping he would realize that she was losing patience.

"Address?"

"Thirty-eight Special Street."

He gave her an even more questioning look this time. "Wow," she thought, "Brown isn't all that smart after all."

"Thirty-eight Special," she repeated and motioned with her eyes for him to look at her concealed hand in the bag on the counter. Brown looked ever so puzzled. After another moment's pause he stood bolt upright and looked like a light had suddenly come on. Now fully understanding the nature of their conversation, he glanced back and forth nervously between her hand in the plastic bag and his notebook.

He pushed the pile of cash toward her.

"No, it would be more convenient for me if you would put it in the Walmart bag and then all three of you can escort me to the door. I find customer service to be very important in my pawnshop dealings."

Brown was now looking downright frightened and was fumbling in his attempt to get all the money into the bag quickly.

"Carefully!" Nervy demanded.

Brown managed to finish filling the moneybag and walked with it in front of her to the front door.

"Curtis, you idiot!" she exclaimed abrasively, resuming her conversation with her imaginary child. "I gave you that money to get gas for the trip to Dallas." She gestured angrily with her gun hand, still in the bag. She continued deriding Curtis and Cletus as she accepted the moneybag with her other hand from Mr. Brown while Iceberg held the door open for her in a most unexpected and gallant manner.

"I can't trust you to do a goddamned thing!" she ranted to Curtis, continuing down the sidewalk and around the corner of the building, escaping the surveillance camera's view.

Nervy tossed the glasses and hat in the dumpster as she passed and quickly made it to the car. She drove very calmly out the back exit of the furniture store parking lot and merged unnoticed into the late-morning traffic, becoming just another indistinguishable corpuscle flowing through the veins of Middleton.

Nervy was frustrated by how things had gone down in the pawnshop. She wasn't worried about the pawnshop calling the cops—they hadn't been taken advantage of and were going to make good selling her jewelry. But the experience had been a first. She had never had to force someone to pay her less than what her merchandise was worth. Having to raise tensions or threaten force made her uncomfortable. Seduction was much less dangerous because it didn't frighten people, whereas intimidation frightened people and made them more unpredictable.

Nervy caught the freeway west out of town and turned north, taking a leisurely drive home through the country on back roads. Reviewing her plans, she hoped liquidating the gold coins would be easier than today. She wasn't exactly sure where Walter had bought the coins, but it was somewhere around St. Louis. He brought them home after visiting his kids every month. Walter's divorce settlement with his first wife had cost him his entire savings. Recounting his experiences, he had explained to Nervy that he would never have a discoverable retirement account, savings account, or safe-deposit box ever again. He bought two pistols from a local gun shop and a plastic storage tub at Walmart. He started buying $50 US Gold Eagles with the money they had saved every time he was in St. Louis and stored them in the tub in the closet. Nervy was now reaping the benefit of Walter's plan, but she was going to have to hide the coins from the Adairs' malpractice settlement. No matter what the courts or the law said, she didn't owe them her financial security.

After she arrived home, she sealed the jewelry money in two layers of ziplock freezer bags and hid it under about six inches of rock salt for the driveway in a plastic five-gallon bucket that sat out in the garage.

CHAPTER 11

Wednesday morning found Nervy back at the office with Griff, working on charts and answering phone calls—if she felt like it after looking at the caller ID. There was really nothing she had to offer anybody in terms of psychiatric care anymore, except Jules. She wondered if he had called yesterday while she was in Middleton. If he had, she assumed her unavailability had just increased his eagerness to get hold of the promised script today. Throughout the years of his getting his medications from their office, Nervy had learned that if Jules was told that his next Valium prescription was ready, then he would be there to pick it up before the end of the day. Jules's thirty pills were supposed to last thirty days, but Nervy thought he usually used them up by twenty days, because that was when he would start calling the office to check if Dr. Corvus had written his refill yet. She wasn't sure if he called so much because he forgot he had already called or because he was trying to annoy her into asking Walter to refill his Valium early.

The door to the office opened and Nervy looked up, thinking the most likely visitor would be Jules. Instead she saw a medium-built man in overalls, lace-up work boots, a denim shirt, and a ball cap carrying a pie pan. "Woodrow?" she wondered aloud.

"Yeah, it's me. I'm surprised you know'd me 'cause the years haven't been too kind."

"Kind or not, I would have recognized you anywhere, but I am surprised seeing you here in my office."

"Well you're right to be surprised about that. I'm come 'cause Bertha made this here apple pie and ordered me to deliver it to ya so's you'd know you was on her mind a lot since Sunday."

"You drove all the way into town by yourself to bring me one of Bertha's apple pies?"

"No, me and her was comin' into town to go to Aldi's anyway and we stopped by here to drop this off." He held the pie a little higher.

"Did you leave her at the store?"

"No, she's right out in the parkin' lot waitin' for me in the truck."

"Well put that pie on the counter there and let's go out and say hi to her," Nervy scolded. Telling Griff to stay in the office, Nervy headed out the door. Despite an assortment of twenty or more cars, pickups, and SUVs scattered throughout the parking lot, there was no mistaking which vehicle Nervy expected to find Bertha in.

The red Ford was at least thirty years old, a half-ton farm truck with a black flatbed and a blue heeler in the back. It had to be the chariot holding the prophetess of Greenbriar. As she approached the truck, Nervy noticed that its exterior was textured with paintbrush marks from having been repainted by hand during its long and rugged life on the farm. She briskly finished the remaining distance to the truck's passenger door and greeted the eccentric and generous oracle. "Hello, Bertha. Thank you for the pie." Bertha was sitting stiffly upright in the passenger seat with both hands securing her large purse in her lap. She stared straight ahead, a pink scarf tied firmly on her head.

"Well, God's been putting you on my mind a lot lately, child. He says you been messin' with some dangerous ideas and dangerous people," Bertha proclaimed with prophetic condescension.

"Well, Bertha, I'm facing some hard times and I'm not sure what I'm supposed to do," Nervy responded defensively.

That made Bertha finally turn and face Nervy straight on. She tore into her. "Just because you don't know what to do doesn't mean you forgot what you're not supposed to do! You're waterin' weeds and they're gonna put down roots and you'll wind up the worse off." Bertha paused, then added, "I'm bringin' you a good old apple pie to remind you that you ain't alone—God's got me an' all of Greenbriar Assembly a-prayin' for ya."

"Well thank you again for it all," Nervy said. She tried to ratchet down the conversation to the immediate here and now and deflect its condemning tone. "What's your dog's name?"

"Number Three," Woodrow answered from behind Nervy as he joined the conversation.

"Number Three?"

"Number Three!"

"Because . . . ?" Nervy continued to inquire.

"Because she ain't my first dog and she ain't my second dog!" explained Woodrow, clearly exasperated at having to explain the self-evident.

"Blue heeler?" Nervy continued, trying to calm the tone of the conversation while she began a closer examination of the short, muscular, bristle-haired dog who maintained direct and unflinching eye contact, never lifting or moving its head a bit.

"Best and bravest bitch I ever seen!" Woodrow bragged. "Last week I sent her into a pen of three boar hogs and she had all three of 'em cornered together in about thirty seconds.

Held 'em there all by herself for five minutes. Fifty pounds of gutsy bitch scaring the shit out of seven hundred fifty pounds of meanness with three heads." Woodrow was cut short by Bertha, who had evidently heard enough and seemed satisfied she was done with her business here.

"Nervy, enjoy the pie. Them's good apples and God's been telling me that you only been around bad apples lately. Woodrow, time to go get the groceries and head back home." Without moving a hair, Number Three glanced back and forth between Nervy and Woodrow.

Nervy waved goodbye as they exited the parking lot, but she immediately lost interest in that truck as she saw the late-model Cadillac pull in. Jules wasn't bothering with the phone today; he was coming in person. Quickly thinking through the approach she would try on him, she settled on "secretary professional" because she didn't want to seem too eager. She walked halfway to his car and stood there observing him. As he stood and closed the Cadillac's door, she began a new appraisal of him as a prospective partner. She had never done that before, and if last Wednesday hadn't taken her husband she wouldn't have permitted herself to be looking at him the way she was on this Wednesday. He stood straight, with a dignified posture acquired as a lawyer and perfected as a judge. He exuded a slight aura of superiority, but it was not really alienating, because he remained as friendly and engaging as if he were still campaigning for office. Nervy had known him since she was a teenager, when her father brought him to their home as one of her "visitors." Throughout the years of their acquaintance, she had seen him attempt to display his superiority while so inebriated that he couldn't walk straight. Those experiences had forever protected her against his charm.

He looked financially prosperous, but she doubted that he had much money left, having gone through three divorces. Each one had successively reduced his remaining wealth by fifty percent. He put the best face on his divorces that he could, jokingly referring to himself as serially monogamous. His sense of humor could be enjoyable when he was sober because of his intelligence, but there was a tipping point associated directly with his use of alcohol that inverted his sense of humor and transformed his intelligence into a dark, sinister, destructive weapon. She had repeatedly seen him use it mercilessly.

Nearing her on the sidewalk, he appeared to be sober and in good spirits.

"Allow me to say how truly sorry I am for your loss. Dr. Corvus was a good man, and the marriage the two of you shared appeared beautiful to all who saw it."

So smooth, she noted to herself. As they walked into the building, their informal conversation flowed much too nonchalantly for Nervy's comfort.

CHAPTER 12

By the time Nervy and Jules reached the office, she had determined that he was completely sober and in full control of his faculties. She had hoped to find him at least partially inebriated and therefore more receptive to her advances. Her intentions were to entice him into a disadvantaged partnership where his incessant desire for controlled substances could be exploited by *her* provision of five more months of Valium using the blank prescriptions the late psychiatrist had signed. She had no strategy in place for the sober and intelligent retired lawyer who showed up.

She walked behind the counter as he remained on the patient side and noticed him look at the recently deposited apple pie.

"Where have you found the time to bake a pie in the midst of all you're going through?"

"It was a gift from a friend. They just dropped it off a moment ago. It's apple. Would you like a piece?"

"I'm a little confused. Are you going to begin my temptation with a variation on the biblical apple, or lead off with your womanly wiles, or go straight to the ever-so-effective offer of drugs to the addict?"

"They are all on the menu today," Nervy replied, deciding she had no choice but to go with the direct approach. "I have no idea about your tastes in apples, but as for sex, I've known your tastes since you used to come visit when I was a teen. I think you still sometimes show a taste for me. As for the drugs, I don't know if you lust for them more than me, but we might negotiate conditions where you wouldn't have to make a choice."

"Thank you for not being coy," Jules said. "I knew that Walter's death would activate your devious survival skills. I wondered who you would try to use first, and not so surprisingly it turned out to be me. Your call on Monday initially scared me, but when I thought about it I decided that we both know each other so well and have had our paths cross so many times that I would come and ask you if we could address your situation together in a direct conversation."

"Speaking directly, I need a new marriage where I can hide some assets, specifically gold coins I don't want discovered and taken as part of Walter's malpractice settlement. I need the security of a fixed address with familiar inhabitants whose price for partnership is affordable. I expect to pay the rent in currency of the landlord's choosing, but I would require that it be an exclusive closed system of exchange involving only myself and one other person. You would be my first choice, and honestly that was because I thought you were so hooked on the pills and maybe me that you could be seduced. There's my offer, but I'd be surprised if the sober you took me up on it."

"The sober me is the only one who would consider it, because the intoxicated me would be completely vulnerable to you and I don't believe that you would ever show me any mercy if I were. Surprisingly, I'm not only considering the offer but find myself flattered by it."

Feigning insult and rage to avoid being seen as too eager, Nervy seethed back at him, "How interesting that you accuse me of no mercy when it was you that repeatedly came to my house and paid my daddy to be able to strip me, fondle me, and rape me before I was even fifteen years old. You accuse me of wanting to take the first opportunity to exploit you, but I never mentioned your perversions to the court as you presided over my trial and sentenced me to five years in prison. Did I ever throw you under the bus? You've got quite the arrogance to assume I'm the predator of the two of us! You're the one who has entertained yourself with my scars, my vulnerability, and my mistakes ever since you first laid eyes on me when I was a girl." Nervy paused and collected her breath. "I'm not asking for a favor here. I'm making an offer to a preferred customer, so don't get too damned flattered."

"So why haven't you exposed me?" he asked, calmly accepting her observations of him.

"You didn't make me run drugs for Fatty. You weren't the first and certainly not the only 'visitor' daddy brought to the house. You didn't give me the maximum sentence or use my case as a backdrop for your Crime-Busting Judge reelection campaign. You're just another predator, higher on the food chain than me, and I learned how to stay alive in my particular location on the food chain a long time ago. Besides, I'm no narc. You and Fatty both know that."

"Explain some things to me," Jules interjected, hoping to stem her tirade. "You still have your daddy's farm and you could bury the gold out there where no one would ever find it. Why complicate things and risk the betrayal of someone like me by bringing the gold into a new marriage?"

"Because I don't want to have to worry about all the uncertainty and risk the possibility of harm transporting gold to hidden locations in the middle of nowhere. If I marry you and present you as the source of the gold instead of Walter, then it becomes your and my marital property and would be immune to the malpractice settlement. I'm more than willing to safeguard my gold by providing you with sex and drugs. I've been dealing in that kind of currency for a long time, and so have you," she reasoned.

"Well, let me *directly* tell you how I see myself as a prospective partner," Jules offered. "I have stage four prostate cancer, with a couple of years left. My male plumbing doesn't work for business or pleasure dependably. My only child despises me. I'm a known drunk with three ex-wives and very little money. On the plus side, I own my house outright and my car outright and get a decent social security check. I admit it, I still often think of engaging in sexual activity with you, but I have no desire to degrade you as I once did. I don't want to be seen or see myself as an abuser of women as I face the end of my life. I don't need money from you—I can afford to cover the routine expenses of daily life, including utilities, groceries, taxes, and the various insurances. I don't intend to let you get a life insurance policy on me or leave you my house in my will. With those off the table I would worry far less about your preference for me dead as opposed to alive. I haven't forgotten that the last two men you lived with died while they were sharing a house with you."

Nervy picked up the negotiations quickly. "You seem awfully concerned with Daddy's tragic death. I wasn't charged with anything, and I'm not going to take the blame for that. If that worries you, that's your problem. As for me, what I want is to be legally married. I keep my dog, he's permitted to be a house dog, and you help me shelter the gold that I don't want connected to Walter or his estate. I need you to specify in your will that I am the sole beneficiary of one hundred fifty gold coins that 'you have been collecting since shortly after your last divorce.' You can exclude anything else you want to with a prenuptial contract. The papers have to be drawn up by Raleigh Baggs and include stipulations that your will cannot be changed without my documented notification thirty or more days preceding such changes."

"Did you ever think of becoming a lawyer?"

The office fell quiet, but she smiled as she thought of her response the last time she was asked that question.

"So, tell me about the prescriptions."

"I have thirty blank prescriptions Walter signed before his death. Some of them were intended for you at your regular dose, but I haven't filled any out because I've been busy. I can fill them out for anybody and any substance of any dose I want; they just have to be dated before he died. The scripts are valid for six months from the date they are written."

"Aren't you the evil little temptress. I'm actually a little surprised that you reverted to your criminality so quickly amidst your grief. Don't you feel some guilt profiteering from the death of your husband?"

"What have you done with the Jules I used to know? Don't try to distract me! We are doing business, not therapy. My morality and mourning are my business, and I don't believe in or care about your concerns for my grief. Walter's dead. I'm alive. Walter is room temp and I'm feverishly desperate. Walter's gone to wherever, but I'm stuck in the here and now! If you're not interested, then move out of the way so I can find somebody that is. Are you on board or not?"

"Yes, I'm on board," he answered. "But I didn't know I had to leave my humanity at the door and ignore your loss."

"Drop the *humanity* bullshit. My 'humanity' never mattered to you or anybody else except Walter, and he copped out on me, so excuse me if 'humanity' is not part of our deliberations! I'm offering five one-month prescriptions of Valium. I write them so that you can only have a refill every twenty-eighth day, but the dose will be most generous—Walter gave you 30 per month; I'll give you 60 per month. I hold on to the scripts and release them to you one month at a time so that I remain *interesting* to you. We live together as husband and wife within sixty days from now, and sex comes with the deal at a frequency of your determination, as does cooking, housekeeping, and all the other little wifely things that I've learned the past several years. I'll provide you the first prescription tomorrow as a good faith deposit, and, to get our arrangement really rolling, I'm willing to show up at your place for 'entertainment' at a time of your choosing."

Jules raised his eyebrows and nodded his assent to her offer. He invited her to his house the next evening at 7:00 p.m. and told her he would prepare dinner.

CHAPTER 13

Thursday morning Nervy was already at the office with Griff and typing by 8:30 a.m. She was creating "addendums" for several specially selected patient records as part of her plans for life after Walter. This particular task had been on her to-do list since shortly after his first trial, and her intentions had been reinforced by her experience at the last trial. It was clear to her that the patients she observed during the jury selection phase of the last trial had no regard for Walter's professional vulnerability or appreciation for his commitment to their privacy and dignity while under his care. Initially, Nervy had admired Walter's caution in not including his patients' revelations in therapy of sexual fantasies, extramarital affairs, drug abuse, shady business dealings, etc., in their psychiatric records. He wanted to avoid his records being seen as tantalizing weapons for use by lawyers in divorces, custody disputes, and the like. Now, in retrospect, it was obvious to her that his sensitivity to the privacy of his patients had come back to bite him in the butt. "No good deed goes unpunished," she mused under her breath as she typed, "but maybe it can be avenged or leveraged."

Nervy wanted revenge for what had happened to Walter professionally, emotionally, and financially. She also wanted to punish a few patients she had met in her life before Walter for her own reasons. Selecting the records of people she felt had betrayed Walter during his trials or whom she thought shouldn't be shielded from their own iniquities, Nervy began amending their charts by adding repugnant but truthful details of their lives. Now, with the office closed, she had all the time in the world to change as many records as she wanted. Imagining that her ethics in these chart revisions would be questioned eventually, she planned to base her response on the rebuke that Mr. Shemp, the lawyer for the malpractice insurance company, had lodged against Walter about having too little detail in his patient histories. She was now correcting those deficiencies.

Her knowledge that Walter would not approve of her modification of his patients' records didn't stop her, but as a concession to her conscience, Nervy stopped short of forging his signature to the addendums. Instead, she clearly labeled these inclusions in the medical record as an "addendum" at the top of the page and indicated the actual date that she had written it. The first sentence in each one was a disclaimer clarifying that the information included in the addendum had been obtained by Dr. Corvus and provided to the secretary with instructions to prepare a document for placement in the patient chart to remedy historical deficiencies in the record. The disclaimer concluded with the explanation that Dr. Corvus had died before personally signing the addendum. Nervy placed her own signature at the bottom of each addendum.

Jules's was the first addendum she had written that morning. Her plan for his addendum had been to expose his perversions and addictions to a degree that it would humiliate his son, the judge she despised so much for the harm he had caused Walter. After she completed it and then reread the account of his abuse of her during her teen years, it dawned on Nervy that the tables between her and Jules were now turned. Actually, it was she who was exploiting him for her own reasons. She left his record untouched, still representing him as a lonely, alcoholic widower who frequently contacted the clinic seeking early refills on his monthly Valium prescription. Nervy's intuition was telling her that Jules wasn't her best path for getting even with his son.

Apart from her experience with Jules's record, writing the addendums was feeding Nervy's appetite for vengeance. Now she wanted the involved patients to know the extent of the information that was in their records. She wanted them to feel exposed and powerless just like she and Walter had. Nervy fantasized about sending people copies of their new "complete" records. She enjoyed the idea of their discomfort at seeing the embarrassing chapters of their lives fully documented. In answer to their imagined protestations she quoted Lanny's justification out loud: "It's legal!"

With Lanny now in mind, she decided that the next chart she would turn her attention to would be that of Martha, Lanny's live-in girlfriend for the last few years. Nervy assumed Lanny didn't know about Martha's ongoing blackmailed entrapment in sexual exploitation by her drug dealer. She also doubted that Lanny had any idea that Martha had been seeing Walter for therapy to help manage her traumatizing stress, drug dependence, and fear of losing Lanny. What was a sure bet was that Lanny would drop Martha like a hot potato if he caught wind of her secrets. He had divorced his first wife for far lesser indiscretions, which he had very publicly exposed and exploited during the unfolding of their scandalous divorce.

At 4:00 p.m. she decided to wind down and go home to get ready for her evening with Jules. Planning the evening, she had to accept the fact that she had much less control over him than she had expected. Equally surprising was that he hadn't seemed nearly as needy and dependent in their interactions yesterday as he had as a patient in the office. He made her feel uneasy with his mental faculties intact because when he was sober he was more skilled in deception than she had ever been. Lastly, she had to admit to herself that she was the needier of the two of them. Without Jules's physical and financial shelter, her next option was the drug trade, and there was no safe way to get back in. No one asked Fatty for work without being invited. Before prison, she had been his most trusted assistant. Her last job for him had been to help him ambush two new competitors. Together he and she had gunned them down and disposed of their bodies. She was arrested the next day and sent to prison on trumped-up charges trying to get her to roll over on Fatty. She never did, but she never heard from him again either.

CHAPTER 14

At home she took a shower and groomed herself very intentionally. Cosmetics, fragrances, and jewelry were all consciously selected for the way they complemented her apparel, as well as her body without apparel; she thought the latter to be the more important. Equal attention was given to her selections of lingerie and clothing. She opted for a dress because it gave her a feminine appearance and because she could unburden herself of it in a manner that was at once enticing and simple. The lingerie was selected for its express invitation to look and to touch. She assumed its removal would not be her problem.

As Nervy left home, she thought of running by the store to pick up a bottle of wine to bring in her role as appreciative guest. She also considered substituting a bottle of midpriced bourbon for the wine, since she knew her host's tastes. Ultimately, she opted to bring no alcohol because Jules would probably accuse her of trying to intoxicate him and then she would be on the defensive, which was the last thing she wanted. She did bring Griffin, though, because he was an essential part of her offer, and Jules might as well get used to that fact. She felt silly being as nervous as she was for their dinner. Intimate interactions with men as a business venture were something she had done for many years, before her life with Walter.

After parking her car, Nervy walked Griff to the door, which Jules opened before she even had a chance to knock. He greeted her by name, acknowledged Griffin with a non-critical glance, and stepped back in a welcoming manner. The house smelled slightly stale, which Nervy supposed was the product of an older man's housekeeping. There was also the smell of cooking meat. He was wearing dark casual slacks, a light-colored plaid button-up shirt that was tucked in, and loafers. The house was furnished comfortably with quality furniture representing upper-middle-class decor that had probably been trendy fifteen years earlier. She was surprised at his home's overall neatness, since she imagined him being inebriated nearly all the time. Jules headed toward the kitchen after closing the door. Nervy noticed that he was walking with a notably slow and deliberate gait, probably attempting to hide his slight imbalance from his afternoon's alcohol consumption and avoid stumbling. Mentally registering his impairment, she decided to start their evening pleasantly and not mention it.

"You have a nice home," she offered as a conversation starter.

"Thank you," he replied. "The furnishings are a little dated, but that reflects my third wife's passing several years ago. She had superb tastes in furnishings even if she settled for disappointing men. The place would be a little fresher if it were still under her influence, but a once-a-week housekeeper's involvement keeps things at an acceptable level for me."

"It looks better than I expected," Nervy said, deciding to keep her approach authentic. "The food smells delicious. Is that your doing?"

"Well, if I have my wits about me, I can practice a cooking philosophy that says quality ingredients cooked in a consistently simple manner result in good meals. Tonight we are having steaks broiled in the oven along with baked potatoes and seasoned green beans, all of which I can manage by myself."

"Dessert?" she asked.

"You're out of luck unless you are willing to settle for sandwich cookies or ice cream," he admitted apologetically.

"Or me," she interjected.

"Yes, or you," he muttered unenthusiastically, leaving her somewhat surprised and a little insulted. Without turning or making eye contact, he finished setting the table.

Pulling back the curtain on the back door window, she turned her gaze outside. "May I look outside at the backyard?" she asked, trying to restart friendly interaction.

"Yes, please do. It's not fenced, but I'm willing to put in a fence if that would be more suitable for your dog."

"You're very considerate. Thank you."

"You're welcome. How do you like your steak done?"

"Well done!" she said with emphasis.

"Ugh, the farm girl inside you is very much alive and well."

"I realize that confuses you, since you always liked your meat raw and tender," she rebutted.

"Okay, truce! This was your idea. Don't punish me for providing what you asked of me on terms you offered. I accepted without negotiation. Please have a seat," he requested, setting the steak and vegetables on the table.

Jules pulled her chair back from the table in a gentlemanly fashion, and once she was seated he proceeded to seat himself. The meal was good, actually better than Nervy had expected. No alcohol was served or mentioned.

"Would you like to sit on the back porch for a while?" he asked.

"Well that's your call," she said in a serious tone. "I think this is where it's your turn to begin clarifying what it is I can provide you. I brought a prescription if you would like me to make good on that part of my offer. As for the porch or the bedroom or the living room, that is all up to you—I'm game wherever."

"Wow! You didn't tell me you were going to punish me as part of the price. Does everything have to be so crass, so impersonal?"

"Okay, Jules, I hate to have to explain this to you—I don't care for you emotionally. Drunk old men who live their lives searching for their next prescription are not my thing! I'm not offering you love or closeness. I'm not interested in your redemption or apologies or search for peace at the end of your life. Last week I had the best life that I could have ever imagined ripped from my grasp. I hadn't thought of you for years as anything except a monthly annoyance at the office. Walter had transported me from a life in hell to a life of value and beauty, but then with no warning whatsoever he pitched me right back into my hell and split. So now I'm back in perv-town and tweaker-ville all by myself, trying to survive using my best skill set. You of all people know that I learned my role in hell before I even started high school. It seems I'm back at the beginning. The only difference is now I get to set the price and receive the payment instead of Daddy, so man up and place your order. Is it the regular?" She beckoned him patronizingly. Pushing her chair back from the table and standing up, she rested both of her forearms on the top of her head provocatively, feigning being tied up. She leaned forward at the hips just enough to accentuate her breasts and buttocks invitingly.

"Fuck you, Nervy!" protested Jules.

"Exactly, Jules! Atta boy! Where and how? Speak up!" she taunted.

"You hate me. I understand that, but can you see how much you hate yourself? If being your villain is part of the deal, then the deal with me is off. The only villains you have to choose from are Walter and yourself. Write the script for Valium, ten milligrams two times a day, leave it on the table, and get lost.

Your dog was better company than you. He managed not to soil himself or my carpet."

Nervy wrote the script angrily and slammed it down on the table, rattling the plates and silverware. She scooped up Griffin, shushing the grumble-growling he had begun during her scourge of their host. Jules had the door open for her by the time she had finished writing. Neither one said a word as she walked out. On the drive home, she wondered what had happened at dinner, why it had wound up the way it did. As she replayed the evening, she had the first glimmer of recognition that she was acting out her anger at Walter.

CHAPTER 15

The next morning Nervy returned to the office to resume her records additions. Her sleep the night before had been fitful, her mind continuously focused, whether asleep or awake, on the evening's conversation with Jules. She went to bed recognizing that even somewhat inebriated he had pegged her predicament and emotional response so accurately she couldn't deny it no matter how much she wanted to. Jules's role as a villain in her life had passed its expiration date—that role no longer really applied to him. Tormenting him at this stage in their lives really wasn't called for and could cost her the opportunities he offered.

After finishing a couple of addendums by 10:00 a.m., Nervy took a coffee break and was walking Griffin outside when the familiar Cadillac parked in front of the building. Wanting to avoid any interactions in public, Nervy walked into the office's back room, where she set Griffin on the floor and tried to collect herself, wondering what Jules was here for. He entered the office and waited patiently for her at the front desk.

She came out from the back room and greeted him with "Hey."

He paused for a minute and then asked, "Do you want the script back?"

She smelled alcohol on his breath and noted that he was wearing the same clothes as the night before.

"I don't know, why?" she countered calmly.

"I don't think this deal is going to work out," he explained.

"Look, last night went sideways and it was my fault, I'm sorry," she offered.

"That's your best apology?"

"Okay, the best I can do is admit that you understand me better than I do at this time. I didn't see what I was doing last night in terms of dumping anger on you that didn't belong there. My problem is I'm not seeing myself real clearly right now. I'm terrified, and I'm only beginning to see that I'm over-reacting. Let me make it clear that what I said about not wanting to be your love interest is completely true, but I am capable of keeping a promise to be consistently respectful."

"Thank you. That seems genuine, and I can only imagine the loss you felt for Walter. I don't want your love; it would be wasted. I have never reciprocated love in my entire life. I was never a man like Walter. Walter was a good man and a good doctor, and anybody who knew you knew that when you found him you found the antidote to all the previous poison of your life. I don't say that to impress you. I needed to say it to clarify for both of us that I know who I am and what I can and can't offer you. Do you want the script back?"

"No, keep it. I was going to string you along with these scripts, but when I look at that plan in the light of day it doesn't show any respect for Walter, me, or you," she explained, mainly for her own benefit. "Walter really did pre-sign some of these scripts for me to write for you, and if he had lived you would have continued receiving your usual amount. Why don't I just get the script issue off the table between us and write you five more scripts matching last night's? You can have them all.

Beyond that, if you want to try living together in a partnership, then great, we can try, but if it goes south, then we call it quits that very day."

"I'm willing to give a partnership a go under those circumstances," he said. "All the same stuff holds about the will, the coins, etc.?"

"Yes, with Raleigh writing the whole thing," Nervy replied.

"So, what keeps you at the office all the time nowadays?" Jules wondered aloud.

Nervy told him of her work adding the sordid details of people's lives to their psychiatric records.

"To what end?" Jules asked incredulously.

"To let them know they can be just as vulnerable as Walter was. His respect and dedication weren't valued by the community he diligently provided psychiatric care to for over two decades. The gratitude he got for his effort was the community and its courts repeatedly hoisting him up as a public spectacle and auctioning off his dignity and empathy to the highest bidder three times," she fumed.

"So how are you going to illuminate these people about the new additions to their psych records?" he asked, appearing worried.

"Mail them a copy," she boasted.

"Honest to God, Nervy, you are off the leash! You are going to get yourself killed. You don't get to mess with people's secrets for free. That is emotional torture—no, no, it's blackmail with no payment. You want to mind fuck whoever suits you in secret so you can sit back and entertain yourself with fantasies about how their vulnerability and shame will torment them the rest of their lives and that you unleashed it on them to avenge Walter. Even if you had the balls to pull off this blackmail, the best of criminals—which you aren't—can only manage one or two blackmail scams at a time. You can only rack up so many enemies at once and expect to survive. You—you're planning to take on a large part of a community."

"Well, what am I supposed to do with Walter's legacy, just forget about it? He loved me. I loved him. He changed my life for the better like no one else ever had and no one is left to defend him."

"What a crock!" he argued. "Your self-righteousness is unbelievable! Defending the dead must be some kind of award-winning paradox, but it is a completely inadequate reason to jeopardize your safety!"

"I can't do *nothing*. It's not in me. I loved him and I want vengeance for him!" she protested.

"Are you listening to the shit you're saying? I'm drunk, but even I can hear the lies you're telling yourself. Wake up! You're not doing anything for Walter or his legacy except using it as a lead pipe to assault the community and wreak havoc for the misery and shame you've endured all your life." They both paused to let the accusations and defenses settle in. After a moment's silence Jules resumed. "Right now I seriously have to take your anger and chaos into account. If you have to write addendums about the living to avenge the dead, then more power to you, but count me out if you start mailing this stuff and intimidating people. I want to die in my bed, not dangling at the end of some log chain down by the river."

Nervy was simultaneously incensed by his casual insensitivity and stunned by the implications of his comment. "You son of a bitch!" she shouted, trying to drown out the voice of reality that she desperately wished she hadn't heard.

"Hey, don't tell me you ever seriously thought that Walter's *suicide* was a suicide," he shouted back. "You knew him better than anybody, and even I could tell from my faraway vantage point that the way he died was completely at odds with the way he lived."

Nervy collapsed into her chair, having finally glimpsed what she had been using every shred of mental energy to avoid seeing. The possibility of murder surged like a lightning strike through the past week's confusion, doubt, and uncertainty. She immediately revised all of her theories of Walter's death. He wouldn't have wanted to ruin the riverside woods for her, he wouldn't have involved his beloved '51 Chevy pickup, and the brutality of using a log chain to hang himself was not consistent with his self-respecting, gentle character.

The likelihood of Walter's not having committed suicide provided an end to Nervy's distress that Walter's last act was a selfish abandonment of her. But as she realized he had been murdered, she was also realizing how deeply she had unknowingly sunk into the dangers of the criminal world she thought she had left behind. She was now frightfully aware of how far behind the power curve she was in preparing for the violence which was already stalking her.

Reacting to her sudden illumination, Nervy helplessly reached out to Jules with questions that begged for a partnership that they were still struggling to establish. "Who? Why? What's the payoff? Who wins what?" she stammered as the questions ricocheted around in her mind.

"Well, was he behind on debts to any major players?" Jules asked, sounding like his lawyer brain was kicking into action.

"He had nothing like that in his life at all," she answered.

"Are you?" he asked Nervy.

"Absolutely nothing," she replied calmly and convincingly.

"Anybody have any reason you know of to want to send you a signal or warning? Maybe from the past?"

"Nope," she replied.

"Well, the brutality of it all gives the appearance of retribution or a major warning. If that wasn't the reason, then that leaves us with simple undisguised brutality as the most likely," he reasoned.

"Yeah, but who?"

"It certainly seems to have been premeditated: bought a chain, had a location, had a method all thought out ahead of time. Seems to have been motivated by a lot of hate too. Any crazy patients from the past come to mind?"

"Not in the fifteen years I've been involved, and I open all the mail and answer all the phone calls. The biggest drama that I've witnessed is the Cindy Adair lawsuit, but they don't look like underworld-killer types to me." She paused. "But that sister . . . Candy . . . sure tried to glare holes through me at the trial. And she's a loose cannon, from what I'm told," she mused.

"I don't think that his hanging sounds like woman's work," Jules said.

"Women get plenty of work done that they don't have to do themselves if they got a bad man under their thumb. She got real dressed up for the trial, and even though that's the only place I've ever seen her, the tweaker in that girl showed right through the skirt and blouse. She's got plenty of access to plenty of crazy lawless manpower," she said, brooding over the possibilities that began opening up in her mind. "I hate to connect these things, but just the other day—on the walk home from the funeral—one of Fatty's up-and-coming recruits turned his pit bull loose on me and blamed me for Cindy's death because I didn't keep Walter on a chain."

"That's too spooky to be coincidence."

"Yeah, and I was so blinded by believing the whole suicide thing that the threat was wasted on me. Wow, I'm losing my edge," she admitted, trying to ignore the fear and rage taking root deep in her heart. Jules was standing straight up and staring unblinkingly at Nervy, letting the connection between the players sink in, with all its implied dangers.

"What's next?" he asked.

"First things first," she clarified. "Us? Are you up for being connected—married—to me in light of this? If you are, I want to move in tonight. If you're not, then it's been nice knowing you."

"This sense of danger is only new to you; I thought Walter's death was a homicide before you even called me about the scripts," he explained. "I've been willing to join you in your suggested partnership since day one. The issue for me isn't that there is an unexplained murder, but that you are so set on creating trouble or suffering for others, as if their pain would somehow lessen yours. If you'll quit weaponizing people's medical records and quit trying to torture me about our past, then I'm ready to let you move in."

CHAPTER 16

Agreeing with Jules's conditions, Nervy said she would meet him at his house at about 2:00 p.m. and asked to be able to pull into his garage to unload her belongings. With that decided, Jules left, and Nervy shut down her computer and headed home. Walking in the house, she felt twinges of sorrow and self-pity knowing that when she left again her relationship to this house and all that it had sheltered would never be the same. Nervy pursed her lips in an attempt to suppress those feelings, fearing they would deplete the strength she needed right now to turn a corner in her life and not look back. Refocusing, Nervy inventoried her reasons for leaving: she couldn't afford this house without Walter; she didn't want this house without Walter; she didn't need this house without Walter. What she needed was a hiding place, a hole to bolt to for safety while she was being hunted, and this house wasn't suitable.

After she had a bite of lunch, she loaded her car with what she needed to begin life at Jules's house. Finally arriving, she found the garage door invitingly open and his Cadillac parked obligingly in the street. She parked in the garage and paused, taking a deep breath, before she finally got out with her dog.

She pounded twice on the door to the house before letting herself in, not waiting for a reply. "After all," she told Griffin, "this is our place now too." Then she called loudly, "Hey, you here?"

"Yeah," came a reply from deeper in the house. Nervy went looking for the source of the voice and found Jules in the living room recliner watching TV with a half-emptied tumbler of ice cubes and whiskey sitting on the lamp table beside him. "I was beginning to wonder when you were coming," he offered.

"It took a while to grab the essential stuff and get it all in the car. Is there a room I can have?"

Jules cocked his head and made a questioning face as he processed the question. Nervy responded, "Look, your bedroom can be a destination for us as often as you request, but it's not going to be my primary living space. I want a place for my stuff and personal privacy."

"Okay, if you insist," he mumbled, putting the recliner footrest down and getting up. He escorted her to a guest bedroom that appeared to have not been inhabited for quite some time. "This is *your* room," he grumbled. With a slight but notable slur he inquired, "So, when might I get to start enjoying my benefits of our arrangement?"

"I thought you'd never ask." She turned and faced him, giving him her full attention. "Before or after I unpack the car?"

"Let's go to *my* room before you unload," he replied.

"Just let me close the garage door and I'll be right back. Pretty much all my life is in the car, and I'd be more relaxed if the door were down."

"Okay. Meet me in the living room. The button for the garage door is on the garage wall next to the kitchen door."

Returning to the living room, she found the TV had been turned off and Jules was sitting attentively upright in the recliner, sipping from the tumbler. "Shall we retire to the bedroom?" she invited.

"Let's don't," he commanded. "Let's begin here with you disrobing while I watch!" Nervy felt the situation was unfolding as she had expected. Without a word or a moment's hesitation, she reached down and grasped the hem of her shirt. She lifted it at a deliberately measured pace, progressively revealing her bare midriff, bra, chest, shoulders, and neck before finally lifting it over her head and dropping it on the floor. Next, she used each foot to nudge the shoe off the other foot and scooted the shoes next to the shirt. She then unbuckled her belt and her jeans in one continuous action. Slowly she unzipped and opened the front of her jeans, then slid both hands around her hips on the inside of her jeans, freeing them to submit to the pull of gravity. With the jeans in a crumpled pile around her feet, Nervy was able to step out of them.

She reached behind her back for the clasp of her bra and Jules interjected. "*No*, I'll finish. Come over here and stand closer." Nervy moved toward him and waited calmly until he clumsily released the clasp after three or four attempts. After he removed her panties, he informed her he would follow her into the bedroom. She went ahead, providing the implied entertainment of walking naked for his viewing. Once in the bedroom, she undressed him as he demanded and lay down beside him on his bed. She was aware that her scars didn't surprise him, since he had gained familiarity with them years ago. Instead she was the one who was surprised by what she saw. Jules had no erection. Avoiding a giggle, which could be disastrous, she decided to let sleeping dogs lie and see what came up.

After a moment, Jules gruffly urged her in a matter-of-fact voice, "So surprise me."

"Do you have any oil or lotion?" she asked.

"No," he said flatly.

"Well, I would suggest Mazola then."

"Who?"

"Mazola, canola—either of those ladies will work in a pinch!"

"You gonna fry me?" he asked, feigning alarm.

"I was going to begin with a generous basting, then play it from there—unless you want to continue getting pickled."

Jules rolled over and looked at her. "In the cupboard on the right side of the exhaust hood over the stove." Nervy got up and retrieved the oil.

"I couldn't find the fork or the spatula," she said apologetically. Jules smiled weakly and rolled onto his back. After the application of canola oil and a series of massages and caresses with various parts of her anatomy, Nervy received the signal from Jules that her first rent payment was satisfactory.

Nervy showered without the luxury of her own soap or shampoo in a bathroom that was unfamiliar. After putting on the same clothes for the second time that day, she started unloading her car. Jules refilled the tumbler and returned to the recliner. After bringing in all the items she needed and putting the salt bucket in the garage, she went into the living room and sat on the couch. "I need to tell you a few boundaries that I have," she said, overpowering the TV volume.

"Fire away."

"Number one: Turn down the TV while I'm talking to you."

Jules obliged without hesitation.

"Don't mess with my dirty clothes, don't mess with my ironing, don't look into or open closed boxes or containers. If you have a question, ask me. Don't go through my stuff. I put a plastic bucket of driveway deicer salt in your garage. Don't throw it away or mess with it."

"Sounds easy to me. Is that all?"

"Yeah," she assured him.

"Will you show me the same respect?"

"Yep. Can I move stuff around in your garage so that there is room for us to keep both of our cars in there? It would make my presence a little less conspicuous and make me feel a little more secure."

"Knock yourself out," he offered passively.

"Can I ask how much Elijah Craig bourbon you go through a day?"

"No!" he responded less passively.

"May I set up an appointment with Raleigh for us to talk to him together about the prenup and the will?"

"Yeah, any time works for me."

"Do you have any guns here?"

"I feel safer with you not knowing for sure."

"Okay . . ." she responded, a little unsure of the implications of his answer.

"Do you?" he asked.

"Absolutely. More than one!"

"You're a felon," he observed.

"Yes, and fully armed. One who will fully protect herself as she deems necessary. Do you intend for me to do all the cooking or do you want to share it?" she continued.

"I'll pay for the groceries, and you can go to the store and do the shopping and then do the cooking. Ask for help as you think you need it. Try to be careful about the amount of noise you make of a morning. I'm usually a late sleeper and hung over for an hour or two after I do wake up. Your dog seems like a reasonable creature, but he's your responsibility, and I wish no involvement with him at all."

The afternoon continued in meaningful negotiations and clarifications as the new co-travelers accustomed themselves to each other and their arrangement. Supper found Nervy familiarizing herself with the appliances, utensils, dinnerware, and cooking supplies—and lack thereof—in Jules's kitchen.

CHAPTER 17

This was as cold a mid-November as Nervy could remember and she felt that it was mirroring a lot of the adversity that she was immersed in emotionally. For his part during their two months together, Jules had fully followed through on their agreements. He secured a safe-deposit box at the local bank and placed the 150 gold coins safely inside. Nervy's name had been included on the contract so she could have free and equal access to the box. In fact, he gave her both keys to the box so that she would know he wasn't going to abscond with the coins she valued so much. After their first month together, Jules had settled into an alcoholic routine of consuming two fifths of Elijah Craig bourbon every three days. This schedule produced a perpetual buzz and profound apathy. Any expectation that he might have any interest in or concern for something other than himself elicited immediate defiance, which Nervy learned was best to avoid if possible. In the course of her various domestic chores, she had discovered that he kept a 9mm Glock in the drawer of his bedside table. She didn't mind his having a gun and figured that his intoxication would compromise his effective use of the weapon if he even remembered he owned it.

Drafting their prenuptial contract and his new will had turned into a battle with Raleigh. He was overtly hostile toward Jules and vigorously challenged Nervy's plan to marry him. After much back-and-forth squabbling, he eventually complied with their requests and, two revisions later, finally drafted the requested documents to Nervy's satisfaction. The process had taken so long that Raleigh had only filed the documents with the court a week ago. Jules immediately contacted a fellow judge and longtime friend in Middleton and asked if they could stop by that afternoon for him to officiate their vows. Just for old times' sake, Mazola was invited to the honeymoon in a motel in Middleton.

As Nervy's relationship with Jules was consolidating, her remaining connections with Walter were fraying. The state coroner ruled Walter's death a suicide, opening the door for Nervy to ask for the hundred-thousand-dollar life insurance policy he had maintained. His personal belongings that had been held as evidence by the police department pending the coroner's finding were released back to Nervy. She had expected the return of his clothing, cell phone, and vintage pickup but had been shocked that they included the chain that he had been found hanging from.

Besides managing the stress of husband transitions, Nervy continued to accumulate additional disappointments. The first was a subpoena requiring her to testify at a discovery deposition scheduled in Lanny's office. Even though they had already collected three million dollars in out-of-court settlements from the other suits connected to Cindy's death, she was being personally sued by the Adairs, who were seeking money they thought she was hiding from them. No doubt she owed them the title to the restored pickup, but she decided to throw in the deed to the house to boot. Although she wasn't obligated by law to surrender her home, she hoped doing so would appease them enough that they would leave her alone, and maybe even satisfy the killer hunting her. Giving them the house was not really the sacrifice for her that it appeared. She had absolutely no desire to keep it—that chapter of her life was over.

The second disappointment occurred when she went to the social security office to sign up for Walter's survivor benefits. The benefits counselor informed her that she had been eligible to receive Walter's social security benefits, but because she had remarried before she turned sixty years old she had forfeited her right to ever receive them. Devastated, she immediately inquired about her rights to Jules's social security. She was told they would have to be married at least nine months before he died and that she would have to be sixty years old before she could begin collecting his benefits.

Yesterday had delivered her third disappointment. Nervy had stopped by her and Walter's house to retrieve the deed to the house and the title to the truck to turn over to the Adairs at the deposition meeting. When she opened the garage door, she found the contents of the garage to be wildly scattered about. She parked in the driveway, then walked with Griff into the garage and put the door down. Once beyond any of the neighbors' prying eyes, she took her gun out of her purse and set Griff free to roam at will. She and her canine companion examined the chaotic garage quickly before turning their attention to the house. They worked their way room by room as a team, searching for any imminent danger, and found none. The disarray they did find throughout the house was overwhelming, exceeding anything that a law-enforcement or even burglary search would have created. It had been a rampage, an exaggerated nonverbal tantrum denouncing reason and refusing negotiation. It had been the rape of a home left to be found in its debauched misery. Nervy was not surprised she found the deed and the title in their respective locations unmolested. Unfortunately, she wasn't able to say the same for her clothing. All her garments had been strewn about the house and defaced. After she examined the first blouse she picked up and registered the red marker scrawling of "bitch," "slut," and "cunt" amid the various slashes that adorned it, she decided to forego close inspection of any of her other clothing.

"Message received!" she said. She called to Griff and proceeded to the garage. Getting back into her car, she thought of how the storm she had been anticipating was closing in on her quickly.

Nervy's departure was blocked by the arrival and precise positioning of a red flatbed farm truck with an uncannily motionless blue heeler in the shade just behind the cab.

"What the hell, Griff! If it's not one thing it's two!" Nervy uttered far too loudly. She stayed in her car as an act of defiance and to show her rejection of any moralizing missives. The standoff lasted three or four minutes until, exasperated, Nervy got out of her car and walked back toward the vehicle. The heeler's astute eyes followed her without her head moving a bit. When Nervy finally reached the truck, she asked the woman with a sky-blue scarf tied over her head, "What do you want, and why did you come here? Your timing is unbelievable. Do you have radar or something? Is this about another pie? Is it peach season?"

"I know you don't want me involved in your affairs, but God keeps running a picture show of your life through my mind," Bertha answered, about as sensitively as Nervy had ever heard her speak.

"Well, I feel sorry for you—that really has to suck!" Nervy shot back.

"He told me to meet you here today and tell you to be certain how you want to walk your path—"

"Yeah, do what's right, be good, blah, blah, blah. Why don't you tell me exactly what doing right is, because it seems to be escaping me right now?"

"Don't fight fear with hate or falsehood! Don't hold Satan's hand to get out of the ditch! Listen to your momma's voice—I know she's still there in the back of that scared mind of yours. God put her there!"

"God!!!" Nervy screamed back. "God. Why don't you just leave me alone and tell God to cut me some slack . . . please?"

Nervy turned to walk away, but Bertha continued, talking to Nervy's back. "Nervy, you're so busy protecting yourself that you're forgetting to love and value your own self, and you're trying to chase off anybody that tries to."

With her message delivered, Bertha motioned to Woodrow to pull away from the driveway and head to their next destination. Nervy made it back to her car and closed the door before she released the sobs that were being wrung out of her by anger, fear, and sorrow. Griff climbed into her lap and stayed there until she regained her composure twenty minutes later. At that point Nervy hugged her faithful terrier and redirected him back to his place in the passenger seat. Then they drove to Jules's house.

Nervy didn't bother to tell Jules about the events of the afternoon but retreated to her room. Late in the afternoon she did tell him she was nervous about her pending deposition and had no appetite. She said he could fix any supper he wanted, but she wasn't cooking. She then spent the evening obsessing about how events might unfold in court and couldn't escape a feeling of impending doom that she blamed Bertha for. She repeatedly wondered how Bertha had shown up at her house at just that time.

"Man, you can't write this stuff," she muttered aloud to Griff as she began getting ready for bed. He wagged his tail at the first sign of her attention in over two hours.

CHAPTER 18

After an excruciatingly fitful night slipping in and out of sleep, Nervy got out of bed the next day. She had no concern for her attire or grooming for the deposition. There was no fight to take to the hearing today, no sense of anything to lose. This was just another station on her personal Via Dolorosa, and she was going to bring her own special cross to the hearing because it was so fitting.

Drinking her morning coffee, she revisited a new strategy for her life that had come to her during the night. Instead of trying to be somebody or something that would be of recognized value to herself or anyone else, she would attempt *being nothing*. Nothing for anyone to attack, nothing for anyone to fear, nothing for anyone to loot or pilfer—this would be her new strategy. Today she would go to the deposition, surrender the title to the house and pickup, and give the Adairs the remaining joint property she had owned with Walter. Practicing this new outlook, she decided she didn't need breakfast because she didn't need the energy. With a look at her coffee cup, she conceded that caffeine would be required for the new life in order to maintain wakefulness.

After dropping Griff off at Susie's spa, she arrived at Lanny's office and parked as close to the door as she could to save herself the trouble of worrying about whom she might wind up parking next to. Today everybody here would be hostile and hateful. Nervy got out of the car and opened the trunk. She paused, summoning her maximum strength to lift out the heavy-duty canvas tote bag she had placed in the trunk the night before. After lifting and tugging her bag out of the trunk, she set it on the ground and caught her breath. She lugged it to the front door of the lawyer's office and carried it into the waiting room. She was greeted with an emotionally cool but professional attitude by the secretary, who asked if she was going to be represented by Raleigh today. Nervy informed her equally calmly that she would be present without legal representation.

"Well then, why don't I have you wait with the others, and Mr. Peltor will join you all in a moment?" the secretary said, motioning Nervy to follow her to the conference room where the deposition would be taken. Nervy was ushered into a room with five people already sitting around an imposing wood-grained conference table. The door closed with an authoritative thud that Nervy barely registered as she began identifying each of the room's occupants. An unknown individual surrounded by recording equipment was in the corner of the room—obviously the court recorder. Then there was Mr. Adair, followed by Mrs. Adair, Candy Adair, and Cooker Grant. Suddenly Nervy's intended nihilistic persona completely vanished.

Seeing Cooker there provided Nervy all the verification she needed to finally know who had killed Walter and was hunting her. Empowered by her new certainty, Nervy picked a chair in the middle of the opposite side of the table, directly across from the Adair gathering. She carefully set her bag on the floor and took her seat all alone. "Good morning, Adairs," she announced clearly. "And to you too, Killer," she announced equally calmly, staring a hole through the incarnate evil sitting there in a flannel shirt.

"Fuck you, bitch!" he seethed back at her.

"Candy, are you and Mr. Killer exclusive, or would you let him have me as he is suggesting?" she said, turning her direct inquiring gaze to the young woman. The whole family seemed stunned by the unexpected assault on their collective dignity. Capitalizing upon their silence, Nervy continued her interrogation. "He does belong to you, doesn't he, Candy? Why else would he be here?" It was more of a statement than an actual question. "Did you bring your little doggie, Meth, today too? I didn't know you two were separable." She turned her attention back to Cooker, who had pushed his chair back from the table and was standing up, obviously contemplating coming at her over the top of the table. "Mr. Adair, your team doesn't seem to want to wait on the bench until the ref gets here," she said matter-of-factly, still eyeing Cooker.

"I'm not going to dignify your chatter, Mrs. Corvus. I didn't come here to talk to you; I came here for some answers from you." Mr. Adair was doing his best to seem disdainful but appeared clearly uncomfortable being the one impugned in the legal processes he had set in motion.

"Well your guest here today, Mr. Killer, and I met on the day of my husband's funeral as I walked home. He turned his pit bull loose on me and then called him off at the last minute, telling me that I should have kept Dr. Corvus on 'a chain'—did you get that part Mr. Adair, on a chain?—and if I had, Cindy wouldn't have gotten hurt. Did you give him that message yourself or did you leave him to improvise in his own criminal fashion? He also spoke of his girlfriend and her children, so, Candy dear, if you don't have at least a couple of kids, then you need to know Killer here has a girlfriend besides you. Now comes that part that I hate to tell you but I must. Whether you already knew that Cooker was a killer or not I don't know but now that I've told you that he is your lives are all in danger! He is not the kind of man that will let anyone live if they know of his killing. He would willingly murder anyone of you or me to avoid being arrested. Turning back to Cooker, she cocked her head and demanded, "By the way, how did you really kill Walter, and who helped you hang the body in the tree?"

At that moment Lanny walked into the room. As he joined the assembled group in his opulent conference room, he offered a general, somewhat overly familiar greeting given the adversarial composition of those gathered and then followed with overly ingratiating apologies for his delay. He recounted having gotten home very late last night from an important court session down at the state capitol. He laid his designer leather briefcase on the table and took off his silk suit jacket, hanging it over the back of his rolling wingback leather chair as he went on to further justify accidentally sleeping past the alarm. He then rolled his chair to the prearranged space that joined him with the collection of the Adair-related attendees confronting her from across the table. Nervy noted that his was the only wingback chair, and it was slightly taller than all the others. Lanny then asked the court recorder to have Nervy swear to tell the truth, which the court recorder promptly and monotonously did. He then began talking in generalities about the hardships of the Adair family as he rolled up his shirtsleeves to his mid-forearms. Lanny then leaned forward, clasping his hands together as he placed his elbows on the table, striking what appeared to be the most earnest of human postures.

Lanny looked Nervy directly in the eyes and asked in a practiced hushed and solemn tone, "Mrs. Corvus, do you understand the gravity of the circumstances that demand today's deposition?"

Nervy seized the unexpected moment and responded with a solemnity fully matching Lanny's. She leaned toward him, placing her elbows on the table and clasping her hands, and said, "I'm not Mrs. Corvus."

CHAPTER 19

Lanny leaned back in his chair, appearing to have no comprehension yet of what he had inadvertently stepped into, and in a self-righteous voice loudly demanded, "May I remind you that this is a deposition to be used in an important court proceeding seeking the legal rights of this bereaved family and that you just swore to tell us the truth, Mrs. Corvus?"

"My name is Minerva Tucker," Nervy replied calmly. "My new husband, Jules, and I have been married a week today." She was satisfied that her answer was having the desired effect on Lanny as she watched him awaken to the implications of this new information.

"Are you telling us that retired judge Jules Tucker is your new husband?" Lanny asked.

"Yes," she answered, "father of Judge Justin Tucker, who I believe is a very close friend of yours."

"Is Judge Justin Tucker aware of this *marriage*?" Lanny asked insultingly.

"Are you soliciting hearsay evidence, Mr. Peltor? I don't know what Justin Tucker knows about my marriage, and I didn't know that my statements about other people's knowledge or understanding of things were admissible in courts in Missouri."

"Well, this unexpected change of circumstances overrules any further meaningful proceeding in this case until Judge Justin Tucker's suitability as a judge in this case is determined," Lanny opined. "There is no need to continue this meeting. Thank you for your attendance, everyone. You are dismissed."

Nervy cleared her throat loudly and then suggested they could still use the time productively in regard to the monetary damages that had been awarded to the Adair family. She said that she had come prepared and intending to surrender deeds and titles to valuable property as part of her obligations in that settlement. Mr. Adair looked questioningly at Lanny, who motioned the court recorder to go ahead and leave. As the recorder was closing the door behind himself, Lanny resumed control over the conversation. "Tell us more, Mrs. Tucker."

"I have brought the deed to Dr. Corvus's and my former home to surrender for partial payment of the award. I have also brought the title to the restored 1951 pickup that belonged to Dr. Corvus," she said as she dug both documents from her bag and pushed them across the table toward Lanny. "But I also wish to make a statement to this family in follow-up to what I was beginning to say when you walked into the room, Mr. Peltor. Cindy's death was a tragedy, but it was not Walter's fault. I don't begrudge you Adairs your sorrow, but Mr. Peltor exploited your grief for money, and you were foolish and confused enough to follow him into the charade of a trial that was staged in Judge Justin Tucker's courtroom."

Mr. Adair leaned toward Lanny and motioned that he wanted Nervy to be silenced and dismissed, in response to which Lanny started to address Nervy, but she proceeded and cut him off by raising her voice. "In the blind rage of her sense of vengeance, Candy, on behalf of all of you, incited this drug-fueled killer to murder my husband, who was guilty of nothing more than trying to help your emotionally troubled daughter. The actions of all of you resulted in my good and gentle husband being repaid for his concern with the vicious placement of a log chain around his neck and being hanged from a tree down by the river, where he had gone to take a walk. He was left to dangle, swinging and struggling his way through a slow, cruel, suffocating death."

By this point Nervy was tearful and fueled with adrenaline, which she effectively utilized by hoisting the heavy tote bag from the floor. With a deafening clatter, she poured out the twenty feet of log chain on the enormous wooden conference table. "This is the last 'Corvus property' that you will voluntarily receive from me. Trust me when I tell you that I believe this single piece of property is the only thing that the court should have awarded you, because it is the one item which you truly deserve to have! In closing, let me warn you again that the killer in your midst will not spare any of your lives when he begins feeling afraid of getting caught. If you don't think he is the murderer of Walter, go see if this isn't the identical chain that his dog is secured with outside his drug house." And with that she stormed out of the room.

After picking up Griff and going back home to Jules's house, she parked in the garage and went into the house carrying her dog. Hollering so as to be heard throughout the house, she called out to Jules, "Okay, so how did you keep our marriage licenses from being public knowledge down at the courthouse? Lanny was completely clueless today! Justin must not know yet either."

There was a thirty-second silence and a sleepy-sounding voice called back, "I have a few favors still owed me at the courthouse, and maybe even an old friend or two."

"Well, even old dogs can surprise you with their old tricks," Nervy hollered back.

"Well, I've been short on surprises myself lately. Why don't you get naked and come back here and surprise me?"

"Be there in a minute." She reached into the cabinet next to the stove. "Let me get Mazie so we can have our usual threesome."

After supper was over, Jules was watching TV and Nervy was cleaning up the kitchen and putting away the washed dishes when she was struck with an awareness of a new but unwanted obligation. Now that she was sure that Cooker was Walter's killer, she had to find out directly if he had killed Walter with Fatty's sanction or not. If Fatty sanctioned the murder, then she would have to ask if he had further intentions for harming her as well. If he hadn't sanctioned it, then she would ask why Cooker was remaining alive and unpunished. The gnawing reluctance she had about talking to Fatty was that she would have to go onto his turf to talk to him. He was dangerous, his office was dangerous, and she hated going past the mental milepost that having to talk to him in person represented in terms of how far she had sunk back into her old life. Like it or not, she needed to get her questions answered, and the sooner the better. She decided to go out the next day.

CHAPTER 20

Saturday morning was cold enough to be classified as a "hard freeze" by the weather service. Nervy was glad because the last few miles to Fatty's place were dirt roads—no gravel, no pavement. If the roads were muddy, there was no "bottom" to the road, and your car could easily get stuck in the mud up to the axles. A hard freeze meant no danger of getting stuck.

While fixing her requisite two cups of coffee, scrambled eggs, and toast, she formulated her plans for the day's meeting. She would definitely take her cell phone with her today so that her travel would be tracked as far as the cell towers reached on the way out to Fatty's. She would also take the .38 Special but would surrender it to one of his henchmen before she could see him. It would be given back on her way out with the bullets removed. Informing Jules about her trip would serve no purpose; if Fatty had her killed, Jules couldn't intervene and shouldn't. Griff could go along because she could use the company on the drive out and back, if there was a drive back. "Besides," she thought, "if they kill me they will kill my dog too, and then all my affairs that really matter would be in order and over." She was gone by 9:00 a.m. The drive to Fatty's place was essentially the same one as to Greenbriar church, except he was on a road that turned off two miles before the church.

The closer she got to the salvage yard where Fatty did business, the more deeply rutted and scarred the dirt road became. The salvage yard was the site for several operations—making and distributing meth was just one of them. Fatty also bought semitrailers of wrecked cars from insurance companies out of Kansas City. Occasionally a truck would come from St. Louis or Chicago with stolen cars to be traded for drugs. All the cars got chopped into parts that were channeled back into the car parts market. The delivery trucks were too heavy for the dirt roads to support, so over time and subject to the weather the roads surrendered to the trucks' overbearing weight and were compressed into dirt trails scarred by four- to eight-inch-deep ruts.

Nervy was now within a mile of Fatty's hideout, and her memory told her she was in binocular range of the sniper posted in the barn loft. When she arrived at the welded pipe gate blocking Fatty's driveway, a heavily bearded man in jeans and a denim jacket was waiting at the gate with a walkie-talkie held in front of his mouth while he waited to see if she would stop. When she did, he motioned her to roll down her window and hollered, asking what she wanted.

"Tell Fatty that Nervy wants to talk to him," she hollered back. Further explanations at the entrance to the compound would make things worse; Fatty would make his own decision for his own reasons, and your explanation just made you more suspicious by the syllable. The redneck talked into his walkie-talkie and then grabbed the gate and walked backward, an invitation for Nervy to enter. He offered her no further greeting and leaned down, squinting, to examine her and the inside of her car as much as he could while she drove past. Nervy approached the house and parked among the half-dozen four-wheel-drive pickups, all with custom high-lift suspensions and oversized tires, giving them the clearance to cover uneven terrain whether on the road or off. The modifications made the trucks high enough that the bottoms of their doors were about the height of the bottom of her car doors' windows. All of the trucks also had brush-buster bumpers, which were imposing metal frameworks on the front of the trucks made of welded heavy-gauge metal pipe that would protect the truck's radiator and engine from weeds, saplings, animals, or people in the truck's path. She left Griff grumble-growling about her departure from the car and walked up the porch steps, where another bearded one stood blocking further passage. She handed him the .38 Special and told him it was all she had. He then let her pass, which Nervy understood as an indication that Fatty had instructed them not to hassle her.

Nervy walked in through the filthy antique door with plywood nailed onto it where an oval of frosted glass had once graced the home's entrance. Fatty was sitting behind a desk about ten feet to the right of the front door. He was already awaiting her arrival, leaning back in his chair as far as it could tolerate his exaggerated mass.

"What interest would a fine doctor's wife have in a salvage yard?" he asked Nervy with a sort of familiar and taunting tone.

"Fats, I'm a doctor's widow and we both know who killed him," she answered without hesitation or apology.

"Only my friends call me Fats."

"Three and a half years in prison earned me the privilege to call you anything I want to, *Fats*. The task force offered me probation and witness protection for any info on the McCullum boys' bodies, and they never got squat out of me."

"Well, I knew we'd have this meeting sooner or later after you went down to my pawnshop in Middleton. Selling off all that jewelry for so cheap was a sure sign of desperation," he told her, revealing more information than she had ever imagined he could have.

"So that's your place. I should have known, with a name like Smithson. You looking to get out of salvage and drugs?"

"Nope. Pawnshops give me a window on the activity of other criminals—like you," Fatty explained.

"Your man Brown didn't seem all that bright," she offered.

"Well you scared the shit out of him, banging your gun on the counter and all that foolishness. You made him a juicy offer, and he doesn't have my permission to make juicy deals without checking with me. You nearly had everybody in there crapping their pants. You still got your bad-girl shit working!"

"So how did you figure out it was me?"

"Your daddy's ring. My daddy always liked it," he explained.

"They were both first-class assholes."

"Enough small talk. Why are you here?"

"Cooker killed my husband. If you gave him permission, you owed me more than that, but I don't think that's how it went down. I think Cooker is off your leash and you need to bury him."

"I won't touch him. He's kinfolk, my brother's kid. You know I always stick up for family."

"Well, I *had* family and he took it away from me. He *is* gonna pay for Walter's murder!"

"You sure you want to say that to me right here and right now?" he replied, narrowing his eyes and focusing a glare directly at her.

"You need to fry Cooker! If you don't, you'll look pretty weak when I go and kill your blood right under your nose."

The meeting was over. Nervy turned and walked back onto the porch. Once outside, she held her hand out to Mr. Whiskers and received her revolver and a handful of loose .38-caliber bullets, which she put in her coat pocket to deal with later.

Back in the car with Griff, she maneuvered out from between the big pickups and headed for the gatekeeper and the road beyond.

"Well, boy, that went like shit. There was no way it was going down different. If I'd pretended I understood he had to leave Cooker alive, he'd have seen I was lying. It's game on now."

She assumed Fatty had left her alone all these years due to her silence in prison, but as of today, that was over. Their last chapter had begun, and Fatty would end it quickly. He had dealt with the McCullums the very next day after he heard they were in business.

The immediacy of her peril demanded a plan. Being at home with Jules would not sharpen her thinking, so she decided to spend time alone and drive past her old home place since she was this close. She reasoned that maybe stirring up old memories would awaken some of her childhood survival instincts to assist with today's dilemma.

The road stretched on cold and lonely and further than she remembered, but eventually she arrived at the site of her old home. Having not been by here since she married Walter, she only recognized the place because the old garage was still standing. It was fifty feet back from the road and looked lonely standing there a few feet from a cinder-block foundation outlining a cluster of weeds and saplings growing from a bed of ashes left from her family's house. When she reached the driveway, she was disappointed to find the fence she had placed across it years ago was now just a tangle of wires among the brown and broken winter weed stems beside the road. It had been knocked down and repeatedly driven over by trespassers gaining access to her garage. The wooden pole for the driveway light still had an electrical line running from the transformer at the road and still supported the light fixture, but the bulb had been shot out, leaving a few glass shards protruding from the socket.

Nervy parked her car outside the fallen fence. She opened the door and both she and Griff got out. Being quite agile, he maneuvered over the tangle of weeds and fallen fence wire more quickly than Nervy; she finally caught up to him at the garage, where he had begun exploring. Beginning her own exploration, she found the side door of the garage had a ragged hole where the knob had been removed by a shotgun blast. The door stood partially ajar, and she nudged it open with her toe enough to slip in. Inside, the garage had a noxious chemical smell that told her the shelter had been used for making meth within the past week or two. Other evidence included pseudo-ephedrine boxes and foil wrappers, lithium battery wrappers, and Coleman stove fuel cans. Surveying the floor and walls, she saw that there was nothing of value left in the garage. "If this is how it was being used," she thought, "then maybe the property would be better off with no structures at all." Griff left the garage after a couple of minutes and went back outside to track vermin trails he discovered along the outside of the garage and around the foundation of the former house. Nervy followed him, carefully circling the shallow foundation.

The sound of an approaching vehicle snapped her attention back to the present; whoever had been cooking meth here could very well be showing back up to cook more. Realizing that she had never reloaded her .38 Special, Nervy reached into her coat pocket and fumbled with the revolver and loose bullets, doubting that she would be able to have the gun fully loaded by the time the car arrived. At least thirty yards from her car, she wouldn't be able to make it there in time either. She began worrying in earnest—with her car in plain sight on the road, it would be clear to the drug makers that she was here, but maybe her presence would be incentive enough for them to move on for now. She finally quit her anxious fumbling with the bullets and .38 when the flatbed truck and stoic blue heeler came into sight. Woodrow drove past Nervy's car and over the fallen barbed wire before bringing the truck to a full stop with the passenger door right next to her.

"Hey, Woodrow," Nervy greeted in a respectful but unenthusiastic manner.

"Bertha wanted me to run down here and have you stop by for beans and cornbread while you were in the neighborhood. Hop on in. I'll run you and your dog up home and back," he offered.

"Might as well," she responded, finishing the rest of the statement in her thoughts, *since there's no escaping the woman.* She opened the door and motioned Griff into the cab, then climbed in behind him. Woodrow drove at a cautious pace and offered no conversation. Finally surrendering to the question filling her thoughts, Nervy asked, "How did you know where to find me?"

He didn't turn his gaze from the road or make any particular facial expression. He just said in a matter-of-fact voice, "Bertha said you'd be there by the willow tree."

CHAPTER 21

Woodrow pulled into a sparsely graveled dirt driveway. He parked in an alignment of dips that corresponded with his truck's four wheels. The parked truck was at the end of a frozen dirt path that ran from the old truck to the back porch screen door. Number Three and Griff were expected to stay outside to honor the farm code of no animals being permitted in the house. Griff grumbled to Nervy as she went in the back door without him. Inside the farm kitchen smelled of simmering beans and a hot oven. Bertha didn't turn to greet them but did invite her guest to take off her coat and have a seat. The table was already set with three stoneware plates and unmatched silverware and attended by three wooden chairs with chipped white paint. Nervy selected the chair farthest from the stove, assuming the other two chairs were Bertha's and Woodrow's usual spots. She took her seat without asking Bertha if she needed any assistance; to do so in the woman's own kitchen would be the equivalent of going to a ship's bridge and offering the captain assistance in managing his ship.

With the food set on the table and everyone seated, Bertha folded her hands and thanked God for the food, the warm house on a winter afternoon, and His continued protection and guidance of Nervy in her struggles. The gathering remained silent after the prayer as first Bertha and then Woodrow helped themselves to the food. As Nervy figured out that she would need to serve herself, Bertha interrupted the silence. "This is Sadie's cornbread recipe—she gave it to me and Woodrow along with an iron skillet for a wedding present." Nervy was caught short. Her mother, an actual flesh-and-blood saint that she had really known and believed in, had been invoked. Overwhelmed by a sudden flood of affection, she set her cornbread back down and accepted her unseen saint's presence at the table with surprise and gratitude.

Amid the absence of any conversation at the table, Nervy struggled to fit the pieces of her day into a coherent picture: an exchange of murderous threats with a drug lord; a dinner invitation from a clairvoyant; a spiritual reunion with her deceased mother. Either some evil seductive force wanted to unhinge her or some benevolent beckoning force wanted to redeem her. Unfortunately, the one she desired most was the one she trusted least.

With the meal finished, Woodrow drove Nervy back to her car. He stayed and watched while she checked to see that the car was empty of unexpected passengers, let Griff in, got in herself, started the car, and drove back out onto the road. She and Woodrow then drove opposite directions. She looked repeatedly into her rearview mirror and watched him diminish with each glance, weaning herself from the afternoon's connection.

Finally reaching Jules's house, she felt a sense of relief and anticipation at being with someone for the rest of the night instead of being alone. Pulling in the driveway, she saw that Jules had uncharacteristically left the garage door open and the light on. She parked in her side of the garage and put the door down. Uneasy with the unfamiliar homecoming scenario, Nervy reached into her pocket to retrieve the remaining loose bullets and the .38. After finishing loading the gun, she let Griff out and walked behind him to the door into the house. Once inside, she called loudly to Jules and got no reply. She cautiously made her way back to his room and found him lying fully unresponsive on his bed, his face an ashen color. On the bedside table next to him was an empty bottle of Elijah Craig, an empty tumbler, and an empty bottle of Valium.

The situation caused Nervy to have a very strong sense of self-awareness and intentionality. "First the firearms," she said to herself, grabbing Jules's Glock out of the bedside table, then collecting her .22 from her bedroom. She went to the garage and wiped each of the guns and each of the bullets in each gun free of fingerprints. She then put them in a tool cabinet behind the power tools Jules stored there. She pushed the firearms way back on the shelf, safely beyond the view of a casual observer. Her felon status could threaten her freedom if she was found to be in possession of firearms during the investigation of Jules's death. Only with the guns at least temporarily sufficiently hidden did Nervy call 911 to report that she found her husband dead.

The rest of Saturday and early Sunday morning felt like an eerie replay of Walter's death—long, earnest and empathetic questioning by the police. She unhesitatingly granted their request to search the bedroom and house freely for evidence of foul play. Again, the coroner would order an autopsy due to the appearance of suicide. Questions about unusual circumstances were answered in the negative. She withheld information about the unusually open garage door because she didn't want to attract attention to the garage, resulting in unwanted searches and unwanted discoveries. Near dawn, the police left and the ambulance took Jules's body. Nervy then sat, exhausted and sleep deprived, wondering if she was being punished by

God, hunted by Cooker, or stuck in a spell of Bertha's doing. It was a dizzying parade of possibilities that ultimately spun her mind to sleep.

CHAPTER 22

Nervy awoke later Sunday morning with Griff whining to go out, confused about her circumstances or even what day it was. She sat up in bed, realizing she had to take care of the dog, but she was unsure where she was supposed to find the door to take him out. As she stood up, her full understanding of where she was and what had happened flooded into her awareness immediately, draining her mental and physical energies.

"Well, boy, here we are, just the two of us *again!*" She reached down and pet him; then they walked out the back door into a morning that was brutally cold.

After breakfast Nervy made a trip around the house to inventory her possessions. Her dirty clothes hamper remained full, as did her ironing basket. The driveway deicer salt bucket in the garage was also present and accounted for. Going to Jules's room, she saw that the tumbler, whiskey bottle, and pill bottle had been taken as evidence last night by the police. It appeared that the whole room had been examined carefully, and she had no idea how many other items had been taken by the police. There were no other signs of disturbance through-out the house as Nervy finished her inspection.

Nervy tried to impose some logical explanation on Jules's unexpected death. Whether he was murdered or not was completely unclear to Nervy, but she was certainly not going to exclude it. Yesterday's exchange with Fatty had been ominous, and her car had been clearly visible to Fatty and his gang on her land not far from their headquarters. Maybe they had looked for her there and, not finding her, had gone to town and looked for her at Jules's house. Maybe they were sending her a message. Maybe Cooker was still acting independently and came to the house last night to kill whomever he could for whatever effect it might have. Maybe Jules committed suicide, or maybe he just finally dialed in the right combination of sedative substances and hit the cosmic jackpot. Nervy paused and tilted her head and grimaced as she opened another line of mental inquiry that was more disconcerting. Did Bertha know that this was going to happen? Did she know as it was happening? Did she have Nervy to dinner to save her life? It was all very alarming and made Nervy wonder about Bertha's spiritual power and exactly which direction it pointed on a moral compass.

As the morning progressed, she felt her mind sharpen. How Jules died made no difference. If he was murdered, it had undoubtedly been by the people who already wanted to kill her, so his death didn't heighten her sense of vulnerability; it merely confirmed it. His death hadn't changed her priorities either. Her mission remained simple: protecting herself and her assets. Some adjustments were now required in her plan, but she certainly did not need a new plan. Justin would see to it that she would be evicted as quickly as possible. His being a judge would make that happen more quickly than anyone could expect, so she would protect her valuables by removing them from the house today and asking Bertha if she would keep them for her at her place. Her plan for protecting herself involved spending only tonight in the house and moving to the office tomorrow morning. She would use it as a stopgap shelter until she could find somewhere more suitable for her safety and comfort.

Nervy got dressed, then loaded the car with dirty laundry, the ironing, the deicer salt bucket, and three individually wrapped handguns. She left her cell phone on the kitchen table because she didn't want her travels traceable today. Absentmindedly forgetting her phone on the kitchen table the day after finding her spouse dead seemed very believable.

She collected Griff, then set out for the Greenbriar Assembly. Nervy knew where she would find her oracle, but she wasn't sure if Bertha would offer genuine assistance or just her usual prophetic moralizing. The drive also allowed her to sort through memories of Jules and accept the fact that she would miss him, not because of any affection, but because he was a familiar resource with whom she could predictably barter.

Nervy reached the church before the service was over. She backed into a spot as far from the church as possible but with a clear view of the door. Before long the familiar hand-painted dull-red flatbed truck drove into the lot, with its silent canine sentinel positioned in her usual location. Nervy realized that she was going to be unable to talk with Bertha at church with Woodrow there to chauffeur Bertha from door to door. She might as well go to their house and wait there rather than be seen by any witnesses here.

After arriving at the farmhouse, Nervy sat in her car for another twenty minutes before the truck turned into the drive. While it was slowing to a stop, she opened her car door and let Griff out. Then she got out herself and waited at the back of her car, approaching Bertha as soon as she exited the truck.

"May I speak with you briefly?" she asked.

"Yes, come in and have a bite of lunch," Bertha offered.

Once inside, Nervy directly asked, "Did you know my husband was going to be killed while I was with you last night?"

"Did you lose a husband last night? I thought your husband died several months ago."

"Did you know or not?" Nervy asked tersely.

"How do you think I would know something like that?"

"Because you told me that God's been showing you my life like a picture show. Did you see Jules's death coming? Just answer me!"

"Are you sure you want to know what I know? I told you everything you need to know about your life: you got your crooked path to walk and your path is going to end someday."

Realizing the old woman was never going to condescend to revealing the extent of her gifts, Nervy turned to more practical matters. "Can I store some things with you all? My life is short on people that are dependable."

"You can leave anything you want to in our old chicken coop except weapons," Bertha replied before turning to Woodrow and telling him to help Nervy unload her car.

With the dirty clothes, ironing, and salt bucket placed in the abandoned coop, Nervy asked her helper if she could have a moment alone. After he stepped out, she retrieved half of her money from the salt bucket and reburied the other half for a future withdrawal.

Finished stashing her belongings, she returned to the farm kitchen and found a place set for her at the table. The three of them shared a midday meal of leftovers in complete silence. After the meal was finished, Nervy assisted with collecting the dirty dishes and silverware from the table and depositing them in the dishpan in the sink. Realizing she had no further reason for staying, Nervy thanked her hosts for their generosity. She left by the back door and headed to her car, with Griff following close behind. She made the drive back to town and Jules's house as the afternoon was darkening. Upon arriving, she found a notably plain dark-blue sedan, inhabited by only the driver, parked at the curb in front of the house. She pulled into the drive and then into the garage. She parked and put down the garage door. After Nervy walked into the house, she took off her coat, draped it over a chair, picked up her cell phone, and followed Griff to the front door just in time to answer a detective's knock.

CHAPTER 23

Still holding her cell phone, Nervy opened the door to an officer in business casual attire. He introduced himself as a detective, offered his badge for inspection, and asked if he might come in and ask her a few questions. Nervy stepped back from the open door, gesturing her invitation. As he entered, Nervy offered to take his coat, which he refused. Instead he laid it on the floor beside him as he abruptly took a seat in one of the living room chairs. He stared directly at Nervy without saying anything for a moment and then pulled out a pen and field notes pad from his shirt pocket.

"Were you at home all day today?" he asked, establishing an impersonal and hostile tone for their interaction.

"Cut the shit—you watched me come home just now. What's this in regard to?" Nervy asked abrasively.

"Mr. and Mrs. Adair were found shot dead in their home today and their daughter was seriously wounded and is in critical care in Middleton."

The news slammed through Nervy's mind like a tornado. Feelings of pain for the murdered family swirled amid the terrorizing fears she was feeling for her own safety. Briefly disoriented, she collected herself as she thought of the children.

"What happened to the daughter's kids?" she asked.

"So where were you today?" the officer continued, ignoring Nervy's question.

"What about the kids? What happened to the kids? *The kids!*"

"They were in their beds asleep and were picked up by the social services worker who was on call and placed in foster care. So where were you today again?"

"I went out to an old family friend's house near Greenbriar church and visited for a while. Were you here last night?" Nervy demanded.

"Why? I mean, why did you go visit the friend, and why did you ask if I was here last night?" He continued to scribble into his field notes without even dignifying his questions with eye contact.

"I found my husband dead last night in the bedroom right down the hall and lots of police were here investigating. I wondered if you were one of them. I didn't want to be alone today, so I went out and spent time with a friend. Is there a reason you are treating me this unprofessionally? Do you think I'm good for both deaths? Do you think you'll get me to confess with your bad-cop approach?"

"You're the common denominator in a lot of deaths, starting with your dad's, then your first husband's, then your second husband's, and now the Adairs. They are all people who either loved you or pissed you off. I know your record."

"Arrest me or leave—we're done!" Nervy stood up. "Jared Grant, a.k.a. Cooker, is good for the Dr. Corvus and Adair family deaths. Maybe Judge Tucker's death too. Who sent you my direction?"

"Lanny Peltor is handling the Adair family matters and said that you were pretty angry at the Adair family in his office this week and told them they should be scared of dying or some-thing like that," he said, hoisting his coat onto his shoulders. With his coat on and notes tucked back in his shirt pocket, the officer turned his back on Nervy. He paused in front of her door, buttoning his coat and putting on his gloves. Even then he didn't reach for the knob but instead began reaching deeply into his right-hand coat pocket.

Sensing grave danger, Nervy quickly lifted the phone she had been holding and placed it to her ear. "Hello," she answered in a perturbed tone. "Oh, Raleigh . . . No, I'm not all right. I'm being hassled by some detective guy right here in my own living room . . . Unmarked new blue Ford sedan . . . About six-two with a shitty attitude . . . Medium-length thinning brown hair, no glasses."

As Nervy continued her phone description of the detec-tive, he quickly removed his hand from his coat pocket and let himself out. When the door finally closed, Nervy took the phone from her ear and discontinued her imaginary call.

"If that guy really is a cop, I got a thousand dollars says he's bent," she said as she double-checked the door lock. He definitely seemed rogue to her. She figured him to be a hit man, cop or not. Showing up on a Sunday, late in the day, no partner—if he wasn't trying to score a hit, he was clearly operating independently from the other detectives, maybe for Fatty. The only reason she could figure a real cop might have acted as hostile as he did would have been to try to stir her up and give him some justification for a broader search than they were permitted last night.

She carried on an audible dialogue with herself to try to sort through her feelings as the new developments and their implications swirled through her mind. "I didn't wish them dead. I warned them that Cooker was a killer and that they were in danger letting him hang around like he was family. Either he's left the country to lay low or he's still here hunting me. Lanny gave the cops probable cause or something close to it involving me. That guy has it out for me . . . Anything to add to the stress."

Her mind turned to her guns and the need to temporarily place them beyond the reach of any further police searches of her home, car, or office. As much as she wanted to have a gun available, the consequences of her being found by the police with a gun made the decision to hide them an easy one. After getting the guns from the car and a shoebox from her closet, Nervy began wrapping each gun in washcloths or newspapers to prevent them from banging around during shipping. She taped the box securely and placed an address label on it, listing her name above Bertha's address. The psychiatry clinic address was the return. Bertha had said she couldn't store weapons there, but she hadn't said she couldn't ship them there to be retrieved a day or two after their arrival. Besides, all Bertha would have to do is refuse to accept them, and then they would make the return trip back to the office, keeping them out of the reach of the police that much longer. With the package ready for shipping, Nervy threw it up in the air a few times, catching and shaking it at the same time to check for noise or movement inside the box. After three repetitions, she was satisfied with the quality of her packing job. "Number one on tomorrow's to-do list," she said out loud again to create a sense of partnership in her isolation. "Number two is going to the safe-deposit box."

The rest of the evening was spent loading clothing into the car and packing up her makeup and toiletries. She also loaded up Tucker's dog food, bowl, and toys. She jammed as much in the car as she could but left out her clothes for the next day and enough food for Griff to have breakfast with her. Nervy got ready for bed intending this to be the last night she would sleep in Jules's house. She would feel safer in the office than she would staying here if Cooker was still prowling around. After a final check of doors and windows, she went to bed with a large screwdriver and crescent wrench beside her pillow, since she didn't have her gun.

Monday morning Nervy got ready, fixed breakfast, and concluded her stay at Jules's house by 7:30 a.m., aiming to be at the post office by 7:45, when it opened. Wearing a hooded sweatshirt with the hood up and a pair of sunglasses to prevent any meaningful personal identification, she drove to the post office, where she was the third customer in the door. She had to stand in line for a couple of minutes as the customers ahead of her conducted their business and exchanged brief pleasantries with the mail clerk. The clerk unquestioningly accepted the box Nervy placed on the counter and merely engaged in small talk about the moderation of the morning's weather. She handed the mail clerk her money and received her change back with gloved hands, then turned from the counter to leave and managed to drop her change on the floor. She bent over and collected her change, then walked out with her head bowed, counting the money she had recovered from the floor and never raising her head high enough for the camera over the exit door to get a glimpse of her face.

After getting back in the car with Griff, she drove to McDonald's. There she removed her sweatshirt and sunglasses in the car, then pushed them into the trash can at the lobby entrance as she walked in. Two sausage biscuits and a cup of coffee were her and Griff's reward for a job well done, and they would enjoy them together in the car while listening to the radio for the hour they had to kill before the bank opened. She ate her biscuit first and then entertained herself indulging Griff by finger-feeding him luscious biscuit fragment after biscuit fragment and laughing at the intense anticipation and eager tail-wagging that was a hallmark of her little friend's breed. The hour in the McDonald's parking lot passed pleasantly as Nervy enjoyed her breakfast, coffee, country music,

Griff, and thoughts of taking personal possession of the gold coins waiting for her in the safe-deposit box she was about to empty.

CHAPTER 24

Nervy arrived in the bank parking lot about five minutes before they would unlock the doors. Leaving her dog in the front seat, she busied herself making room in the back seat among her possessions for the storage container she was going to carry the coins out in. The quicker the gold was in the car, the safer she felt, and having a space already prepared seemed like a good idea. When she was done, she closed the back seat door and leaned against the car, letting the morning sun warm her face for a while. Checking her watch after a moment or two, she figured that the doors would be unlocked by now.

Once inside the sliding glass doors of the bank lobby, she paused to let her eyes adjust to the dimmer indoor light and reach for the safe-deposit-box key that she had tucked into her pocket. Her improving vision confused her, as it revealed Lanny Peltor facing her just fifteen feet away. He was standing next to a bank executive, who was standing next to a bank security guard. They stood as a line of defense, shoulder to shoulder. Undeniably outnumbered, and unprepared for this confrontation, Nervy waited silently for Lanny to offer his explanation of the circumstances. She didn't have to wait long.

"Mrs. Tucker!" Lanny abrasively declared as though he were addressing the halls of eternity. "The court has sealed the safe-deposit box held in this institution by your late husband Jules Tucker. Your late husband's will is being contested by his son, Judge Justin Tucker, who believes his father's last will was prepared under duress and the influence of drugs and alcohol, rendering him mentally incompetent and making the will null and void. You are also hereby prohibited from reentering Jules Tucker's residence from this time forward unless permitted to do so by court order and under court supervision."

The other man in a suit then began, "Mrs. Tucker, unless you have further business to conduct in this bank at this time, you are requested to leave." The suddenness and power of the attack left Nervy motionless in the bank lobby. Her mind struggled to avoid being overwhelmed by thoughts and feelings the ambush had unleashed—the unfairness of her gold being withheld, Lanny's unjustified hostility, her accumulating disadvantages. Rescuing her guns and personal belongings from Jules's house was the one victory she could claim at that moment. As she remained stationary before the three bank defenders, she was startled out of her mental processing by their sudden unified approach. Nervy drew back a step and raised her eyebrows reflexively. Recognizing the threat intended by the approach of the men, she turned for the door and was unable to get there before the guard opened it for her in a brusque fashion. Lanny walked out the door uncomfortably close behind her.

Even though Nervy had not uttered a single word throughout the morning's occurrence, Lanny began lecturing her from behind, not even waiting for her to turn her head around. "Listen, Nervy, you're going to find out just how much of a friend to Justin Tucker I really am because he retained *me* when he discovered his father had died under suspicious circumstances. Neither he nor I will rest until we have connected his father's death to you or the late Dr. Corvus or both. There are already search warrants being executed at Jules's house and Dr. Corvus's office looking for records or *any* kind of evidence of malpractice, elder abuse, poisoning, or other foul play in the matter of Jules's death."

Nervy kept walking as fast as she could to the safety of her car, trying not to break into a full-fledged run. Still trailing her, Lanny continued his tirade. "But, Nervy, there's more. I'm just *beginning* with you. There are also search warrants being executed at those same locations by additional law enforcement officers looking for evidence of planning or participation in the homicides of Mr. and Mrs. Adair and the attempted murder of Candy Adair, on whose behalf I will testify to having personally heard you threaten. I've already scheduled another deposition for you to attend later this week seeking those assets that you've hidden and that are owed to the Adair estate as part of Dr. Corvus's wrongful death conviction. You have no one left to run to and nowhere left to hide, and you will have nothing left at all when I'm through with you."

With his full inventory of threats delivered, he stopped still in the middle of the sidewalk, allowing her to continue to her car alone.

In the parking lot, Nervy opened the car door to the enthusiastic greetings of Griff. Finally in her car, she exhaled deeply and let Griff climb into her lap. Petting him and allowing herself to release the tension from the surprise attack she had just endured, she began refocusing herself. "Well, boy, it's back to the post office. I'm glad you weren't there; you woulda gone for Lanny's throat and got us thrown in jail. He's so arrogant he didn't even realize he told me his plan, that Justin Tucker is his partner, and that this is personal with me, but I don't have a clue why."

On this trip to the post office, Nervy was much more casual and visible to the security cameras as she conducted her business. She filled out a change of address card so that Justin and Lanny would have less opportunity to examine or with-hold the mail that would have been delivered to Jules's house. She walked out of the post office and tucked her copy of the verification for the address change in her wallet and tossed the receipt for the gun shipment in the trash. She smiled as she recognized that Lanny's threats were already benefitting her. Now that she knew she was being investigated, she would ditch any info about her shipment of the guns and their destination. She would be more careful about everything. She rejoined Griff in the car and announced, "Next stop, Raleigh!"

At the lawyer's office, the secretary was cordial but reported that Raleigh's schedule was full all day. Nervy explained that she was facing a barrage of legal attacks from Lanny and she was willing to hand over a twelve-hundred-dollar retainer in cash today if she could meet with him. The secretary held up an index finger and gestured to the nearby chairs. Nervy took a seat in the small waiting area and overheard the secretary make a phone call cancelling Raleigh's lunch meeting "because of unforeseen developments in an urgent case."

CHAPTER 25

As Raleigh spent his lunch listening to the laundry list of legal assaults Nervy was facing, he shook his head, acknowledging the magnitude of the onslaught. His facial expression showed a certain pessimism, and Nervy figured he wanted to remind her of his opposition to her involvement with, let alone marriage to, Jules and was surprised that he was able to refrain from actually telling her "I told you so!"

After thinking quietly for a while, he said, "This is an enormous amount of legal work. Twelve hundred dollars is a drop in the bucket of what it would cost to fully fight the string of battles Lanny has constructed. Do you have a lot of money to spend on all this?"

"Besides what I just gave you, I only have another twelve hundred and fifty dollars to my name. I have the gold coins in the bank, but I can't promise those to you at this point. I have forty acres out by Greenbriar, but it's not worth a fortune. I have a life insurance policy on Walter that I haven't collected yet and it's worth one hundred thousand."

"Where will you live?" Raleigh asked.

"I'm going to try camping out in the office. I have the rent paid up there for a year, but the contract specifically prohibits living in the office, so it probably won't be a long-term option. There are some old family friends out in the Greenbriar area that might let me stay with them for a while."

"Which of Lanny's attacks do you think you could handle by yourself?" Raleigh asked.

"I think I can manage the deposition this week about the monetary damages in the Adair case," she said. "And any legit investigation of me as a suspect for Jules's death or the Adair deaths is going to go nowhere, so neither one of us needs to bother with that, at least not yet. But I think that the business about contesting Jules's will requires you to fight it. If the twelve hundred retainer doesn't cover it, would you consider taking a percentage of the coins if we win?"

"Yeah, I'd consider doing that, but I'd want twenty-five percent of the coins," he offered.

"Twelve hundred dollars and five percent of the coins or twenty-five percent of the coins and you give me back my retainer. Your call."

"I think Jules's will can ultimately be verified as legitimate, and I'm willing to take the risk for the payoff, so keep your cash and I'll take twenty-five percent."

"Okay, the first thing then is the police are probably going through the office files right now and probably have Jules's medical records in their possession already. They are going to find out that Walter provided Jules with six prescriptions for Valium, each good for a one-month supply and each with instructions informing the pharmacist as to the date at which it can be filled and to refill none of the prescriptions sooner than twenty-eight days."

"*What the hell!* Who would give that old drunk that long a leash with controlled substances?"

"Actually, it was me, not Walter. I used some signed blank prescriptions I found after Walter died and traded Valium for Jules's help, but the record reads like I told you."

"So why did Walter give an alcoholic Valium at all?"

"Well . . . he had an anxiety disorder that had been diagnosed by his family doctor before he ever came to our practice and it was the medicine and dose that had already been started. The family doc didn't care for Jules and was uncomfortable with using Valium, so he referred him to Walter."

"Does his record have him diagnosed as an alcoholic?"

"No, he denied excessive use of alcohol on direct questioning in the office."

"Didn't Walter suspect it?" Raleigh was incredulous.

"Documenting suspicions creates risk for the doctor. You can't treat suspicions. You often can't explain them, and they may make you seem judgmental, so it's best that the documentation stick with what the patient says or what the doctor can observe," Nervy said.

With an obvious expression of alarm about everything that he had just heard, Raleigh concluded their meeting with his assessment that it was going to be an uphill battle to defend Jules's will from the perception that he had been compromised by Walter's treatment.

Nervy left to go examine her own office and assess the aftereffects of the searches that she was sure had been executed and probably completed earlier that day. Parking in her customary spot, she looked for any unusual cars or those that appeared to be either fleet cars or official vehicles. She saw none. She got out of the car and walked Griff into the building. The office door was intact, relieving her worry that it might have been battered down out of spite. She assumed the landlord had been asked to open the office. Nervy's key still worked in the lock. She entered to find the office less disheveled than she had expected. Walking through and taking stock, she saw that the contents of her desk had been completely removed and piled on the floor fairly neatly. The office checkbook was gone, as was the computer on her desk and the fax machine. Further checking revealed that Jules's medical record was missing, as was Cindy Adair's. Her phone had been repositioned on her desk and all the furniture throughout the office had been scooted out of its normal location. As she surveyed the changes to the office, Nervy concluded that trying to take overnight shelter there was a bad idea. The investigators might have left listening devices, cameras, or God knows what. She would also probably be on the landlord's radar now that a search warrant had been executed.

Nervy spent a couple of hours replacing the contents of her desk and straightening up the office. She took two pictures that she had a special attachment to off the wall and laid them on the floor next to her desk to take with her. Making another circuit through the office's rooms, looking for items that could benefit her current struggles, she consciously suppressed her emerging memories of the collaboration she had valued so much with Walter as her partner. With her pictures from the wall collected, she turned out all the lights and left with Griff in tow, locking the door behind her. In the car she shook her head as she told Griff, "Boy, you better get ready to be a farm dog because we're headed out to ask Bertha for a favor. Seems like life just keeps bouncing us back to the country no matter what."

CHAPTER 26

The stairway was narrow, with unpainted worn wooden steps, and the faded wallpaper smelled like old library books. Upstairs were two small bedrooms with ceilings shaped by the slope of the roof. They had no heat or electricity. Nervy's room was furnished with a bed, a chest of drawers, a hanging mirror on the wall, and a short length of metal pipe affixed to the wall with brackets that was holding a dozen empty wire hangers. A porcelain-covered three-gallon bucket with a matching lid sat on the floor in the corner in case she didn't want to go all the way to the outhouse at night. Two pillows, two handmade quilts, and two wool blankets were on the top of the chest of drawers.

Nervy had shown up unannounced at Bertha and Woodrow's house in the late afternoon, but she figured that the old woman's gift of prophetic foreknowledge prevented her from being caught unaware. A slight smile crossed her face as she entertained the idea that Bertha had already prepared a room for her and planned on her being there for dinner. Nervy didn't see herself as having any other options for a place to stay, other than her car, which could be a death sentence at the moment.

By the time she had reached the old couple's driveway, Nervy had nearly convinced herself that Bertha would be reluctant to grant her request for sanctuary, but the response was quite the opposite. She was waiting at the door as Nervy walked up and invited her in. Upon hearing the request, she immediately offered her a bedroom for as long as she needed it.

With all her belongings upstairs, Nervy surveyed her new circumstances. Though Spartan, her accommodations at Bertha's house were not demoralizing. The feelings she remembered having when she moved into her cell in prison were much worse. Nervy felt valued here and had no concern for protecting herself against the other inhabitants. She did worry about her canine companion though. His change in accommodations would be much greater than hers. He was going to sleep in the old chicken coop because she didn't trust him to find his own shelter outside like Number Three did, nor did she trust him to know who or what to avoid in his explorations of the hills and gullies of the farm, since coyotes and badgers were common in these parts. Nervy dug his bowl and food out of the car and bribed him into his new nocturnal quarters with his supper. After she locked him in and then carried the sack of food to the back porch, she was surprised that he hadn't started barking or howling. Returning to the house, she found Bertha in the kitchen fixing supper in a large floral print apron. Nervy asked if she could set the table and Bertha gave her hurried instructions about where the plates, glasses, bowls, and silverware were. She also tasked her with placing a small glass of buttermilk where Woodrow sat because he liked it with his supper and felt it aided his digestion. As she helped, Nervy felt the simplicity of this life and these people offered her a window on a better existence than any she had experienced since Walter died.

Her gratitude to Bertha overflowed. "I can never repay you for your generosity in allowing me to stay; I want to thank you again. I know it must be an imposition on your usual routine, but I really believe you're saving my life."

Bertha paused her activities at the stove, then turned to look Nervy straight in the eyes as she wiped her hands on her apron. "I'm glad to do it; you matter more to me than you know. I loved your momma, and she loved and cared for me during some tough times in my life. The wheels of life just keep turning, and we do what we can for others when we're on the top, and we ask for what we need from others when we're on the bottom." Nervy noted tears beginning to collect in Bertha's eyes just as the old woman turned back toward the stove and resumed shepherding supper to its destination on the table.

The next morning Nervy awoke under the pile of quilts and wool blankets to the smell of bacon cooking. She hustled to get into her clothes and make it to the outhouse in time. It had been years since she had had to use unheated, nonflushing outdoor facilities in which the main component was a board with a hole. Once back inside, she went into the kitchen and found her aproned, overweight benefactor busily preoccupied in the kitchen, finishing breakfast. Nervy got busy herself, repeating the same task she had performed last night. She inquired if Woodrow required buttermilk at breakfast and was informed that it was required only at supper "for his digestion." When all three of them were seated, Bertha bowed her head and asked her Lord to bless the food, bless the challenges of the day for everyone gathered at the table, and proclaimed an assertive "Amen!" Bertha fell silent and set about filling her plate, Woodrow followed suit, and Nervy, now knowing the routine, served herself.

After the dishes were put away, Nervy went outside to let Griff out and feed him. Opening the door to the coop, she found her terrier curled up next to the door, resting comfortably with his face and front legs covered in dirt. Beside him lay two dead rats, whose fur looked to have been slathered with dog saliva and rolled in dirt. Far from being dejected, Griff acted as satisfied as if he had spent the night at the finest of hotels. He was reluctant to come out of the coop until Nervy grabbed both rats by their tails and carried them out. Griff followed along, appearing proud that his evening's labors were worthy of her attention. Walking a few steps into the pasture behind the coop, she awkwardly flung both rodents as far as she could and then went back to the house to clean up.

Nervy checked her cell phone and found it blinking an announcement of a waiting text. Raleigh had left a message telling her to call his office as soon as she could. She checked the cell signal strength to see if she could expect a call to go through without breaking up and decided to give it a try. On the second ring the secretary answered, and upon hearing Nervy's identity she immediately transferred the call to the lawyer.

"Nervy, all hell's broke loose. Lanny and Justin have manipulated the court schedule and got a hearing set for today on challenging the will, and a hearing scheduled for tomorrow on finding you in contempt of the court's ruling on the damages for the Adair estate," he breathlessly informed her.

"Are you at all ready for this?" she asked.

"Well, I've got a strategy that I'm intending on using for the will. I think that speeding things up is their strategy to force us into court before we're adequately prepared, but they haven't had time to be as prepared as they should either and are as open to surprise and mistakes as we are. Do you want me to try to stall them and ask for a continuance?"

"No, it's time to just face whatever is going to happen. The sooner the better! I've got nothing to prepare for in terms of the Adair estate deposition. I've turned over everything that was part of Walter's and my shared property, plus the house."

"Have you asked the life insurance company for the payout on Walter's life insurance?"

"Not yet. There is no way that the insurance is something the Adairs are entitled to anyway. By the way, how is the girl doing, the Adair girl? Have you heard anything lately?"

"I haven't heard anything. Everybody expects her to be in the hospital a long time; she got shot up pretty bad. Look, today's hearing is set for 1:00, so if you want to sit at the table with me to defend the will, then show up a little after 12:30."

Nervy immediately set about getting ready for the afternoon's court hearing. She informed Bertha of her urgent need to go to town today and then went upstairs to change into clothes for court.

CHAPTER 27

Leaving Griff to run loose for the afternoon, she made the drive into town, lost in thought about the various approaches that Lanny and Justin might try to use to invalidate the will and simultaneously vilify Nervy's sudden presence in the final weeks of Jules's life. She made it to the courthouse by 12:20 and sat in the empty courtroom for ten minutes before Raleigh arrived. He set his briefcase on the table and motioned her to join him.

Sitting together at the table, they pulled out the copy of Jules's psych records and, shaking his head, reported rather grimly, "This record looks bad. It basically displays Jules as a person who probably shouldn't have been given Valium."

"Well I think it is fairly defensible."

"Listen up, Nervy. I'm telling you that I'm going to let the other team push the narrative of Jules being overmedicated and intend to fail miserably at presenting Jules as being of sound mind at the time of this will's filing with the court. I have knowledge of Jules's prior will, which preceded the one being contested and will be Jules's fallback will if this one is thrown out. I don't think that either Lanny or Justin know about this previous will because it was never filed with the court. It was kept in the safe of the lawyer who prepared it. The two witnesses to Jules's signature of that will are both impeccable and are both still alive and available for court today." As Lanny, Justin, and the others began filing into the courtroom, Raleigh finished in an urgent whisper. "This earlier will is *much* more favorable to us than the one you and he asked me to draw up for you, so don't blow this with one of your outbursts!"

An unfamiliar judge entered the court, and the bailiff announced the presence of the Honorable Judge Bailey and pronounced the court in session. As the proceedings began, Nervy found herself confronting a flood of memories from Walter's last trial and was drawn to stare at the presidential pictures behind the judge once again.

The judge requested Lanny address the court first, since he was the petitioner in the matter. Lanny began building the foundations of his case against the will by highlighting the very likely greedy motives and emotionally manipulative influence Nervy had subjected the frail, elderly widowed judge to. He skillfully layered on the undoubted additional mental compromises the unfortunate man had experienced due to the unnecessary mind-altering drugs provided by the disgraced psychiatrist Dr. Corvus, Nervy's prior husband, who had also died unexpectedly while married to her.

Raleigh rose abruptly from his table before the judge. "Your Honor, I object! I fail to see how opposing counsel's malicious innuendos smearing Mrs. Tucker bear on this case."

"Objection sustained. Mr. Peltor, restrict your observations and evidence to the matter of the will's legitimacy."

Lanny resumed his presentation by entering into evidence the three unfilled Valium prescriptions discovered by the police in Jules's home when they executed the search warrant investigating his unexpected death.

"Your Honor, I object to this evidence being entered into the court's consideration in these proceedings. This is not a murder inquiry. The deceased's will and its fidelity to the deceased's true and rational desires is in question today, not his cause of death," Raleigh argued.

"Overruled! The medications the deceased was taking are relevant." Judge Bailey motioned for Lanny to continue.

Lanny then reported to the court that the will in question had been written in complete opposition to many years of repeated promises the elderly judge had made, assuring his beloved son that he had collected the gold coins expressly for the purpose of passing them on to successive generations of heirs as a hedge against any financial hardship that might befall them. Dramatically turning toward Justin, who was sitting at the table behind him, Lanny gestured Justin's presence to the court and suggested that, should the court wish, the esteemed young judge himself would testify to the promises made by his father before he fell under the pernicious influence of his fourth and final wife. Judge Bailey declined the offer of testimony and accepted as fact the statement the counselor made on the young judge's behalf. Lanny thanked the judge and sat down, indicating it was Raleigh's turn.

Beginning by identifying himself as the counsel for the deceased's wife, Raleigh clarified to the court that he had been retained by the deceased himself to prepare the will in question. Raleigh reported to the court that the expired judge had unambiguously outlined his wishes for the will and then actively participated in the careful crafting of each of the specific provisions present in the will now before the court. Continuing his case, he reminded the court that he had been a professional colleague of the deceased for over twenty years and had a long-term familiarity with the deceased judge's mental acumen, especially professionally. Raleigh affirmed that in the course of their repeated meetings preparing the will he never witnessed Jules display any cognitive compromises. Reviewing the principal stipulations of the will, which gave both the surviving child and surviving spouse relatively equal portions of the estate, Raleigh challenged the opposing petitioners to point to any particular provisions in the will that made it seem suspicious or irrational. Lastly, he argued that the will had in no way been produced utilizing stealth or deception; it had been filed publicly and its provisions had all been a matter of public record. With his main points presented, Raleigh sat down.

At the request of the judge, Lanny rose and began rebutting Raleigh's defense of the will. His first focus was on the brevity of Jules and Nervy's courtship. He then connected the brief marriage with the suddenness of the deceased's suspicious demise. Lastly, he referenced Nervy's criminal past and her current status as a felon.

Raleigh erupted. "Your Honor, I *must* object! *This is not a murder trial, and Mrs. Tucker is not on trial today.* As for the matter of Mrs. Tucker's status as a felon, her deceased husband was the judge presiding over her trial and he sentenced her to prison himself. Need I present any further evidence that her prior criminality was of literally no concern or threat to him?"

"Objection sustained. Mr. Peltor, restrict your attention to the matter before the court. Please proceed." The judge nodded toward Lanny.

Lanny resumed by turning his attention to the matter of the Valium Jules had been prescribed for years and the well-reported danger its long-term use represented to older people.

"Your Honor, I object. This is not a malpractice case, and the doctor in question is now deceased anyway."

"Overruled. Please sit back down, Mr. Baggs. The deceased's mental state and his psychiatric medications *are* an important component of the court's consideration!"

Lanny, looking exasperated by Raleigh's repeated objections, called the court's attention to Jules's psychiatric records. He enumerated the number of one-time-per-month Valium prescriptions Jules had received from Dr. Corvus over the course of the past ten years. He then dramatically reached under the table his briefcase rested on and retrieved a plastic five-gallon bucket, which he hoisted as high as his arm could reach, displaying to the entire courtroom that it was heaping full of medicine bottles. He then loudly proclaimed that the bucket was filled to the top with 120 medicine bottles so that the court could have an understanding of the quantity of Valium that Dr. Corvus had provided Jules during the past decade. He prominently rested the bucket on the tabletop in full view of the courtroom and took his seat.

Accepting the judge's instruction to conclude his case, Raleigh rose and awkwardly paused for an uncomfortable moment, acting somewhat overwhelmed by Lanny's showmanship. He limply excused Dr. Corvus by relating that he was not the first doctor to prescribe Valium to Jules and had provided the Valium merely as a continuation of another doctor's treatment. Valium, he explained to the court, had been used in the US to treat millions and millions of patients since 1963, especially for Jules's diagnosis of generalized anxiety disorder. Raleigh then quit talking and took a deep, audible breath while looking around the courtroom dejectedly. Appearing to be bereft of any remaining arguments, he sat down.

CHAPTER 28

The judge ordered a thirty-minute recess during which he would attempt to reach a ruling on the validity of the contested will. Lanny and Justin both stood up and smiled knowingly at each other. Nervy and Raleigh sat motionless for a few moments, avoiding eye contact. Without warning, he leaned down and reached into his briefcase. He took out a legal pad and began writing.

He scooted the pad over to Nervy to read and poured himself a glass of water, staring blankly into the distance as Nervy read the note. *Don't show any signs of confidence during the recess! How do you think I did?* Nervy pushed the pad away in a disgusted fashion and passively looked around the room as though she couldn't be any more disappointed with Raleigh right now than she already was.

She then quickly grabbed the pad and furiously wrote a note and pushed the pad back at him aggressively. It read, *I'm glad you explained your plan before court because you did a really good job of letting them use those records in a damaging way. I hope you are as good at winning as you are at seeming to lose!*

He shook his head, gesturing disapproval of her written note, and scribbled a note back to her, seeming to appear defensive. Nervy reached over and took the pad from him and read, *Watch me! By the way, those records really are indefensible. I could never win this case trying to defend Walter's psychiatric treatment using those records, sorry.*

This time after reading the note Nervy really was angry at Raleigh and she discontinued their note writing and sullenly avoided eye contact for the rest of the recess.

At the conclusion of the appointed wait, Judge Bailey returned to the courtroom.

"I have reached a conclusion," he announced. The occupants of both tables stood. The judge then said, "I find the preponderance of the evidence presented today leads to the conclusion that Jules Tucker's last will was produced under circumstances involving the influence of prescription drugs known to have adverse effects upon cognition. I rule the will to be invalid." The judge brought down his gavel, giving an echoing authority to the opinion.

As Lanny and Justin were shaking hands at their table, Raleigh loudly interjected for the entire courtroom to hear, "If it please the court, I would like to submit the most recent will that Jules Tucker had drafted previous to the will struck down today. It was produced by Mr. Barnes, a lawyer in Middleton, whom you are no doubt familiar with in his capacity as the current president of the bar association in our state. He has taken the time to join us today and is sitting in the third row." Raleigh turned and gestured to indicate the distinguished gentleman rising from the third row. "This will was produced approximately three years ago and has been kept in Mr. Barnes's office safe. It was witnessed by Judge Sanders of Middleton, who has also joined us today and is sitting in the fourth row." Another gentleman in a suit stood in the audience. Nervy recognized Judge Sanders as the man who had married Jules and her. "The other witness to Jules Tucker's signature on this will is the bailiff in court today, Deputy Sheriff McDonald," Raleigh said, nodding his head to the bailiff, who nodded back. Raleigh continued to rule the moment. "Because of the urgency of determining the most likely legitimate desires Jules Tucker had regarding the disposition of his estate, this court was convened in an extraordinarily rapid fashion today. Since we have the primary individuals who drafted and witnessed this will present with us, I request that the court use the remainder of today's session to reach a conclusion regarding the legitimacy of *this* will."

The court fell completely silent and all eyes turned to Judge Bailey.

Judge Bailey paused long enough to stroke his chin several times. He looked around the courtroom into the faces of the opposing counsels as well as the gathered professionals all present and ready to testify. Finally drawing a deep breath, he squared his shoulders and announced that he was calling the court to order to consider the legitimacy of the will prepared by Mr. Barnes. Identifying Raleigh as the petitioner, Judge Bailey invited him to begin the proceedings by presenting his case to the court.

Raleigh, who had continued to stand, picked up the three copies of the will he had come to the courtroom equipped with and handed two of them to Nervy to distribute, one to the judge and one to Lanny, so that they might follow along as he read it aloud for the court recorder to document. The essence of the brief document was that Jules was disgusted by the disrespect and disregard his son had persistently shown him over the course of several consecutive years. He wished it to be known that from that time forward he disowned his son Justin and granted all his earthly possessions to his other heirs upon his death, explicitly excluding Justin Tucker. The sole additional provision was that if he were married at the time of his demise, then his spouse was to inherit his entire estate and be given the full authority to dispose of or distribute it at her discretion.

Concluding his recitation of the will, Raleigh then added, "Jules told me as I prepared the will struck down by the court today that with his advancing cancer and worsening loneliness he had softened his anger at his son and wished me to include him in his will as the beneficiary of his house. But as the court has previously ruled today, perhaps the considerations he had me include in that will were merely the byproducts of an excess of psychiatric medicines and should have never been given legal consideration." Finished with his presentation, Raleigh returned to his seat, seemingly satisfied that he had rubbed as much salt and shame into the wounds he had inflicted on Lanny and Justin as was humanly possible. He turned to Nervy and, with a triumphant look, quietly asked her what she thought. He realized as he looked at her that she was exhibiting an entirely unexpected somewhat distant and thoughtful expression.

Looking back at him, she whispered, "Do you know any good malpractice lawyers?"

"What . . . What did you ask?"

"Do you have any recommendations for top-dog malpractice lawyers?" she asked more compellingly.

"Nervy, I'm not getting where your question is coming from. Why do you need a malpractice lawyer?"

She paused, intensifying her eye contact with him, and then spoke slowly and distinctly, as though he might be hard of hearing or have difficulty understanding English. "I am interested in pursuing a malpractice case against Dr. Corvus for the unnecessary death of my husband, Jules Tucker. Because of Dr. Corvus's *negligent* use of dangerous medications, my husband is dead, and I wish to seek *damages* because his death has deprived me of his companionship and financial support." Raleigh stared at her with a blank facial expression.

At that moment Judge Bailey began speaking loudly for the court to recognize that he was ready to deliver his ruling in the will that Raleigh had introduced. "This day has indeed been a day of many surprises and I believe that the matter of Jules Tucker's will is in dire need of clarification. Mr. Baggs's request for a clarification of the legitimacy of the new will that he has presented has merit and seems validated by the presence of the esteemed and respected witnesses to the will. Mr. Peltor, do you have a more recent will than the one presented by Mr. Baggs that you would like to present to the court?"

"No, Your Honor."

"Do you wish to question any of the witnesses Mr. Baggs has presented to the court?"

"No, Your Honor!"

"I have no option," the judge resumed, "other than to accept the will presented and authenticated by Mr. Baggs as the legitimate will expressing Mr. Tucker's last and reasonable wishes regarding the disposition of his estate after his passing." He again brought down the gavel, the bang resounding through the room like an audible exclamation point. Raleigh turned to Nervy and congratulated her on her acquisition of Jules's car, house, furnishings, bank account, safe-deposit box, and state pension life insurance benefits.

With his congratulations concluded, he continued exploring the concerns she had triggered in his mind. "Why are you thinking of a malpractice case against Walter?"

"For the principle of the matter. His shortcomings have become some sort of cow that everybody is milking. If anybody should get anything, it should be me. I loved him, but he isn't here with me, suffering the shame and humiliation left behind after he died. I want to sue that damned malpractice insurance company and make them pay, if not him, *then me!*"

Raleigh, shocked and disgusted by what he was hearing, began chastising her. "You just won big today. You have shelter and finances now that you could live comfortably with, but instead of celebrating you are raging about life's unfairness. Count me out of this malpractice business. Even if you win, you'll lose any respect or sympathy from any decent person, and my credibility means more to me than money earned that way. Cash me out." Signaling his departure from their partnership, he hastily picked his papers off the table and crammed them into his briefcase.

"So, you're not up for making a malpractice insurance company pay for the damages caused by a doctor whose records are *indefensible?*"

"*Not* with you, *not* on Walter's grave! Drop my share of the coins off at my office in the next week or two . . . and *don't* call me!" he ordered. Then he turned and left the courtroom, which had already cleared out, except for Justin and Lanny still talking at the table nearby.

After Walter stalked out, Nervy walked over to the opposition's table to offer Justin the invitation to stop by Jules's house and take any mementos he wanted, since she was just going to put the house on the market and sell it. Responding to her approach, Justin quit talking to Lanny and focused an angry glare at Nervy.

"Fuck off. I'm not my dad; I don't want blow jobs from worn-out drug whores."

"Do you kiss your children with that mouth?" she retorted.

Lanny turned and looked straight into her eyes. "We'll do our talking with you tomorrow morning in the hearing, *Mrs. Tucker,*" he sneered. "Save it till then!"

CHAPTER 29

Thursday morning Nervy was back in Clay Center. Walking into the courtroom at 9:00 sharp, she found the same court reporter from Lanny's office when the deposition had been cancelled. The same bailiff from yesterday was present, and Lanny was already there. Nervy took a seat in the gallery, assuming she would be called forward by the judge or Lanny when they wished her to take the stand. She was surprised at how little anxiety she had about the proceeding, but then again, she had already provided the Adair estate with more than they had been legally entitled to.

Judge Bailey entered and was announced by the bailiff. The judge opened court by reciting the case number and invited Lanny forward to begin the day. Lanny called his first witness, who was Nervy. She was sworn in and waited for the first question.

Lanny began, "Mrs. Corvus . . . I'm sorry . . . Mrs. Tucker, do you understand that it is your legal responsibility to honor the court's ruling that the Adair estate be paid the monetary damages awarded them from the late Dr. Corvus's estate?"

"Yes."

"Have you done so to the fullness of your ability?"

"Yes."

"Mrs. Corvus . . . I mean Mrs. Tucker—" He was cut short by Nervy interrupting him.

"Your Honor, is it your habit to permit this repeated disrespectful behavior toward a witness by an officer of your court?"

"No, it is not, Mrs. Tucker. Mr. Peltor, I am warning you to display appropriate respect and professionalism during this hearing. Last warning! Now please ask your question of the witness."

Lanny resumed with a somewhat subdued tone of voice. "Mrs. Tucker, among all of Dr. Corvus's assets that were examined by the forensic accountant, there was no evidence of a retirement account. Were you aware of one?"

Nervy looked Lanny in the eye and answered, "None that I know of. His first wife received the retirement account he had accumulated up to that point as part of her divorce settlement. Walter never wanted a retirement account after that."

"Are you telling the court that a successful and responsible medical specialist set aside no savings for his retirement? What was he intending to live on after he retired from practice?"

Nervy cocked her head quizzically. "Mr. Peltor, you have made a significant amount of money over the past five or six years presenting my deceased husband to the Clay Center community and courts as irresponsible and incompetent. Now, however, you assume that the man who you have publicly held accountable for the death of his patients would be the kind of man who would save for his retirement. Have you forgotten that he didn't even have malpractice insurance during his treatment of Cindy Adair?"

Lanny tried another approach. "Where did the doctor's income go? His lifestyle didn't appear to consume the income he was making."

Nervy responded calmly, "Dr. Corvus would take cash from our bank account and once or twice a month go to St. Louis to visit his children and return without the cash. I have no idea what he was doing with the money."

Lanny appeared flustered before regrouping. "You chose to remain married to a man for fifteen years who you thought was irresponsible?"

"Who I marry and why is not the concern of this court or a matter for discussion in this case, but I will answer your question. I am a felon and have been misused by men for sexual and criminal purposes since I was thirteen years old. Dr. Corvus did neither of those things to me. During my life with him, I always had shelter and food, and there was never any physical or emotional or sexual abuse. Life with him was the best life I ever knew. Not having a retirement account didn't matter to me; a man who squandered his own money and didn't try to pimp me out to get it back was a good enough husband in my book!"

"Dr. Corvus or his estate owes damages to the Adair family for his role in the loss of their daughter. Can you not see the importance of that?" Lanny demanded. "The only surviving member of this tragic family continues to recover from horrific wounds and will be in the hospital for many months to come, receiving rehabilitative treatments and trying to regain her ability to walk. Don't you care? Do you even understand?"

Pausing and softening her tone of voice, Nervy allowed her shoulders to drop as she turned her gaze directly to the judge and answered the question. "Absolutely I care. Even though Dr. Corvus was a good enough husband to me, it has become apparent that as a doctor he caused a lot of people considerable pain and suffering. He robbed me of my second husband, whose death was caused by his reckless prescription of hazardous substances. Yesterday this very court ruled that the substances my husband received from Dr. Corvus were compromising his judgment. Yes, Mr. Peltor, I understand Ms. Adair's entitlement to damages very well, despite the fact that I have nothing left to add to her settlement. I do understand. In fact I'm filing a malpractice case against Dr. Corvus myself because of my late husband Jules's death. If I remember correctly, when the doctor died he had the kind of malpractice insurance that pays even if he's dead."

Nervy noticed as she concluded her remarks that both Judge Bailey and Lanny seemed mentally stunned and distracted from the courtroom as her intended plan became clear in their minds. For a moment the proceedings froze in place. Silence prevailed in the courtroom until the judge took a deep breath. Straightening his posture, the judge reengaged the current matter before the court and asked Mr. Peltor if he had any further questions for the witness.

Lanny responded, "No, Your Honor. I rest."

The judge adjourned the court and was standing to leave the bench when Nervy asked him politely when she might expect to get the original medical records on Jules back, since she was the custodian of the records for Dr. Corvus's practice and his particular record would probably be subpoenaed soon.

The judge stared, silent and unblinking, for a moment and then in the softest tone of voice answered, "I'm not really sure."

Nervy thanked him and promised to return after lunch and check in with his court clerk to see if they might have an answer for her by then. She spent part of her lunch hour back at her and Jules's house collecting nonperishable foodstuffs and various items to contribute to Bertha and Woodrow's household as an expression of gratitude for their sheltering her. With the remainder of her lunch hour, she stopped by McDonald's and got a Big Mac to celebrate the completion of the morning's court session.

After lunch Nervy arrived at the court clerk's office and approached the clerk's desk. Looking up and recognizing

Nervy, the clerk held up the medical record, signaling that she had what Nervy was looking for. She held it aloft until Nervy took it from her. Neither woman said a word, and Nervy's business there was conducted in less than half a minute. She then drove to the office and copied Jules's file. She kept one in her personal possession and placed the other back in the patient files.

CHAPTER 30

Her next stop was the bank that had refused her access to her safe-deposit box on Monday. She opened the trunk and retrieved her heavy canvas tote bag. This time her entrance was much less momentous and there was no welcoming committee. She went to the reception desk in the lobby and made her intentions clear. A bank employee who appeared to be a young management trainee was summoned. He wordlessly led her to the safe-deposit vault, assisted her in locating the appropriate box, and courteously excused himself, allowing her the privacy of conducting her business unobserved. She inventoried the coins and placed 38 of them in her purse; the other 112 were put into the tote. She summoned the young attendant, handed him her key, and showed him the empty box. She informed him that she would no longer be requiring the box and it could be rented to someone else. After exiting, she drove four blocks to another of Clay Center's banks and took her purse and tote bag inside. She opened a safe-deposit box there in her name only and, following the proper protocol, she placed the 112 coins in it. With her share of the coins now secured, she departed the bank for Raleigh's office.

Entering the lawyer's waiting room, Nervy was immediately recognized by the secretary, who smiled warmly. "Congratulations on your court victory regarding the will. Sometimes the good guys—and gals—win."

"Raleigh accomplished that entirely by himself. It was the most dramatic turn of events I've ever seen in court."

"Until someone pulled off an even bigger surprise in court this morning, the way I heard it." The secretary grinned.

"Hard to say how that will work out. I've stopped by today to drop off Mr. Baggs's payment for his services in the matter of the will. I'd be glad to leave them with you if he would rather not see me," Nervy said.

Before the secretary could respond, Raleigh walked into the waiting area and invited Nervy back to his office in a friendly manner. He offered her a chair and initiated an apology for his reprimand of her in the courtroom yesterday.

He began explaining. "Walter's suicide hit me like a rock. He was a decent man, and I've been mourning for him. Having lost my spouse several years ago, I was feeling a lot of sympathy for your circumstances as well, but the business between you and Jules made me question what kind of person you were. I hung in there with you through all the unconventional maneuvering. I was feeling rather proud of myself yesterday after winning the will dispute, and when you didn't seem to appreciate that and then topped it off with what I saw as a slander of Walter, I lost it. I apologize for that response and retract my refusal to do any work for you. I would like to retain your friendship, and I offer you my assistance if you need it for legal endeavors."

Nervy smiled and nodded. "I apologize to you too because I sprang my new strategy on you with no warning. Actually, your emotional response yesterday confirmed just how shocking the strategy is and convinced me that it really is a good idea. Today's court proceedings let me announce my malpractice suit in complete sympathy with the Adairs. You should have seen Judge Bailey's and Lanny's faces—it was a hoot!"

"I'm glad we're friends, because you are frighteningly unpredictable," Raleigh said solemnly, shaking his head and seeming to be talking to himself as much as to Nervy.

"Let me reward you for your friendship." She put her purse on her lap. She then began repeatedly reaching into her purse and pulling out short stacks of two or three one-ounce gold coins and depositing them in a line along the edge of his desk until all thirty-eight of them were removed from her purse. "Payment in full is delivered as promised. I would like a receipt indicating that full payment has been made for services rendered regarding Jules Tucker's will. Please don't make mention of gold coins."

Smiling while admiring his payment, he answered, "You can have the receipt say whatever you want. Is there any other legal business you want taken care of?"

"Would you file the malpractice charges against Walter and the insurance company?"

"I guess so . . ." He appeared squeamish. "It seems to be the next step in the process of me stretching my professional boundaries in an effort to help you with unorthodox schemes."

"Good. The sooner the better. I want the case started while the negative sentiment in town is still hanging on from Cindy's death. Can you file it here in town, please?"

"It'll take a day or two—nothing fancy, just the basic stuff to begin with. Are you figuring to go to trial or settle out of court? And by the way, do you want to pay me an hourly fee or on percentage of settlement?"

"Whichever you think will work out best for you," she answered. "Would you still represent me in probate court while they finish up Jules's estate and throw that in for the gold I just paid you?"

"Yes, on the probate business, and twenty-five percent of the award on the malpractice case, but you know malpractice is not my area of expertise," he countered.

"I'm good with both those terms and I don't think you are going to have to be that good to prevail with the insurance company. Let me know when probate says I can put Jules's house and car up for sale."

Raleigh agreed and they promised to be in touch soon. She walked through the waiting room and wished the receptionist a good day as she headed back out to her country refuge with Bertha and Woodrow.

The drive to the farm was pleasant. She was enjoying a sense of satisfaction about her and Raleigh's defeat of the legal assaults Justin and Lanny had thrown at them. The possibility that she could find a tranquil life after Walter seemed feasible to her; maybe she could park a trailer or put a double-wide on her forty acres and leave the people and hassles of Clay Center behind. After arriving at the farm, she entered the house and hollered a greeting beyond the empty kitchen. Bertha hollered back, letting her know that a package that Nervy must have mailed to herself had been delivered and she put it upstairs on the bed.

CHAPTER 31

Nervy had awakened to a mid-February Sunday morning and had already run outside through the frigid morning air to the outhouse and returned. Now back in her upstairs bedroom, she was selecting clothes to take to the bathroom downstairs, where there was heat and she could get ready more comfortably and change into clothes appropriate for attending church later in the morning. Woodrow had been outside long enough to have his chores half done, and Bertha was in the kitchen preparing breakfast, making the smells of bacon and a hot oven infiltrate the house all the way up to Nervy's unheated bedroom. She felt herself to be part of a completely loving family for the first time in her life. Her time with Walter had been the happy life of a married couple, but somehow different than a full "family." Perhaps the fact that she had a father figure now who showed only respect and fondness for her made things different, or maybe it was that the mother and father figures loved and respected each other unquestioningly. She found herself talking as little as Bertha and Woodrow as she lived at their house because the predictable roles, affections, and simplicity of their lives didn't require much inquiry or affirmation.

Attending Sunday church with Bertha had become part of Nervy's routine, but she had drawn the line on going with her to Wednesday night prayer meeting. There was no way that she could believe that her prayers could carry the influence with God that real church people's prayers did. Nervy thought about God more often now that she lived with the Turners and was occasionally offering gratitude to God in her thoughts when things worked out the way she wanted, especially for the money she got from Jules's estate and Walter's life insurance policy.

Sunday breakfast unfolded in the usual manner, and Bertha prayed her usual prayer, but with an unexpected sentence thanking God for the love that each one at the table had for the others.

As they ate, Nervy noticed that Bertha had not begun her usual preparations for Sunday dinner. She thought of asking Bertha about it but knew that the old woman never operated by accident or inattention, so she decided to wait and see what would unfold when the time came.

Going to church had developed its own routine, like so much of the rest of life had on the farm. Woodrow went out, started the truck, and turned it around so the passenger door was closer to the back porch. When Bertha was ready to leave, she would walk out the back door and wait for Nervy at the truck's door. Nervy would climb in and sit in the middle of the pickup's bench seat, and Bertha would sit next to the door and hold her purse on her lap. At church Nervy sat next to Bertha in the back row. The services were becoming familiar: the most likely songs to be sung, which men prayed the longest, when the pastor was likely to shout, and when the congregation was likely to offer amens. Sermons were irrelevant to her, so she read the Bible and was surprised by how the bad guys had been trying to exploit and kill people even back then. When the altar call came at the end of the service for people to come forward and kneel at the edge of the pulpit to conduct *special business* with God, Bertha went forward this Sunday for the first time since Nervy had been attending with her. She wondered just how usual this was for her, but like so much of Bertha's life, her worship was something Nervy didn't feel comfortable or entitled to directly investigate. After the closing prayer the other members began mingling and engaging in pleasantries, but Bertha made a hasty departure and direct beeline out the door for Woodrow's truck. Nervy hurriedly followed, barely keeping up.

Halfway home from church, Nervy saw a pickup riding high on oversized tires with a big brush buster on the front approaching them at breakneck speed. It shifted its path to their side of the road, aiming right for them. Woodrow frantically veered to the left side of the road. Nervy was watching the other vehicle, hoping that it would avoid them, and as she looked out Bertha's window she glanced at Bertha and saw that her benefactor was calmly facing straight ahead with her eyes closed and her lips moving in silent prayer. Her purse was held tightly in her lap and her woolen winter scarf tied securely in place.

Nervy regained consciousness as the pain of being pulled out of the mangled cab of the truck and placed on her back on the ambulance gurney awakened her. She realized that her head was being secured between two blocks of foam, and then she felt her legs, her torso, and her arms all being strapped down securely. A deep part of her memory told her to never submit to being restrained, but her body and mind didn't seem to be working cooperatively and she lay there passively. Her next conscious moment was in the ER, where she became aware of a bright light being shone in first one eye and then the other while both of her eyelids were held open. People were in motion around her, and there was more talking and more voices than she could follow, so she let go of consciousness again, not really wanting to be a part of the pain she was feeling or the surrounding confusion.

A headache was her next awareness and, as a distraction from the pain, she decided to open her eyes. She was in a dark room and in a bed with a hard mattress. She took a consciously deep breath and felt immediate sharp pains in her rib cage.

She gasped with pain and a voice from the darkness asked, "Nervy, are you conscious?" She felt the question to be a burdensome intrusion into her suffering and wondered who would bother her like that.

"Who wants to know?" she forced out in a whisper.

"Raleigh," he said softly. She let the answer sink in slowly. One idea connected to another and began forming a hazy understanding of how she had gotten here. "Damn ambulance chaser." She grimaced, having failed at forming a smile.

Following her invitation to engage in mutual insults, he responded, "I thought maybe you would want me to get another malpractice case started tonight."

"Not tonight," she replied. "How's everybody else?" His pause in answering told her that she needed to prepare herself for bad news.

"The old lady was killed outright by the impact. The old man is hanging in there but is a lot worse off than you," he told her bluntly.

"Go home, Raleigh." She sighed. "Really, thanks for being here, but please go home, and send the nurse in on your way out—I'm hurting."

CHAPTER 32

The next morning's wakefulness brought Nervy a clearer understanding of the extent of her new physical and emotional injuries. She was quickly subject to a bustle of clinical activity, including blood pressure, temperature, and pulse rate measurements. As she sat up in bed to cooperate with the nurses, Nervy felt pain in every area involved with the effort. She felt her face grimace, but she suppressed the cries and groans of pain that her muscles were demanding. The nurse replaced the IV fluid bag hanging from a pole at the head of her bed. Morning pills were presented with a Styrofoam cup of ice water, which she sipped through a straw with an elbow in it. Breakfast was on a tray set on the adjustable table and included a cup of black coffee apparently made by a non–coffee drinker who had been too generous with the water. There was also a small disposable container of orange Jell-O that had the aluminum foil cover partially pulled back so that she could access the Jell-O with the accompanying cheap plastic spoon. Almost every interaction and movement had its own special discomfort, but she decided to conduct herself as someone who was too tough and proud to complain out loud about the cost of still being alive and functional.

Shortly after finishing her clear liquid breakfast, she asked for assistance to use the bathroom. She was told that the doctor wanted her on full bed rest and that they would have to bring her a bedpan. At this point she decided it was time she took control of her own care. She instructed the nurse to either help her get to the toilet or leave the room so she wouldn't have to participate in Nervy's rebellion. Luckily the nurse proved herself to be the type who had more interest in caring for patients than following the orders of a doctor who had not yet examined the patient himself.

Within an hour of Nervy's illicit bathroom excursion, the doctor did show up for morning rounds. At first glance Nervy estimated him to be fifteen years younger than herself. Besides his unbuttoned white coat, he was wearing blue jeans, an open-collar plaid shirt, and Docker-style boat shoes without socks. His attire was complemented by a stethoscope draped around his neck.

"Minerva, I'm Dr. Rutledge and I'll be caring for you while you are in the hospital," he said. "How are you doing this morning?"

"I feel like I was hit by a truck! Do I have any serious injuries?"

"No fractures and no internal bleeding. You had a hard knock on your head, so my diagnosis is a concussion," he explained.

"Are you taking care of the older gentleman that was in the wreck with me?" she asked.

"I don't have a release of information to talk to you about his care," he replied with a remarkable air of unconcern, not even looking up from her medical chart. "I'd like to keep you in the hospital for another day to allow you to rest physically and not move your head around too much."

"I'm leaving as soon as I can get my clothes and belongings together."

"As you wish," he answered, foregoing any argument at all. He turned to the nurse, who had come into the room with him, and told her, "Get her the AMA forms to fill out." Then turning to Nervy, he said, "Watch for headache for the next few days, and don't take any sedating substances because you are likely going to be groggy for the next couple of days due to your concussion, and they would just make it worse. If you start vomiting or have any symptoms you think are serious, just come into the ER and get them checked out. You are going to have a lot of aches and pains all over your body, and they will probably be at their worst tomorrow or the next day. I wish you well. You are a lucky woman to have come out of that wreck alive." With that he turned and left.

"That went easier than I figured," she said to the empty doorway.

Having already had the experience of getting out of bed and limping on both legs, she expected the pain, but she was amazed by the distress in her back when she stooped over to pick up her shoes and the resistance each of her knees screamed as they bent to bring her feet in reach of her hands to put her shoes on. Her last awakening was the pain of reaching her arms backward to get them in her blouse. With her clothes from yesterday back on and her personal belongings collected, she went to the front door of the hospital, but rather than exiting, she stopped at the reception desk and asked for Mr. Woodrow Turner's room number. Told that it was 416, bed A, she went back to the elevators and up to the fourth floor. She knocked on 416's closed door and received no answer. Nervy pushed the door open and saw Woodrow in bed with his eyes closed. He had casts on both legs and his left arm. He had an IV bag hanging overhead that was connected to his right arm and a urinary catheter bag hanging on the side of the bed that was half filled with fluid that was more orange and pink than yellow. He looked very tired and was breathing quickly and shallowly, with a slight snore every few breaths. She decided not to bother him. It was clear that he would be in the hospital long enough that she would have plenty of opportunities to visit him in the coming weeks and didn't need to wake him now.

After painfully navigating her way back to the elevators and down to the lobby, she called Raleigh's office and asked his secretary to ask him if he could pick her up from the hospital, since she was being discharged. The secretary told her that he was in court all day but that she could run by herself over the lunch hour and pick her up. Nervy accepted the offer and sat down to read a three-year-old *People* magazine in the lobby. She dozed off and was awakened an hour and a half later by Raleigh's secretary, who was gently shaking her shoulder and calling her name. Nervy profusely thanked her for the ride and apologized for not having been at the curb in front of the hospital waiting for her. Once they were in the car, the secretary asked where Nervy wanted to be taken. Thinking that a ride clear out to the Turner's farm was inappropriate, she asked to be dropped off at the closed psychiatry office, which was a ten-minute drive from the hospital.

As she dropped Nervy off in front of the office building, the legal secretary asked if Nervy needed anything else, to which Nervy replied, "Have Raleigh stop by to check on me before he goes home tonight."

"Will do," the secretary confirmed with a smile. Nervy maneuvered out of the passenger seat, feeling a dozen different aches and pains, and to an upright standing posture in the parking lot beside the car.

The secretary backed out of the parking space and waved briefly, leaving Nervy to navigate into the office building as best as she was able. The walk seemed to loosen up the stiffness of her limbs and resulted in a diminishment of her aches and pains, but the more she moved, the more she noticed a recip-rocal worsening of her dizzy, headachy feeling. As she reached the office door, she realized that her limit for tolerating the dizziness had been reached. She managed to make it into the office and shut the door. Then she leaned her back against the wall and slid down, until she was sitting on the floor under the light switch, which she had not bothered to turn on. She immediately drifted into unconsciousness and slumped over.

CHAPTER 33

Nervy became aware of an increasingly vigorous pounding sound, and at first she thought that perhaps it was her pulse. Then she accepted the idea that it was a part of her headache pain. But she gradually recognized her name was being called in a pattern with the banging. Four pounding sounds and her name called, four pounding sounds and her name called. She opened her eyes to a completely dark room. The pattern persisted. With the significance of the racket just beyond her mental grasp, the announcements of her name became increasingly urgent. A fuzzy idea of her being behind a closed door began forming in her thoughts—she could stop the pounding and calling of her name by opening the door. Her attempt to stand upright awakened pain in every limb as she successively recruited each one of them for her effort. The pain cleared her consciousness enough that by the time she was able to get hold of the doorknob she remembered how to unlock it.

The door opened, letting in light from the hallway, and a man's shadow flowed into the room with the light. The calling of her name now continued with no pounding. Instead, her name was now incorporated into a pattern of gentle shakes to her shoulders.

"Hands on my shoulders is against the rules!" she mumbled nearly incoherently.

"What rules?" Raleigh asked, raising his eyebrows in surprise.

"Nobody gets to know the rules," she said, affirming her autonomy to herself.

"Okay, can I turn on the lights? Is that allowed in the rules?"

"Sure," she said, "but no touching unless I say so!"

"Sounds like a good rule. I can live with that," Raleigh said reassuringly. "How about helping you get set down in a chair? You up for that?" Operating within a concussion fog, Nervy reasoned that sitting down might lead to lying down, and that could lead to God knows what else.

"What you want, mister? Did Daddy send you?"

"No, Nervy, it's me, Raleigh, your lawyer."

"Yeah, but did Daddy send you?"

"No, Nervy, you've been hurt. You were in a car wreck and Mrs. Turner was killed and Mr. Turner is in the hospital with lots of injuries." He had pierced the fog, and Nervy hated him for restoring her clarity by using what she wanted most to not know.

"Damn you, you damned lawyer—God damn. Turn out the lights!"

"No, I won't turn out the lights. It's against the rules."

"Why?" She slowly pondered his unexpected response. "Whose rules?"

"Mine," he said authoritatively. "I won't help people in the dark. It's too shady and I'm not that shady."

"Well, how shady are you then?" She asked what she thought was the obvious question and then slipped into a conveniently waiting lapse of consciousness.

The smell of pizza invited Nervy to awake. She was lying on her back and staring directly into a ceiling fixture containing two pairs of four-foot-long fluorescent bulbs. Turning her head to the left, she saw Raleigh sitting in a chair and eating a piece of pizza. On the floor beside his chair were a large carry-out soft drink and an open Domino's pizza box with half the pizza missing. Looking down at herself, she saw that she was covered from the shoulders to the hips by Raleigh's suit coat as a sort of blanket on top of her other clothing. The pain of lying on the hard floor made her shift her position in an effort to get some relief. Her movement drew Raleigh's attention.

"You back among the living?" he asked.

"Is that who you are?" she challenged sarcastically. "I figured this might be hell, sleeping under fluorescent lights on a hard floor beside a half-empty pizza box."

"Why, is that against your rules?" he challenged back.

"Oh shit, I didn't tell you the rules, did I? I must really have been messed up."

"Yes, you were messed up, but no, you didn't tell me the rules. Are they interesting?"

"Wouldn't you like to know," she retorted. "Can I have some of the pizza?"

"Sure, if you can sit up and feed yourself," he said, then added, "and if you don't complain about the anchovies."

As Nervy ate, she felt herself gain mental clarity and connection with the world.

"Thank you for the pizza and babysitting."

"You're welcome."

The exchange was followed by an awkward silence that was finally interrupted by Raleigh. "Do you have any idea who ran into you?"

"I have no doubt who it was! Was he killed in the wreck?"

"It was a hit-and-run. The sheriff has no idea who it was. Their main theory is that it was just a reckless redneck probably still drunk from Saturday night," he explained.

"It was Jared Grant, Fatty's nephew. He killed Walter. He killed the Adairs. He shot Candy Adair. He is the father to her kids. He knows I know all this and Fatty knows I know all this too. The wreck was a failed hit on me and killed Bertha instead."

"That is a pretty fantastic story. Are you sure you're thinking straight? You were in a bad wreck and hit your head pretty hard."

"Believe what you want. It doesn't matter to me, because I'm going to take care of it by myself. I'm sorry I even bothered you with it."

Seeming displeased by being so easily dismissed, Raleigh reopened the issue of Nervy's explanation. "If this is true, shouldn't you take it to the authorities?"

She reached for the last piece of pizza and looked up at him with the same kind of tired compassion a mother might have as she explains an ugly fact of life to her innocent child. "Raleigh, I'm a criminal—a felon." As she continued, she redirected her gaze into the empty pizza box to relieve herself of the burden of eye contact as she revealed dark parts of herself. "I'm a criminal with a problem, and the 'authorities' won't solve my problem because they don't like to help criminals. If I go to them and they actually do decide to take me seriously, their investigation will drag my problem out longer and make my enemies harder to deal with. I need to solve this problem myself the way criminals solve their problems. I have to be a better criminal than the ones causing my problem. In the end I usually am." She expected him to look at her with a shocked innocence, but instead she saw that he was looking away from her and seemed deep in thought.

"So, you have rules and you are an especially successful criminal. Can I assume that your rules are the key to your effectiveness?" He looked into her eyes unflinchingly.

She returned his eye contact and asked, "Who are you, and what have you done with the Raleigh I know?"

"What have you done with the Nervy I know?"

"You knew I was a criminal; we just never got into the specifics before. And no, you don't get to know about the rules or their purpose, at least not today, because I'm not up to it."

A quiet settled between the two of them. After a few moments Nervy asked, "What time is it?"

"Four a.m."

"I need to get back out to the Turners' farm and take care of my dog and look for his dog. It was in the back of the truck when we were hit. The old man has livestock chores that somebody needs to do too. Could you give me a ride out there . . . please?"

"Absolutely. Do you think you are going to feel like being in court tomorrow morning for the malpractice insurance company's settlement presentation?"

She pushed herself up from the floor, answering in a muted voice, attempting to stifle groans of pain, "So long as you are there I won't need to say much."

The predawn drive out to the farm Tuesday morning was generally quiet. By the time they passed the church, enough light was available to dimly see the mangled wreck of Woodrow's flatbed pushed off the gravel road into the grader ditch. She turned her head, looking at the carnage and trying to see as much as she could. Raleigh drove past without slowing down. Once at the farm, Nervy slowly agonized her way out of his car and, feeling a sense of debt to him that she rarely felt toward anyone, she thanked Raleigh for all his help and concern the past couple of days.

CHAPTER 34

Watching Raleigh's car back out of the drive and turn toward town, Nervy felt the full weight of being alone and at war with her past life. Tackling her first chore, she let Griff out of the chicken coop. He jumped up on her again and again. Despite the discomfort his exuberance was causing her legs, she was accepting the deepest affection available to her in the emptiest moment she had ever lived through.

Next, she began her search for Woodrow's heeler. The morning light was strengthening enough she didn't need a flashlight. First searching the yard, then the barn lot, she found no sign of a lost or injured dog. Nervy went back to the driveway, got in her car with Griff, and headed to the wreck. When she neared the location, she pulled onto the shoulder of the road and inched forward, scrutinizing the roadside. She parked twenty feet short of the wreckage. Intending to methodically search a ten-foot-wide perimeter around the truck, Nervy had taken her first few steps when Griff's whining called her attention to a large clump of weeds next to the truck's flatbed, which was now perpendicular to the ground. Curled up and covered with a crust of dry grass and clotted blood, Number Three was silently, motionlessly monitoring the movements of her two rescuers with one eye, the other eye being swollen shut. Nervy's respect for Number Three grew as she realized the extent of the blood the wounded creature had lost and that her usual stoic resolve was completely undiminished. She started her triage of the heeler by talking to her softly to see if human attention would result in defensiveness or acceptance. The injured dog lowered her head a little, so Nervy reached her hand toward Three's muzzle to see if she would flinch. Instead she extended her nose and licked the hand weakly. Nervy called her, but Three's attempt to stand resulted only in a feeble rocking motion. Nervy moved closer to her and rubbed her hand down the full extent of the dog's back, trying to feel for discernible injuries to the bones, skin, and muscles under the thick crust of debris. The dog accepted Nervy's examination and licked at her hand again. Next, Nervy attempted to lift the dog, but her own muscle and joint pain caused her to set Three back down again quickly to avoid dropping her. Realizing now that she only had the stamina for doing this one time, Nervy opened the car door to have everything ready before trying to lift forty pounds of limp farm dog again. She took a deep breath and mentally steeled herself for the coming exertion, then with as much self-sacrificing discomfort she could remember ever mustering, she waddled the dog to the back seat of her waiting car. Nervy shut the door and leaned heavily against it, allowing herself to catch her breath and let some of the pain in her back and limbs subside. When she was sufficiently ready, Nervy opened the driver's door and called for Griff to jump in.

Once in the car, she drove up to the church to turn around and head her canine ambulance back toward the house. Three cars were in the parking area, and three women were walking from them into the church. They were obviously gathering in response to their shared love for Bertha, but Nervy felt no community among them; not because she didn't share their love for the dead woman, but because it was her personal badness and criminal choices that had gotten Bertha killed. No doubt the church people viewed her in the same condemning light. Her pause while lost in thought attracted the women's notice, and one of them, someone Nervy recognized as a regular attendee at church, walked to her car. The woman stooped down and spoke through the window.

"Mrs. Tucker, I didn't know you were out of the hospital yet. Are you doing okay?" the woman asked.

Nervy was emotionally overpowered by the woman's simple and sincere concern. Tears welled up in her eyes as she answered, unsure of what to say. "I'm as good as I can be right now . . . I just picked up Woodrow's dog from the accident scene. She looks hurt pretty bad, so I'm taking her home . . . There's chores need doing around the place . . . It just wasn't in me to stay in the hospital . . ."

"You and Woodrow are in all of our prayers. Tell me what we can do to help," the woman persisted.

Nervy was again emotionally overwhelmed, but this time it was by her realization that she had no answer for how someone could help her. Asking for help was foreign to her. The idea that she might ask for help from someone else had been beaten out of her early in life. "I'll get along okay," Nervy heard herself lamely say.

"You're welcome to join us—we're here to pray for strength and peace to accept Bertha's going home to Jesus. We're also finishing the plans for her funeral tomorrow. Please join us. It would mean a lot to us, and I know it would have meant a lot to Bertha."

Nervy bluntly replied, "You're very kind, but I don't have the strength to pray for strength right now. I've got to stay busy, so please excuse me." Nervy waited for the woman to step back from the car window and then pulled back onto the road to seek more familiar shelter in her loneliness on the farm.

CHAPTER 35

Nervy's foremost worry as she pulled into the Turners' driveway was that she was going to need sleep, but sleeping alone in a location known to her enemies was risky. Addressing her options as analytically as her injured mind was able, she figured the best place for her to live right now was here at the farmhouse. The office in town was an option, but if her hunter tracked her down there, a gunfight in town would add immeasurably to her problems if she lived through it. The quiet of the farm setting would permit her dogs to hear intruders approach and raise an alarm. Any attack or counterattack involving assassins here would jeopardize the fewest number of uninvolved people.

Along with her new plan for living in the house alone, she suspended the Turners' rule about no dogs in the house. Number Three couldn't defend herself from predators or attackers outside, as injured as she was. Nervy got out of the car, stepped onto the back porch, and grabbed Bertha's hooded zip-up sweatshirt from its hook. She placed it on the floor, folded in a particular manner to form a multilayered dog bed. After much painful struggling, Nervy eventually nestled

Number Three on her new porch bed. She then let Griff in the Turners' house and allowed him to follow her around as she fetched the three handguns from her upstairs bedroom and distributed them strategically. The .22 she put in the outhouse behind a couple of rolls of toilet paper sitting on a shelf on the wall. She went back outside and put the .38 between the driver's seat and driver's door in her car. The Glock that Jules had posthumously contributed to her arsenal was selected to be her new carry piece. She intended to never be without the Glock unless she was entering some location where she could expect to be searched. Her next task was to hunt through the house to see if Woodrow had a rifle and shotgun like most farmers kept for dispatching terminally ill livestock or getting rid of annoying vermin, such as possums and coons. After searching the porch and the kitchen and finding no long guns, she went to the old couple's bedroom and looked in the back of Woodrow's side of the closet, where she found a pump-action .22 rifle and a double-barreled 12-gauge shotgun leaning next to each other. Nervy checked and found that both of the guns were unloaded. She took the double-barreled 12-gauge up to her room and placed the .22 rifle in the kitchen behind the door.

With her canine patient in her hospital porch bed and her weapons positioned tactically, Nervy focused on feeding the dogs. For Bertha and Woodrow, dog food had always consisted of scraps and leftovers, so she searched the kitchen for something the dogs could eat. She needed to feed them both the same thing to avoid conflict or jealously between them. Finding enough scraps to equally fill two soup bowls, Nervy served the canines their separate lunches in opposite corners of the porch. "Well, guys, I hope you don't mind that I mixed breakfast and lunch all together," she mused aloud as she left the porch and headed for town.

She made it back to Clay Center by midafternoon. Her first stop was Clay Center Motors. A clean-cut, tall, and slender young man came out to the used car lot, where she had begun looking around at pickup trucks.

"May I help you, ma'am?" he asked. She had expected someone older and more patronizing, which made his respect and transparency refreshing.

"I want to spend around twenty thousand dollars and get a full-size, four-wheel-drive pickup for hard farm-type work."

"Everything we have on our lot would cost more than that, but we can go inside and look through the listings on the computer from our sister dealerships," he respectfully replied. Perusing the computer listings, Nervy and her assistant found a suitable ten-year-old Ford F250 with a hundred thousand miles on it at a dealership in Des Moines about a hundred and fifty miles away. After checking with his manager, the young salesman came back and told her the price on the truck was twenty-one thousand, and the fee for having it delivered to Clay Center would be eight hundred dollars.

Nervy replied, "Thank you for your assistance today. Tell your sales manager I'll be back Friday with a certified twenty-one-thousand-dollar check from my bank, and that's what I'll pay for everything if you've got the truck here." With that she returned to her car.

The next stop was Walmart, where she got twenty pounds of hamburger, forty bounds of dry dog food, a large jar of crunchy peanut butter, a loaf of bread, a jar of instant coffee, a two-battery Maglite aluminum tube flashlight and a four-pack of C-cell batteries, a box of fifty high-velocity .22 bullets, and a box of 12-gauge shotgun shells filled with #4 buckshot. Placing the ammunition in her cart, she remembered that she had never found Jules's 9mm ammo for his Glock, so she picked up a box of those as well. After checking out through the express lane and paying with cash, she was in the car and headed for the farm.

Back at home with her purchases unpacked and her phone in the charger for the night, she boiled a pound of the hamburger and divided it between the two dogs for their supper. Nervy was sure that the wounded heeler would dependably eat hamburger and that it would be good nutrition for her healing. The plan was to feed hamburger to Three until she had mended enough to walk on her own and then switch her over to dog food. In the meantime Nervy wasn't about to make Griff witness another dog getting better meals than he did.

After feeding the dogs, she made herself a peanut butter sandwich and then ate it while opening the flashlight packaging. Two C-cell batteries fit perfectly into the flashlight handle, resulting in a reassuring heft to the light as she held it and hit it against her other hand. The beam was bright and could be adjusted. Deciding to test the effective distance of the narrow beam outside, she stood on the back porch steps and found that it illuminated her car in the driveway about as much as daylight did. When she shone it at the barn a hundred yards away, it put out a spot of light four feet wide and bright enough to clearly illuminate a human form if one were standing there.

Before going to bed, Nervy wanted to make sure that today's two additions to her armaments were loaded and ready for action, so she went to the kitchen and retrieved the .22 rifle. She slid ten bullets down the magazine tube, then cycled the pump once and then again to make sure it fed the bullets in and out of the firing chamber. The .22 passed the test and she picked up the ejected bullets and placed them back in the rifle's tubular magazine. With the .22 back behind the kitchen door, she went upstairs and turned her attention to the double-barreled 12-gauge. She opened and closed the barrels to check that the shells would fully eject when the barrels were opened and that the triggers would be reset by the closing of the barrels.

CHAPTER 36

The first night in the house alone passed without incident. Nervy awakened somewhat tired because Griff couldn't resist exploring his new surroundings periodically throughout the night. Nervy got up, collected her Glock from under her pillow, and went down to check on Number Three. The heeler seemed more alert and held her head higher than yesterday. Smiling to herself, Nervy considered the possibility that Three was more alert because she was checking to see if breakfast would include boiled hamburger.

While making breakfast and boiling meat for the dogs, Nervy called Raleigh to let him know she was going to Bertha's funeral instead of the malpractice hearing. She made the call to Raleigh's office and left the message with the secretary. Nervy was portioning out the boiled meat for the dogs when she heard the sound of tires on gravel. Reflexively ducking away from the window, she drew her Glock and checked to see that the loaded chamber indicator was sticking out. She then released the magazine and verified that there were fifteen rounds of ammo in the clip. Only after pushing the magazine back up into its fully seated position did she peek out the edge of the window. A man had parked his pickup in the driveway and was walking toward the barnyard gate with his back to the house. Nervy kept a firm grip on the Glock as she slipped out the back door and eased it closed. She walked unnoticed to the cab of his truck, keeping the gun low and close to her side while she looked inside to make sure no one else was hiding in there.

Securing herself in a well-protected stance behind the truck, she hollered angrily, "What are you doing here?" The man turned around and looked for the source of the call. As he was looking, Nervy saw that he carried no weapon.

Seeming to be talking in the direction of the house rather than the truck she was hiding behind, he hollered back, "I'm Bill Long. My wife talked to Mrs. Tucker yesterday down at the church and told me that she would need help getting Woodrow's chores taken care of. I came by this morning to see what kind of chores needed doing." Recognizing the innocence of the circumstances, Nervy was instantly glad she had not brandished her weapon and slid the gun in her coat pocket as she stepped from behind the truck.

"I was just getting around to go out and check on things myself when I heard you pull up. Since that accident I'm being careful about keeping an eye on people and situations that I don't expect. Sorry that I yelled at you."

"Well I could honk or holler or something when I get here so you know that I'm here and not trying to surprise you." The longer he talked, the more she remembered seeing him at church and increasingly accepted his sincerity.

"If you've got any way of moving those big bales of hay from the barn lot to feed the cattle over in that east pasture, it would be a big help."

"I got a bale stabber on the back of my truck here—use it every day to feed my cattle, so it won't be no big deal for me to feed Woodrow's cows."

"I can take care of the pigs myself. There's only five of them, and I can handle one or two buckets of feed for them by myself. I thank you for your consideration for me and the Turners," Nervy told the young man.

"They were awful good to my wife and I when we were getting our start on our farm," he explained.

"Listen, Friday I'm bringing Woodrow a replacement truck out here for when he gets out of the hospital. Would you be able to go to town and help me drive it out here?"

"Glad to."

"Thanks, that'll be a big help."

Turning her thoughts to Bertha's memorial, Nervy asked, "What time is the funeral?"

"Two this afternoon."

"How's the funeral being paid for, anyway, Woodrow being in the hospital and all?"

"Church," he answered. "She's given so much of herself and their money to the church that it was the least we could do. The doctor told the pastor that Woodrow was too weak to be able to leave the hospital for the funeral and said he wasn't sure Woodrow would even be able to know what was going on yet if he did attend . . . Said he's still out of it a lot."

The mention of Woodrow's continued suffering stirred a mixture of renewed sorrow and regret in Nervy's mind.

"I'll see you at the service later." She dismissed herself and returned to the house to give the dogs breakfast.

Nervy made it to the church at 1:45 and found the parking lot full of the mourners' cars. The hearse was backed up to the front door as close as possible, which caused Nervy to smile when she realized that was the exact location Woodrow always parked while picking up Bertha.

Inside the church, Nervy found that every pew was filled, as were the extra folding chairs the funeral home had brought and set up in any open spaces in the church's sanctuary. Despite the extra seating, there was standing room only when Nervy made it inside. She edged her way along the back wall of the sanctuary toward the corner, out of the way of the various people talking and reminiscing with one another. She was settling into a leaning position against the convergence of the two walls, trying to avoid any undue attention, when she thought she heard her name called. She ignored the thought but then unmistakably heard her name called again, this time loudly enough that the chatter in the room dropped to a whisper. The pastor was calling her name and motioning for the crowd to make way for her to come to the front pew where he was waiting. The crowd obligingly parted, and Nervy found herself facing a direct path to the front of the church. She went forward feeling very self-conscious and kept her gaze to the floor, worried that all the eyes in the church were watching her. When she reached the front of the church, the pastor guided her to an empty seat in the front pew next to a woman she had never seen who looked to be in her thirties. The pastor introduced the seated woman as Bertha's closest relative, a niece, her deceased brother's daughter. The pastor then introduced Nervy as Bertha's best friend's daughter and a friend of Bertha's in her own right. He then seated Nervy next to the niece as the two guests of honor.

The funeral was begun by the pianist playing an intro to Bertha's favorite hymn, which the congregation picked up and sang with the strength and passion of people who believe that their dead loved one was living and listening just out of sight above them, standing next to her Savior. The service transitioned to a sermon memorializing the faith and accomplishments of a woman whose life touched all of those gathered and many of their parents' lives as well. Both men's and women's voices repeatedly and loudly accented the pastor's narrative with their emphatic amens as he compared Bertha's life and ministry with the lives of faithful women mentioned in the stories of the Bible. With the singing of two more hymns the pastor called forward six deacons, who were each asked to express a prayer of thanks for the woman's life they were laying to rest and to pray for strength for the church and loved ones who would be mourning Bertha's death in the days and weeks to come. Each man spoke to God plainly about his gratitude, his sorrows, and his hopes for the ones that Bertha left behind. With the prayers finished, the pastor stepped to the head of the casket, and each of the deacons took their positions along both sides, lifting and carrying it to the waiting hearse. The funeral home director solemnly stepped toward Nervy and the niece, motioning for them to follow directly behind the casket. The remaining mourners were dismissed row by row to go to their cars and turn on their headlights and join the funeral procession to the cemetery.

Nervy and the niece were driven to the cemetery in the funeral home's limo, but even being among so many attendants, the ride down the road from the church was still somewhat of an emotional trigger for Nervy when the procession passed the fateful spot. She had collected herself emotionally by the time they reached the cemetery. Again, she and the niece were ushered to the seats of prominence and each was asked to throw a symbolic handful of earth onto the casket after it had been lowered into the ground. After the close of the service, and having accepted the condolences of at least three dozen people, Nervy took a few moments to walk to her mother's nearby grave. She paused and felt her love for her mother deepen as she connected the love that her mother had had for Bertha with the subsequent love Bertha had shown to her these past few weeks. She found herself thanking God for the intertwined lives of these two women, whose bodies were both laid to rest on the same patch of ground. She then rejoined the remaining mourners and rode in the limo back the church.

Back home, she evaluated Number Three's recovery. The dog was still lying in the nest that Nervy had made using Bertha's sweatshirt, but she was facing a different direction than when Nervy had left earlier. Nervy figured Three had probably moved herself around under her own power; it was a good sign.

CHAPTER 37

On her way to town for meetings with bankers and lawyers on Thursday morning, Nervy thought of Woodrow and intended to provide him an extra measure of comfort by taking him a picture of Bertha and him together that she had found on the dresser in their bedroom. She hoped he would be awake when she visited and know who she was. Her other hope was that he would be willing to have her live with him when he was able to go home and let her care for him until he could live on his own, if he was ever able to.

Once in town, her first stop was the bank. Nervy walked in, expecting her transaction wouldn't take long. Nervy approached a twentysomething teller at the counter and asked her for a certified check for $21,000 made out to Clay Center Motors. The teller asked Nervy to wait and then departed her station to confer with a gentleman in a suit who was sitting in an office with a glass wall, through which he oversaw all the tellers and lobby activities. The teller returned and asked for Nervy's account number. After another consultation with the supervisor, the teller returned with a check she handed to Nervy and a receipt indicating the amount of money that would be deducted from the indicated account to cover the cost of processing the certified check. With a smile and a courteous wish for her to have a good day, the teller concluded their transaction. Walking out of the bank, Nervy calculated that the check in her pocket reduced her holdings in the bank to about $210,000. She had deposited the $100,000 life insurance check from Walter's death as well as the $130,000 from the sale of Jules's house and $10,000 from the sale of his Cadillac. Of course, her calculations didn't include the value of the 112 Gold Eagle coins in the safe-deposit box, because she didn't know the market value of the coins at this particular moment.

Her next stop was Raleigh's office, where the secretary said that if she would wait for another twenty minutes he would be finished with the client in his office and they could have lunch together until about 1:30, when his next appointment was scheduled. She told the secretary to have Raleigh meet her at Ruby Tuesday's. Arriving early, Nervy asked the restaurant hostess for the corner booth. With her back to the wall and having a good view of the door, she was drinking her second cup of coffee when Raleigh walked in and scanned the restaurant for her. She waved for his attention. He reached the booth smiling and extended his hand in a pleasant greeting.

"How did the funeral go yesterday?"

"It was sad and beautiful and comforting," she answered. "The love that church had for that woman was amazing. How does that happen?" she wondered more to herself than to Raleigh.

"Maybe she loved them first?" he suggested, seeming to find her question surprising.

"Well, how did the hearing go yesterday?"

"It was very good in general. The company wants to settle out of court and offered seven hundred thousand dollars on one condition," he reported.

Nervy raised her eyebrows inquisitively. "And that is?"

"That you divest yourself of the psychiatric records from Dr. Corvus's practice within the next sixty days," he explained. "And that they be placed in the custody of a responsible individual. Off the record their lawyer pulled me aside and said that he had never been involved in any case like yours. When he found out that you had been married to the treating doctor and the injured patient both within the same six months, he said that he thought of fighting the case by attacking your credibility or maybe even hinting at your having committed murder. But then he realized that the case was the third lawsuit in which they'd had to defend Dr. Corvus. They were well aware of the recent Adair suit even though they had been uninvolved in it. Ultimately, the company realized that there were so many hazards for them in the case that it decided not to get tangled up defending a doctor that had already lost three malpractice cases or take on a 'wildcard plaintiff,' as he called you. They offered you a settlement they thought would please you but required that you surrender custody of the records in the hope that they can avoid having to ever deal with you again."

Nervy squinted her eyes and slowly shook her head. "Do you know of any laws outlining eligibility for being a medical records custodian or maybe restricting who can be?"

"None I know of, other than being trustworthy with handling confidential medical information and having a willingness to provide a safe and secure storage location for the records."

"And all they said was that I had to get rid of the records, get them out of my possession . . . no restriction on how I do it?"

"Now you're worrying me again." He glanced around the restaurant and lowered his voice. "What are you thinking?"

"How about an auction, a silent auction? One buyer with the highest offer gets to be the custodian of all the records. I get paid a settlement and I get paid to get rid of the records.

Satisfying the terms of this settlement agreement sounds like a win-win for me."

"It isn't legal."

"Are you sure that you are not confusing what's respectable with what's legal?" she challenged him. "I just asked your legal opinion on whether there were restrictions on who could be a custodian of medical records, and you said none you knew of. Then I asked if there were restrictions on the means I could use to meet the requirements for getting the records into someone else's custody," she clarified, "and you told me you didn't know of any."

"It is illegal to sell patient medical records. They can be transferred to another doctor if the practice is purchased, but a practice can only be purchased by a doctor. If you wanted to sell the practice, you could, but its value is now nil to any doctor or hospital group because Walter has been dead long enough that any of the patients that needed ongoing care have found another doc to take care of them."

"So, do you have advice on what to do with the records?" she asked in a tone of disappointment.

"Giving them to another doctor's office would be the easiest solution, but in reality the records would just be a burden to them and you would probably have to pay them to take them off your hands."

"Pay them?"

"Yeah, they would have to find space to store them and then have the hassle of copying them when people ask for their records."

"After all the years of therapy and work that went into those records, aren't they worth anything to anybody?" She tilted her head in thought. "Lanny has always found value in Walter's records. I wonder if he would be willing to be the records custodian. What do you think?"

"Why would you even consider that?"

"Why not? I've got nothing left to lose in terms of his suing Walter's estate—that's all covered with the tail policy I got from the malpractice company. Plus the thought of Lanny continuing to harass the malpractice company doesn't bother me at all either. I figure he's so greedy that he wouldn't be able to resist getting his hands on the records, especially if it is for free," she explained, feeling full confidence that his greed would make the offer irresistible.

"You should notify all the patients that you are transferring the records to a new custodian and give them a chance to ask for copies for themselves if they wish, as well as to know where to request copies in the future should they need them," Raleigh added.

"Get the insurance company's offer on paper and get Lanny a letter offering him custody of the records for free, contingent on his accepting the responsibility of notifying the involved patients of the transfer. Throw in the remainder of this year's prepaid contract on Walter's office so he has somewhere to store them for now, and throw in the remaining office furniture so I never have to go back there again," she said, ending their conversation and their meal.

CHAPTER 38

Nervy parked at the hospital and grabbed the picture she had brought from the house. When she arrived at room 416, she found the door open.

Nervy knocked on the doorjamb to announce her presence. With no response, she peeked around the corner and saw Woodrow lying on his back, asleep. He was still the only occupant of the room, so she went in and pulled a chair over to the side of the bed. She sat quietly for a moment and watched him. Eventually she touched his shoulder and called his name. His breathing cadence paused for half a breath, then resumed, with no signs of his waking. She shook his shoulder again a little more firmly and leaned closer to his ear and said his name loud enough to be heard out in the hallway. There was a pause in his breathing, which then resumed with a deep gasp, accompanied by movements of his head and eyebrows as he attempted to open his eyes. Calling him again, she encouraged his efforts. With his eyes finally open, he took a minute to turn his gaze toward the sound of her voice. He fixed his gaze on her eyes and didn't say a word. Despite no facial expression, his eyes began tearing.

"It's Nervy," she said reflexively, trying to divert her own suppressed sorrow and avoid drowning both of them with it. "Can you hear me?" she asked, fearing to ask him deeper questions like whether he knew her or not. He nodded feebly that he could hear her. "I brought you a picture for your room. It's you and Bertha," she explained loudly. "Can I put it here on the counter behind your sink?" Again, he nodded.

With the photo placed on the counter by his sink, Woodrow stared at it for a moment and clearly said, "Tenth wedding anniversary."

Nervy's eyes teared up and overflowed down her cheeks. "It's so good to hear your voice," she said, returning to the chair and placing her hand on his shoulder.

"I've been waiting for you to show up."

"I went to the funeral yesterday and met Bertha's niece. It was a beautiful service," she explained. Woodrow looked away at that point and became silent again. "Has the doctor told you how long they expect you to be in the hospital?"

"A long time . . . weeks," he mumbled softly.

"I found Number Three, and I'm doctoring her with bed rest and cooked hamburger. She eats it pretty good."

"Bring me some of that—sounds better than what they're giving me here. Is she going to make it?"

"I'm betting on it," she said confidently.

"She's a tough bitch," he commented emotionlessly. "Saw her hold three boar hogs all together in one corner of the barn lot one time for twenty minutes . . . tough bitch," he said, his thoughts seeming to wander.

"Well, I don't want to tire you out too much, so I better go," she said.

"Don't take so long to come visit next time," he scolded. "I need to see you, Nervy. Bertha's gone and I don't have anyone else."

"I'll be back sooner, I promise," she confirmed as she backed out the door and into the hall.

On her way to the elevator she passed the nursing station and saw Dr. Rutledge typing away at a computer. He looked up. "Minerva, wasn't it?" he asked directly, but then a quizzical look passed across his face. "Nervy . . . that's it! I bet you're Nervy!" he exclaimed as though he had just discovered penicillin.

"Yes, I'm Nervy."

"He has been asking for you every day. Are you like the third something or other in Mr. Turner's life? He keeps asking about number three."

"No, that would be his dog, Number Three. She was badly injured in the wreck too, and I'm caring for her at Woodrow's house," she clarified. "Can you tell me whether or not you are Woodrow's doctor?"

"I can tell you. I am his doctor."

"Why the sudden flood of information? You wouldn't tell me anything the other day," she reminded him.

"Seems like he's got no living relatives that the social worker can find and he knows his wife is dead and he keeps asking for Nervy. That seems to put you at the top of the list for loved ones that need to be included in the treatment and discharge planning of his hospital care."

"So, what is the plan for Woodrow, Dr. Rutledge?"

"Probably another week in the hospital getting his pain under control, getting his nutrition stable, and making sure his kidney functioning is stable. Then he goes to a rehab facility to regain muscular strength and his ability to perform activities of daily living like getting out of a chair and walking unassisted. Probably about a month there, so maybe get back home to the farm in about five or six weeks, but even then he will need somebody close by twenty-four hours a day to make sure he doesn't fall or get into some sort of crisis."

"That'll be me," she affirmed, and then gave the doctor her phone number in case Woodrow's condition took a turn for the worse.

As she turned to walk down the hall to the elevator, the doctor asked, "How are you doing?"

"Your warnings about the pain and concussion symptoms were dead-on, but I'm doing well now. I'm sure we'll be in touch," she said without turning.

CHAPTER 39

Even though it was the first day of April and six weeks had passed since the hit-and-run, there was never a day went by that she didn't wonder if that was the day that Cooker would make his next play. He wasn't done with her and she sure wasn't done with him. Nervy had fallen into a routine of visiting Woodrow at the rehab center every day. He had just begun walking with a four-legged walker, which he found challenging and often exhausted him. During her visits she would tell him about the dogs, the livestock, the weather, his new truck, and her new Toyota 4Runner, which she had bought because country roads were too hard on her Avalon. She reminded him that the men at the feed store always asked about him and said to say hi to him. She complimented him on his progress at walking and getting out of bed and out of chairs more and more under his own power. Visiting the rehab unit so frequently had acquainted her with all the staff and many of the patients there. She occasionally brought in doughnuts or pizza for the unit.

The rehab unit received a new patient, who was expected to be staying for several weeks. Candy Adair had finally stabilized enough to be transferred from the university hospital to a rehab unit nearer to her home. Nervy had avoided any contact with her because she didn't want to cause any unnecessary stress for the young woman.

Readying for town that morning, Nervy dressed in business attire because she was going to Raleigh's office to sign the settlement the insurance company had offered. Raleigh was also going to review the contract he had drafted for the patient records transfer with her and call Lanny to schedule the signatures on the contract for later that afternoon. Nervy was looking forward to getting the transfer behind her and focusing her life more fully on farm living. Her intentions were to care for Woodrow at his home as long as he needed her and then put a double-wide on her forty acres and live as simply and cheaply as she could.

Nervy entered Raleigh's office shortly before 10:00 and the secretary sent her straight back to his office. "First things first," Raleigh began. "Here is the insurance company contract for you to sign." He laid papers on the desk and offered her a pen. As Nervy began signing the forms, Raleigh moved the conversation on to the next matter of business. "Like I told you earlier, when I called Lanny about the custody of Walter's records, he took the offer with no hesitation."

"Like a moth to the candle," Nervy quipped, completely unsurprised.

Raleigh then began going over the details of the contract he had drafted for the transfer. Nervy listened superficially and nodded her assent to the contract when Raleigh finished. With the contract approved, he picked up the phone and rang his secretary and then asked her to call Lanny's office.

"Hi, this is Raleigh Baggs. I'm calling to let Mr. Peltor know the contract for transferring custody of Dr. Corvus's medical records is complete, and I was wondering if he could find a time late this afternoon or early this evening to stop by my office and sign it." He was quiet for a while and then said, "Five would be fine with me. Tell him I look forward to seeing him then. Goodbye." And with that he hung up.

Nervy arrived at the rehab center carrying a sack with two McDonald's hamburger-and-fry combos, worried she might not have beaten Woodrow's lunch tray to his table. By the time she found him, he was sitting at a table in the commons area of the unit and his lunch tray was already in front of him. It appeared to Nervy he had not even touched his tray, so she scooted it aside and unwrapped the fast food. He smiled appreciatively at her and went for the fries first.

Nervy looked around the room, watching the other patients eat their meals. One of the patients, who was sitting in a wheelchair across the room, was staring back at her. The woman looked thin, pale, tired, and intensely angry. Nervy stared back for a moment and then diverted her gaze as she realized that the patient was the new version of the hateful woman who had stared so aggressively at her throughout Walter's trial. Candy's survival of her gunshot wounds had taken such a severe toll on her that Nervy would never have recognized her except for that glare.

Wishing not to cause any additional distress to Candy, Nervy avoided eye contact and refocused on Woodrow's eating.

Within a couple of minutes Candy was being wheeled past Nervy by a staff member taking her back to her room. As she passed, Candy clearly but weakly said, "Fuck you, I know who you are."

The staff member said, "Candy, that's not very nice!"

Candy replied, "Fuck her, she got my family killed."

"No," Nervy interjected, "we both know that Cooker is the one and only killer in this story, but I'd say the runner-up for fucking your family over is a tie between you, for getting involved with a homicidal tweaker boyfriend, and Lanny, who got your family all stoked up on self-righteous vengeance believing your sister's death was somebody else's fault other than her own." The staff member wisely pushed Candy from the scene of the brewing battle.

All eyes in the room were on Nervy, and she felt the effect of the adrenaline that had taken hold of her. She turned to Woodrow and put her hand warmly on his arm and said, "I'd probably better go now. It seems I've made a scene."

"Sort of like Bertha used to, except she didn't use your kind of words." He smiled back at her with an expression of compassion, which she hadn't expected.

Nervy left the rehab unit, and on her walk through the parking lot she noticed that the sky had darkened a lot since her drive to town this morning. She got into her SUV and went for a drive both to kill time before having to go back to Raleigh's office and to calm herself down and remind herself that the death and destruction in her life the past six months had not been her doing. The first hour was spent driving past the houses she had lived in with Walter and Jules. Then she circled around the psychiatric office and the courthouse before deciding she had the time to make the long drive out to the Greenbriar cemetery, where she planned to talk to the two women who had most tried to save her soul.

At the cemetery her intended visit was cut short by a spring rain that quickly developed into a deluge, driving Nervy back to her waiting car. Anger and sorrow consumed Nervy's thoughts on her drive back to town. All the unnecessary deaths and tragedies weighed on her mind. Mile by mile as she drove to the appointment at the law office, the rhythmic motion of the windshield wipers drummed her anger deeper.

CHAPTER 40

Both of the lawyers were already engaged in a review of the final contract transferring the records. Nervy took a seat but didn't scoot her chair up to the desk with the lawyers and instead sat back as a sort of audience. When the questions had all been deliberated and the answers agreed upon, Raleigh had Lanny signed the contract. With the conclusion of the deal awaiting Nervy's signature, the men turned to Nervy at the same time and signaled her need to get involved.

She looked back and forth between them and, with a complete lack of expression, said to Lanny, "You are about to take possession of more power and information than you have the strength to handle safely." The two men looked at each other questioningly, as if she had lost her mind. "Your addiction to manipulating people and the information contained in these records has poisoned your soul and caused at least three murders," she continued. "And now you are taking the fire into your own bosom."

"Are you threatening me?" Lanny asked.

"Far from it—I'm warning you. You do what you want, but you have no idea what these records will allow you to do to yourself. It's you that you need to be afraid of, Lanny. I'm going to stay as far away from you as I can. You've got nothing to fear from me." She stood and walked to the table and signed the contract.

Lanny gave Raleigh a perplexed look and then turned to Nervy and said, "You better leave me alone if you know what is good for you!" He took the office key from Raleigh and his copy of the contract and left without another word.

Raleigh looked at Nervy after Lanny had left the room. "What the hell was that about?" he asked. "You nearly ruined the deal. You need a records custodian for the insurance deal, and he is the one you told me to reach out to."

"I won't even bother trying to explain it to you, but let's just say that I had a shitty afternoon."

"Whatever," he retorted. "Just don't ruin the deal at this point."

"*Whatever* indeed," she responded. "Give me a bill for your work on the contract when you're ready and I'll pay you." With that she left and headed back out to the farm and the solitude of the country.

Following supper, Nervy found herself emotionally exhausted by the day's events. Deciding to turn in, she took Griff out on his leash an hour earlier than usual. Once outside the terrier caught a scent that provoked such a vigorous tug that he pulled the leash from Nervy's grip and disappeared into the night, barking wildly. Frustrated, Nervy turned on her flashlight and was searching the darkness trying to locate him when she heard the yelp of a coyote. She began running and pointing her light in the direction of the menacing sound and immediately saw two pairs of reflecting eyes thirty yards in front of her that stood their ground as she approached. She switched the flashlight to her left hand and drew the Glock from her jacket pocket with her right. Still running, she searched the ground ahead with her flashlight beam and illuminated Griff to assure herself of his position. Believing herself to be within her range of accuracy, she took a shooting stance, bracing her right wrist on top of her left wrist. With the beam of the Maglite still reflected in a pair of coyote eyes twelve yards ahead, Nervy sighted the pistol and opened fire. After four shots the eyes no longer reflected back in the flashlight beam and there was only silence. She ran forward and scanned the area with back-and-forth sweeps of the light. One coyote silently struggled on the ground, dragging its hind legs in a desperate attempt to escape. Nervy walked to within one step of the animal and placed three more rounds in its back. The animal stopped struggling. Continuing to explore the field to her left, she hoped to find the other coyote. With no success, she began sweeping the area looking for Griff, whom she found vigorously licking blood off the dead coyote. The terrier made no attempt to stop his activity as Nervy approached and seemed unaware that she had taken hold of his leash until she firmly jerked him away from his dead antagonist and took him home. Back in the house, she got a rag and washed the blood off her excited terrier's paws and muzzle and reloaded the Glock.

CHAPTER 41

Nervy hustled to get out of bed a little earlier than usual the next morning. Besides going to town this morning, she hoped to be able to dispose of the coyote carcass before Bill arrived. Outside she grabbed the back leg of the dead coyote and dragged him out to the hog pen, where she hoisted his carcass over the fence, giving the hogs a meal and saving herself the need of getting a bucket of hog feed. All five hogs converged on the carcass at once and squealed deafeningly as they argued for their share of the newfound feast. On her way back to the house, Bill arrived and honked a greeting.

Having rushed through her and the dogs' breakfasts and then through her getting ready, Nervy left for her trip into Clay Center right on her intended schedule. Raleigh's office was her first stop. She went in to inquire about when to expect the insurance settlement check, but she found Raleigh standing next to the secretary's desk. He stood still and silently stared at Nervy with a blank expression.

Feeling the uncomfortable mood in the office, she filled the silence. "I just stopped by for the bill."

"Martha shot herself in the head last night in Lanny's front yard. She left Lanny a note that told him she couldn't live knowing the disgust he would feel for her now that he could read about her history of sexual exploitation in her psychiatric record," Raleigh reported. The secretary and Raleigh continued staring at Nervy, waiting for her response. She remained silent, remembering her admonition yesterday. She had nothing to say.

"What have we done?" Raleigh asked, seeming to address the circumstance more than the people in the room.

"What do you mean?" Nervy began. "Yesterday's transaction was just business as usual for lawyers. You deal in pain and suffering all the time, but it's almost always from arm's reach, not up close and personal."

Raleigh finally responded. "Did you set this up on purpose?"

"You mean like make Lanny sue Walter three times? You mean like make Lanny so damn greedy that he had to own the details of other people's secrets? You mean like make the courts make me get rid of the records? Yeah, Raleigh, I'm in control of all that shit, and more!" she retorted. "How dare you accuse me of causing last night! Everything I've done has been a reaction to what was done to me or demanded of me! I didn't plant these weeds, I just watered 'em!"

"Okay . . . okay. I know you're not in control of what happened, but you knew that something awful was going to happen to Lanny. How?"

"God? Law of averages? Karma?" She paused and shrugged her shoulders. "What goes around comes around. You were there at the end of Walter's last trial when Lanny sanctimoniously lectured me about those who do harm having to pay for it. Can I pay my bill?" she concluded. She took out her checkbook, paid Raleigh, and reminded the secretary to call her when she could pick up the malpractice settlement check.

Back in her car, Nervy headed straight for the drive-through at McDonald's.

Woodrow was in the physical therapy room doing gait-strengthening exercises. Maintaining a respectful distance, she observed her friend give his best effort at making his painful, weakened legs support him. She wanted to shout praise and encouragement from the sidelines, but his struggle was not a spectator sport. In that moment she was watching a sacred struggle, a refusal to surrender, the sacrifice of painful persistence no matter what. The nursing director called to Nervy and asked her to step into her office. The director invited Nervy to have a seat and began talking about Woodrow's progress in his therapy.

"I saw today that he's come a long way," Nervy offered.

"Well, he can get on and off the toilet by himself and get himself out of bed, so insurance won't pay for continuing inpatient care," the director explained.

"So, what's next?"

"He gets to go home and have in-home therapy and nursing visits if he needs them."

"When does he have to be out by?" Nervy asked.

"We can give you a couple of days at the longest to get things ready at home," the nurse offered.

"Are there certain foods I need to get or certain kinds of furniture or other special items?"

"Not really. You need to sleep where you can hear him if he calls for help in the night," the nurse said, adding, "I heard about the incident at lunch yesterday and wanted to say I'm sorry. That young lady is very angry and worried about ever seeing her children again. She lashes out emotionally at anybody or anything that frustrates her."

Nervy remained silent for a moment and then responded, "She's been through a lot and has a long way to go before she gets to be a mom again. That has to be tough. Does she have any visitors?"

"None, not even the kids. Family services is undecided about reuniting the kids and mom. The extent of her possible recovery is undetermined. Her kids' dad is on the run and wanted for murder, so the kids are in a special foster care setting. We've had to ramp up our security here too," the nurse explained.

After a brief visit with Woodrow, Nervy left. Driving back to the farm, she thought about the additional responsibilities that she would have once he was back home. Once she'd gotten back, Nervy initiated an inspection of the house, looking for changes to maximize Woodrow's independence. The living room would be converted to her new bedroom so that she could hear and respond to Woodrow during the night. She wondered what Woodrow would think of the changes she'd made in his absence—bed in the living room, dogs on the porch and in the house. He'd wonder what she'd done with the guns in the closet if he looked in there, but she figured he hadn't used the guns for years.

CHAPTER 42

Two hours later Nervy had already begun rearranging the house in anticipation of Woodrow's return. She was surprised to hear her phone ringing in the charger. She answered the call, and after a moment's silence Lanny Peltor identified himself and asked if he was speaking to Nervy. After she confirmed her identity, he politely asked if she had a couple of minutes to talk.

"It depends on what you want to talk about," she replied. "You said for me to leave you alone and now you're calling me. I heard about Martha and I'm genuinely sorry for you."

"Nervy, I read her chart and I want to know who had her under their thumb. I don't know what possessed you to put the addendum in her record, but that's a matter for later. My interest now is only in knowing who had Martha over a barrel!"

"Lanny, would you tell me if I asked you the same question? It's a dangerous world we live in and narcs don't live long."

"I think I already know who it is and I would tell you if you were in my shoes. In fact I'll do it right now because I think the same person is behind the suffering that you and I are both stuck in. Fatty is the answer I'm offering," he volunteered.

"What do you mean, 'answer'?" she wondered.

"Fatty wants you dead. He sees you as a direct and immediate threat. He expects you to either rat him out for the murders you witnessed or come for him and kill him yourself because he didn't get rid of Cooker for killing Walter. He's so afraid of you that he's given Cooker free rein to do whatever is required to take you out. The hit-and-run that killed the old lady is just the beginning. There! Does that convince you that I'd answer your question if you were me?"

As Lanny's information was sinking in, she offered, "You had the right answer before you ever called me. Fatty's had his hooks into Martha for a long time." The phone went dead. Nervy was unsure what to make of the conversation's abrupt ending and began worrying that maybe it had been a setup and Lanny had Fatty listening in. Or perhaps he had recorded it and would give the recording to Fatty and let Fatty or Cooker wreak his vengeance for Martha's death on her. She finally decided that it didn't matter, because what Lanny had said about Fatty was undoubtedly true—Fatty had to expect her to avenge Walter in one way or another. From her point of view, it didn't matter whether she was recorded by Lanny or not, because she and Fatty had worked together in the meth trade for years and knew exactly what to expect from each other. It was just a matter of time and chance as to who would strike first.

The next morning Nervy went straight to the rehab unit and checked in on Woodrow. There was a recreational activity being held in the commons for all the patients, so Nervy walked beside him on his way there.

"They told me that I'm to go home tomorrow and that you'll be staying with me to help me get back into farm living," he announced without even looking at her.

"That's the plan. Are you okay with that?"

"Yep, fine and dandy," he answered, continuing to sustain his step-then-move-the-cane cadence.

Today's gathering for the patients was the "first of the month celebration," at which the patients who had birthdays, anniversaries, or other momentous events would be acknowledged. The patients were being seated in rows, so Nervy found a chair in the back of the room. The director of nursing moderated the celebration and did so with a poise indicating that she had served in this role on many occasions. She would call the name of a specific patient and announce their particular celebration. Then they would be asked to stand or speak, and the audience would clap for them. The celebration was proceeding pleasantly until Candy's birthday was announced. With that acknowledgment, Candy loudly burst into tears, and, gasping with grief, she screamed that she wished she'd never been born. The room was hushed except for Candy's sobs. The director looked to one of the nurses, and Candy was whisked back to her room. Within a moment the monthly celebration was resumed.

That afternoon Nervy busied herself with preparations for Woodrow's return home. She was anxious to show up in his replacement truck with his dog waiting in the back for him. Since she had never driven the truck herself, and Number Three hadn't been in the back of a moving vehicle since her injuries, she decided to take a practice spin over to her property and back. She went outside, stood by the truck, and called the dogs. Both canines converged on the truck at the same moment. She lowered the tailgate of the pickup and called Three by name. The dog eagerly leapt into the pickup bed and sat down directly behind the cab. Nervy walked to the driver's door and opened it as she called Griff, who jumped twice his standing height onto the floor of the cab for a chance at a truck ride. Getting herself in the truck was a challenge for Nervy because of its height off the ground, but after a couple of attempts she struggled up into the driver seat. With the window rolled down, the seat and the mirrors adjusted, she buckled herself in.

"Hold on, you two, this may be a little rough."

She turned the ignition key and the engine rumbled to life. Placing the gear selector in reverse, she backed all the way out into the road, then moved the selector from reverse to drive. Straightening her shoulders and tightening her grip on the wheel, she hollered, "Here we go!" and pushed the accelerator halfway to the floor. Gravel spewed from the back tires as she and the dogs shot forward. Number Three stumbled backward. With a smile spreading across her face, Nervy shouted through the wind blowing in the window, "I told you to hold on!"

The drive with the dogs lifted Nervy's spirits and provided a sense of fun that she hadn't felt for a long time. Arriving at her acreage, she drove the truck over the fallen fence still lying across the driveway leading to the dilapidated garage. She turned off the engine, checked that the Glock was in her pocket, then opened her door and jumped out. She called the dogs out of the truck and began walking around. The area near the garage looked like someone had parked there recently. Inside the garage she found a propane camp stove and three cylinders full of fuel. There was a folding chair with a flashlight lying in it. Empty beer cans were scattered around the chair along with discarded wrappings from snacks, lithium batteries, and cold medicine. The item that froze Nervy in her tracks, though, was a heavy chain anchored with a stake that had been driven deeply into the dirt floor of the garage—she'd seen it before. After racing outside and hurriedly getting the dogs into the truck, she left as quickly as she could.

Heading back to the Turner farm, she hoped to not run into Cooker. It was probably much too early to see him there, since most cookers she had worked with preferred to work late at night, believing their activities were less likely to be discovered then. Now that she knew where to find and hopefully eliminate Cooker, she had just gained an edge on Fatty. Her new dilemma was when to attack Cooker. Tonight would have been her preference, but Woodrow's discharge from the hospital tomorrow took precedence.

CHAPTER 43

The next day dawned with warm temperatures, a high cloud cover, and blustery winds, the makings of one of the spring storms which were often quite violent in north Missouri. Nervy dressed for a celebration; bringing Woodrow home was the biggest celebration she could imagine . . . for this year, anyway. She put on her jacket, stuffed the Glock into her pocket, and piled into the truck with the dogs.

Arriving at the rehab unit, she was surprised to find four law enforcement vehicles with emergency light bars on their roofs silently flashing a dizzying chaos of colors. Two Clay Center police cruisers, a sheriff's truck, and a state patrol SUV were parked haphazardly around the front entrance of the building. Despite the gathering of vehicles, there were no officers to be seen around the entrance to the building. Nervy took the Glock out of her pocket and placed it under the pickup seat on the floor. Not sure why there was such a collection of law enforcement personnel, she backed the pickup into a space at the farthest edge of the lot, making a quick departure easier if became necessary. She left both dogs in the truck and walked to the building with an intentionally confident gait.

Inside, the exit was completely unattended and the hall-way clear of patients. The officers represented by their various vehicles outside were standing in a clump at the nursing station. They appeared to be questioning the nursing director and an aide. Nervy walked to Woodrow's room and found her friend had already packed up his belongings and was ready to leave.

"Quite an uproar," she said in greeting.

"Yeah, some desperado came in last night and grabbed that gal you had words with the other day. They say that he beat up one of the night workers pretty bad, and then he left with the gal and they haven't heard from her since."

"Did he come looking for you too?"

"No, I slept through it until the police came and woke me up and asked if the kidnapper had bothered me. I told them that I had no idea that anything had happened at all—slept like a baby."

"Let's get out of here. You stay here while I get a staff member to sign you out. When I come back, we'll grab your stuff and head for home."

She quickly found a young nurse, who was leaving a patient room near Woodrow's. Nervy hurriedly told the nurse that the director sent her over to have her sign Woodrow out because the director was too busy to. The staff member stopped what she was doing and retrieved some forms from the nursing station. Returning with the paperwork, the young nurse shuffled a few papers under Nervy's nose and asked for a couple of signatures. She then gave Nervy a list of Woodrow's medicines and explained how to use them. As the nurse began to explain more paperwork, Nervy curtly interrupted her with a "Thank you" and went back down the hall and into Woodrow's room.

"Got all your stuff?"

"Yep," he answered, pointing to a plastic bag holding various articles, including the wedding anniversary picture. Nervy grabbed the bag as Woodrow put on his jacket and reached for his quad cane. Being hustled toward the door, the old man turned around for the large plastic water mug and flexible straw on his bedside table. She shook her head and waited for him to make his way out of the room. She walked directly behind him, hoping that the authorities wouldn't see him and want to ask more questions before he left.

The hurried departure from the rehab unit was completely different from the homecoming celebration she had intended. She introduced Woodrow to his new vehicle and helped him up into the cab. Number Three was ecstatic seeing her old friend again and made every attempt to lick the old man as he was getting into the truck. Griff repeated the welcoming ritual in the cab and was petted by Woodrow as he got himself settled in. Nervy left the parking lot with noticeable haste, and as they pulled hurriedly out onto the street, Woodrow said, "It's got lots of power, doesn't it?"

Nervy was completely distracted from any meaningful interaction with Woodrow on the drive out to the farm. Now that he was released and on his way home, Nervy felt she was meeting her responsibilities to him adequately. The afternoon would be spent getting him used to his modified surroundings. She hoped to be the one that would take care of him for many days to come, but other demands could change all that. Nervy gave herself permission to believe Woodrow would get along okay without her, since she knew the Greenbriar Assembly would see to his well-being.

Still driving, Nervy began reviewing her intended violence tonight and the people it would impact. Her life, as well as those of Candy, Cooker, and Fatty, hung in the balance. Cooker and Fatty lived irredeemably evil lives that would eventually end in violent deaths, whether tonight or not. Her own chances of a violent death were fifty-fifty. Her criminal years certainly hadn't earned her a quiet, peaceful death.

Candy was a different story. Nervy blamed her for unleashing Cooker's murderous rampage but didn't view her as criminal. If anybody was an undeserving participant tonight, it was Candy.

Cooker would not keep Candy alive for very long, but he wouldn't kill her until he had her somewhere that he felt very safe. It seemed to her that his choices were the garage where he had been cooking meth lately, or his uncle Fatty's compound. She planned to ambush him at the garage after she got Woodrow set up at home. Nervy's wealth of experience "solving problems" with insubordinate meth cookers and dealers would give her an advantage over Cooker. But killing Cooker was the easy half of the job—she would have to kill Fatty tonight too. If Fatty heard about her actions before she killed him, she would be stuck in a savage battle she would likely lose. Her contemplations continued throughout the entire trip home.

CHAPTER 44

Nervy followed Woodrow into the house and showed him the furniture she had moved so that he could walk around the house with fewer obstructions. She also showed him her new sleeping space in the living room. They went outside and walked around, followed by the dogs, until he tired and asked to return inside. In the house he took a seat at the kitchen table and visibly withdrew into thoughts and feelings mourning Bertha's absence. As the afternoon turned to evening, Nervy fixed a supper that they ate in silence. After supper, Woodrow remained seated, staring passively into space. With the dishes washed and put in the cupboard, Nervy sat down beside Woodrow and touched his arm.

"I have an important meeting to go to tonight, so I'll be leaving in a few minutes."

"What's your meeting about?"

"I'm going to take care of a disagreement with somebody I used to work for."

"Who?"

"Why do you need to know?"

"Because I think you're going to get yourself killed by that fat Smith fella," he said, surprising her.

"What makes you think that?"

"Bertha and I knew that you were involved in his corruption for years, but you got free of him after prison, and since your husband died, lots of bad things have been happening to you. Me and Bertha talked about it and figured that Smith was behind it."

"Well, it doesn't involve you and my business is my business, so don't worry about me, I'm a big girl. Besides, you got a lot to work on yourself, getting back into the swing of things here on the farm."

At 8:00 Nervy took her dog, her Maglite, and her Glock and walked out the back door in her farm shoes, jeans, and a zip-up hooded sweatshirt. She left her phone in its charger and went outside and got in her 4Runner. She checked to see that the .38 was beside the seat on the floor. She picked it up and put it in her left sweatshirt pocket. Pulling out of the driveway, Nervy left Woodrow and his farm behind with feelings of both dread and calm at the same time. Ultimately, the danger she faced tonight seemed an appropriate price for freeing herself from the overshadowing danger she had lived with for several months. She was going to be free one way or another in the next few hours.

Arriving at her property, she turned off the headlights, slowed, and came to a standstill in the road. After watching the garage for several minutes, looking for signs of people or activity and not seeing any, she slowly pulled onto the property and stopped thirty feet short of the garage. She was facing the sagging double-door entrance on the side of the building closest to the road. As she turned off the engine, Nervy checked to make sure that she had a pistol in each of her two sweatshirt pockets.

She opened the door of the SUV and stepped out. Griff immediately strained at the leash the way he had with the coyotes and wanted to head straight for the double doors. An audible growling emerged from the garage, and just as Nervy noticed it, the growl erupted into a spasm of ferocious barking that was silenced by two rapid gunshots, instantly creating two splintered holes in the left garage door. Nervy quickly took cover behind the rear of her vehicle, drew her Glock, and fixed her aim at chest height on the left door exactly where the bullets had exited. She waited silently for Cooker's next move. There was no light in the garage and there were no sounds until the door she was aiming at was suddenly pushed open by the broad shoulders of Smack, who had been turned loose and sent outside to attack the new arrivals. Charging full speed, the pit bull made it to the 4Runner and lunged for Nervy faster than she could aim her pistol. Griff responded to the attack with a speed, agility, and fearlessness greater than the pit bull's. Unfortunately, his strength and size were no match for the larger dog. Griff grabbed Smack's throat and latched on ferociously, causing the bigger dog a moment's distraction. The pit bull easily shook him off with the strength of fifty pounds of concerted muscular dominance and countered Griff's attack by lunging at him instead of Nervy. Smack snatched up the terrier by his torso, squeezing the breath out of him. Griff struggled silently, unable to breathe. Nervy heard the sound of his ribs breaking and while his body went limp, she jammed the muzzle of the Glock into the pit bull's ribs and squeezed off two rounds. Smack's growl became an agonizing moan as he struggled to endure the pain. With Griff still in his mouth, he angrily turned his head toward Nervy, who repositioned her Glock and shot him through the left eye. Smack's muscular body sunk to the ground, completely limp and with the smaller dog still in his mouth. Nervy struck Smack angrily across the bridge of his nose with the barrel of the Glock, but his complete absence of reaction informed her that he would never intimidate anyone else again.

"Smack! Smack! Dammit!" she heard Cooker's scream from inside the garage. Nervy remained silent, keeping her position of cover behind the SUV. She again aimed her gun at the same spot on the garage door and waited. She listened for any sounds from the garage for a minute and heard nothing for sure until a truck door slammed and a powerful engine roared to life. Suddenly the doors splintered apart as Cooker's pickup exploded out of the garage.

He narrowly missed Nervy's SUV as he careened toward the road. Passing her, he made fleeting eye contact and wildly fired in her direction, getting off a couple of shots through his passenger window. Then he fishtailed a turn onto the road toward the Smith salvage yard. He pushed his truck's power to its limit and gained speed as quickly as he could shift through his gears. Nervy estimated he must have reached eighty miles per hour before the sound of his truck faded from her hearing.

A surge of disappointment washed through Nervy as she accepted the reality of Cooker's escape despite her best efforts. She collected herself mentally and did a brief inventory of her limbs and torso to see if she had been wounded in the melee. After finding no injuries, she walked to the garage to look for Candy or evidence that she had been there. She found no body, no women's clothing, no blood. The only things she found were the same kind of items consistent with a meth cooker's workplace that she had seen yesterday. Finding no signs of Candy having been hidden or harmed there, Nervy walked out of the garage and turned her attention to the canine casualties.

Carefully untangling Griff and his leash from the dead pit bull, she placed her beloved pet's limp body off to the side of the garage, away from his killer, and wished he would just grumble-growl at her one last time. If she survived the night, she promised herself she would come back tomorrow and give her canine friend and defender a proper burial. She stood silent, permitting herself a moment to acknowledge the sorrow and gratitude and amazement she felt for her fallen comrade. She finally turned toward her car, checked that her .38 was still in her left pocket and slid her Glock into her right one. With both weapons in place, she got into the driver's seat of the 4Runner and headed for the junkyard, where she was now sure that Candy, Cooker, and Fatty would all be found.

CHAPTER 45

Nervy drove at a reasonable speed on her way to Fatty's junk-yard because she had no ready plan in place for attacking the compound single-handedly and was using the drive time to think through her dilemma, unsure of what she would do upon her arrival. She figured Fatty would be in his office. By the time she got there, Cooker would have already arrived and he would be in the office with Fatty, filling him in on what had just happened. Based on her past experiences watching Fatty deal with prisoners, Nervy assumed that Candy either was imprisoned in one of the junked vehicles in the midst of the junkyard, or had already been shoved into the trunk of a stolen car and transported to some remote location for execution.

As Nervy came to the final stretch of road heading to the salvage yard, her headlights revealed a pickup in the ditch off the side of the road ahead that she immediately recognized as Cooker's. Nervy assumed that his high speed, combined with the perpetual ruts on this section of road, had caused him to lose control of his truck and wind up in the ditch. As she drew closer, her headlights illuminated Cooker in the driver's seat trying to get the vehicle back onto the road. It was immediately apparent to both drivers that she was going to reach his location before he could get out of the ditch. Panicked in the glare of her high beams, he kicked open his door and leapt out, assuming a firing position with his handgun pointed straight at her windshield. Nervy stopped seventy-five feet before reaching his truck and drew the .38 revolver. She pointed the gun toward him out of her driver's side window but held her fire because she knew there was no chance of her hitting him from that distance.

Spotlighted, Cooker stood unmoving for a full minute in his ready-to-fire posture, his gun pointed toward her car. Nervy knew her lights were blinding him to movements outside their glare, so she slipped out of her car as quietly as she could to try to maneuver within effective firing range. She walked a wide leftward swath outside the illumination produced by her SUV. The shrinking radius of her circular path was gradually bringing her closer to her target, but keeping her gun trained on him required her to sidestep over the ruts in the road and the weeds and irregularities of the grader ditch as her path led her into it. With her visual contact fixed on Cooker, she snagged her left foot on a large dirt clod and lost her balance. Tumbling into the grader ditch, she struck her elbow and shoulder painfully. Cooker ran toward her position when he heard her fall, firing blindly, using at least five shots. Nervy raised her revolver, waiting until he was within twenty feet, and then fired three shots in rapid succession. Cooker quickly changed course and made a mad dash for her car when he realized she wasn't in it and that he was much closer to hers than to his own vehicle.

The tweaker succeeded in hijacking Nervy's car and accelerated past her once again, heading toward the salvage yard at breakneck speed. She fired off three more rounds as he passed. Nervy picked herself off the ground, stuck the empty .38 in her pocket, and sprinted to Cooker's truck. She climbed into the cab and strapped herself in as best she could. She shifted the truck into reverse, gunned the engine, and managed to back a full twenty feet away from the rut blocking the truck. She put the truck back in first gear and, clinging to the steering wheel, she unleashed all the power the accelerator would provide. The truck shot forward for the twenty feet she had just gained and hit the rut head-on. The front wheels launched upward violently and then crashed down just as violently as the back wheels took their turn launching over the rut. The front-wheel, back-wheel launch sequence would have shot her straight through the roof, but the seat belt undoubtedly saved her life. Back on the road, she quickly corrected course to prevent a repeat launch into the opposite grader ditch. Now again in pursuit of Cooker and headed for Fatty's compound, she was astounded at the twist of fate that had resulted in their exchanging vehicles.

The possibility crossed Nervy's mind that Cooker's arriving at Fatty's compound in her vehicle, in a rush, unexpected and in the dark, could be fatal for him. She wanted to be as near behind him as she could to increase the compound's confusion. She was driving the vehicle familiar to the guards, he wasn't. She sped Cooker's truck along the rutted road as fast as she was able to control it. Gaining on the taillights of her hijacked SUV up ahead, she saw them suddenly light up as Cooker slowed to turn into the compound. Hoping he wouldn't get through the gate before she arrived, she began sending any confusing signal she could to the gate guard. Repeatedly flashing the high beams of the pickup on and off as she wildly honked the horn over and over, she tried to convince the compound defenders that they were in danger. The SUV had now come to a complete stop. A blindingly bright spotlight suddenly shone down from the barn loft, illuminating the SUV. Now less than a hundred yards from the 4Runner, she heard the sound of a high-powered rifle shot, followed a few seconds later by a second shot. She assumed that Cooker was currently bleeding to death in the front seat of her 4Runner, courtesy of Fatty's sniper.

CHAPTER 46

Not wanting to waste any of the unfolding confusion at the compound's gate, Nervy continued honking and flashing as she approached. She decided to crash the massive pickup through the gate as her grand entrance. Where she should have begun her deceleration for stopping at the gate, she increased to maximum manageable speed and aimed straight for the space between the gate and the stationary 4Runner. She released her seat belt and leaned over to a lying position on the seat while still gripping the steering wheel, keeping the truck on its current trajectory and her foot pressing the accelerator clear to the floor. The cab was suddenly illuminated by the spotlight, and she held her breath as the sniper tried to access a target. A bullet crashed through the windshield. Waiting for a second round, she was surprised instead by the truck crashing into the barrier gate and breaching it. Keeping the pedal to the floor and firmly maintaining the orientation of the steering wheel, she was committed to going as far into the compound as possible, in whichever direction. The truck was still moving forward, and the spotlight was no longer shining in. Finally, the truck crashed with sufficient impact that she was thrown from the seat onto the floor and her grip was torn from the steering wheel.

Smiling to herself with a painful grimace, she thought, "This must be my stop." She checked to see if the Glock was still in her right pocket, and it was. Grappling with the steering wheel and gearshifter, Nervy gained a position from which to look out of the truck. Raising her head, she saw that the truck had crashed into the side of the barn. No one was nearby, but she heard the shouts of men approaching, so she exited the truck by crawling out of the driver's side window, which was completely missing. She hit the ground and pulled the Glock from her pocket. She raced around the barn and pulled open the first door that she came to. She left the door open as a distraction and began running toward a field of wrecked and stripped vehicle corpses.

Cars, pickups, more cars, vans, SUVs, delivery trucks, and more cars—hundreds of them were randomly scattered among twenty acres of winter-dead weed stalks. As Nervy looked around, she welcomed the sight of hundreds of hollow, bullet-deflecting hiding places silently waiting for her use. Wanting to position herself as near the middle of the accumulated wreckage as she could, she began carefully negotiating her way into the jungle of junk, sneaking carefully past wreck after wreck until she was roughly in the fifth ragged row of salvage. Four vehicles away she saw a rusted-out delivery truck with its attached cargo box standing noticeably taller than the surrounding debris.

Nervy carefully crept around to the side of the cargo box opposite the direction of the barn. Fully behind the truck's cargo box, she leaned against it and unconsciously softly bumped her head against its side three times because of her frustration at having no plan. Hearing distant voices discussing the open barn door, Nervy was feeling ever greater pressure to come up with a plan for her attack when she heard a series of three soft bumping sounds coming from the wall behind her. Alarmed, Nervy turned and faced the box with its faded signage. She lifted her Glock, pointing it straight at the place she had bounced her head. She tapped the wall with the muzzle of the pistol softly three times, the first two in rapid succession, the third delayed. Ten seconds later her sequence was repeated identically, with bumping sounds from inside the box. Nervy went to the back of the cargo box and found two opposing swinging doors pushed shut but not latched. Holding her pistol at the ready, she opened the right door a crack, waiting for what might happen next.

"Help me please! Help me!" came a woman's soft but assertive whisper.

"Candy?" Nervy asked, edging the door open far enough to be able to slip in and then pulling the door back to within one inch of being shut. "It's Nervy," she announced. "Let's get you out of here."

Candy was quiet a moment in the complete dark of the box. "Are you shitting me? I didn't think things could get worse. I'm praying to God for a miracle and he sends Nervy! I'm kidnapped, buck naked, hog-tied, and freezing to death. The only thing missing from my worst nightmare is you, and now here you are."

"I'm here to get you and kill Cooker and Fatty so you and I can both be free from them."

"My hands are zip-tied behind my back, I get checked on about every hour, and I got no shoes or clothes. I'm not exactly ready for traveling."

"Do you think they will be here very soon to check on you, and do they send more than one?"

"I figure they'll be back pretty soon, since it's been a while. They only come one at a time. I think they draw straws because I get raped every time," Candy explained. About that time the voices of the searchers grew quite close and obviously they were coming to check on the contents of the cargo box. Nervy withdrew to the furthest corner away from Candy and waited. The door was jerked open wildly and a bright light shone on Candy. She called out plaintively, "Leave me alone, don't hurt me . . . not again. Please give me another blanket. I'm freezing to death."

"Shut up, bitch! We're busy," came the reply, and the door was slammed shut just as vigorously as it had been opened. Nervy waited silently in her corner for a full two minutes before she moved or said a word.

"Okay, I'll be back in a minute," she whispered as she went back out the door to search the nearby area for a piece of loose wreckage suitable for knocking a man unconscious. In the darkness, her hands mostly found small, loose metal parts. Occasionally she came across a larger piece of metal that was still attached to vehicles. What she finally settled on felt like an old brake shoe. It wasn't comfortable in her hand, but it had plenty of heft. If swung with sufficient force against a human head, it would certainly stun and probably knock any person unconscious regardless of their size. She decided to suspend her search and quickly took her new weapon back into her box trap to wait for her prey to come for the bait. Back in with Candy, she said, "Next time they come in, you start whining and begging and act really scared—it really turns them on and keeps their attention. I'll be in the corner here in the dark, and once they are fully in the box I'll take them out. Then we'll wait for the next one. After we bag a couple of them, we'll get you dressed and blow this Popsicle stand."

CHAPTER 47

During the next hour as they waited in the cargo box, Candy quietly whispered to Nervy the story of how Cooker had brought her straight to Fatty's compound after kidnapping her, and how Fatty had gone into a rage about the risks Cooker had created for him by bringing her to his junkyard in the pickup that had been ID'd by the staff at the rehab facility. He told Cooker to get the hell out and hide himself and his truck for a couple of days. Fatty agreed to hide Candy until he thought the time was right for killing her. Nervy whispered back that she had found Cooker at a hiding place and had chased him here. She told Candy that she thought Cooker had died out at the compound gate earlier tonight trying to get in with an unfamiliar car.

After waiting about an hour in the cargo box of the wrecked truck, Nervy and Candy both heard the noise of an approaching person. The door of the box rattled as he grabbed the handle. Candy began loudly whimpering a pathetic "No . . . please . . . no" and began writhing on the floor. Nervy backed as far into the corner as possible and waited for her opportunity. A flash of light illuminated Candy, naked and bound on the floor, backed up against the corner of the van looking like a frightened fawn facing a predator. The flashlight beam moved slowly, exhibiting her body for the viewer's pleasure. The beam paused for a moment on her breasts and then moved down to her hips, where it paused even longer between her legs. Candy continued to scuttle backward, as though she were still trying to get farther away from the intruder.

"Well, well, it's my turn, Candy. By the way, your man is gone. Old Cooker got himself shot trying to crash the gate tonight," the man said, laying the flashlight down and reaching for the belt around his jeans. "Too bad for you, 'cause we're going to bury you when we bury him." Nervy launched herself from the corner and took him out with a blow to the base of his skull. The force of the blow knocked the brake shoe clear out of her hand. The man and the brake shoe both hit the floor loudly. Nervy screamed as though someone had just caused her great pain.

"Had to make 'em think you just got beat up so they won't come checking on the racket," she whispered as she began looting the victim's pockets.

"Nice pocketknife," she observed, using it to free Candy's hands. "Help me strip him—you're gonna need his clothes more than he does."

Candy seemed hesitant.

"They're gonna send somebody to check on him in a few minutes, and we have to be ready. Why don't you stay naked, and let's strip him and lay him on top of you so they'll walk in and not be surprised? I'll take care of the rest."

"What the hell? Are you for real?"

"It's only for a few minutes. If you want out of here, it's our best chance. I don't think he's gonna be telling any stories about you and him anyway," Nervy said as she noticed the villain wasn't breathing.

Together they removed his jeans and jockeys and dragged him atop Candy, where he rested like a sack of potatoes.

With their trap set, they waited less than ten minutes before a man's voice was calling for "Randy" with tones of concern mixed with ridicule outside the cargo box.

"Randy, are you hogging the pussy?"

Candy, now getting into the spirit of the trap, called out, "I think he had a heart attack! Get him off me!" The door was yanked open, and the next victim's flashlight shone on an unmoving man, who seemed to have passed out in the middle of raping his hostage.

"Randy . . . Randy!" the new arrival bellowed as he bent forward to check on his comrade. At that instant, Nervy again stepped into action, swinging her brake shoe and creating a matching pair of unconscious thugs.

"There, that should do it. Let's strip them and you take the clothes you want. Do you know how to use a gun?" she asked Candy.

"No, I don't want anything to do with them."

"Suit yourself. I figure we just acquired a couple of pistols and thought you might want to have one for whatever happens next." Nervy shrugged.

Before leaving, they staged the interior of the box so that the smaller of the naked men was propped in the corner with Candy's blanket covering him except for his bare feet and ankles. The other man was pushed as far into the opposite corner as possible so as not to be seen until any interested party fully entered the box to investigate.

"Two pocketknives, two 9mm pistols, two cigarette lighters, and four hundred and thirty dollars," Nervy whispered, inventorying her booty. Pulling the clips from the guns, she used some of the bullets to reload her Glock. Done with the clips, she wiped them free of her prints and set them on the floor along with the pocketknives. The money and lighters went into her jeans pockets, and after pulling the slides back on both pistols and emptying their chambers, she tucked the unloaded handguns under her belt, one on each side of her abdomen.

"Guess I'll go commando," Candy muttered, selecting the pair of jeans closest to her size and putting them on with no underwear. After she finished dressing from the available wardrobe, Nervy offered her a hat.

"Compliments of Randy and . . . whoever," she said, opening the door.

Once outside the box, Nervy led the way back toward the barn. The spotlight from the barn loft was still passing its beam over the acres of wrecks, but it was shining down a hundred yards away from the fleeing women. Now being used to help the search team comb through the salvage yard wreckage, the spotlight was doing a better job of showing the fugitives where the searchers were than the other way around. Continuing their escape, the women paused twice as Nervy wiped her fingerprints from the two empty guns she'd heisted and hid each of them inside separate junked cars. Nearing the barn, they hid behind the last row of cars. She drew her Glock and surveyed their circumstances. There was fifteen yards of open ground between them and the barn. The barn looked to be about thirty yards from Fatty's house. She counted a half-dozen trucks parked around the house. She also spied a dark-colored sedan almost hidden among them, just like the one the "officer" had driven to her house the day after Jules died. The car reinforced her suspicions about that day, but she refocused on the dilemma she faced here and now. Nervy was confident that every one of the trucks had its key in its ignition and would start on the first crank. She also figured that she had reduced the number of Fatty's employees by at least three that night, so the odds for her and Candy were better now than they had been two hours ago.

Her primary worry was the sniper in the barn loft. He was unassailable with her current arsenal. He had a high-powered rifle, a spotlight, and a military scope. He could take her out before she could pose any threat to him with a handgun. Grabbing a looted cigarette lighter from her pocket, she handed it to Candy. Nervy pulled up a large handful of dry grass and motioned for Candy to do the same. She then led Candy in a brief sprint to the barn door near the corner of the building and opened the door just enough for each of them to squeeze inside before closing the door behind them.

The interior of the room was faintly aglow with dim light that had originated somewhere else in the barn and bounced through several rooms before arriving here. The scant illumination was sufficient to permit the two women to begin searching their surroundings for flammable material. In the far corner of the room were several paint cans and a can of paint thinner. The two women collaborated in accumulating everything within eyesight that had flammable potential and heaped their gatherings and the dry grass together in a pre-bonfire pile. Nervy sprinkled the pile with some of the paint thinner and then splashed the rest of it on the walls. She lit the pile and, as the fire greedily grew, consuming more and more of the waiting fuel, the two fugitives fled the room. They waited just outside the door for the fire to fully establish itself and start spreading. A full three minutes of quiet passed before they heard an alarmed voice scream, "Fire! *Fire!*"

With the distraction triggered and the sniper no doubt fleeing the barn loft, Nervy started her dash for the nearest of the big pickups. Candy was following as fast as she could but didn't have anywhere close to the speed that Nervy did. Men came running from the house to fight the fire in the barn and were on an exact collision course with the two women. Nervy had the advantage of expecting to run into them and opened fire first. She felt that she could be generous with her use of ammunition, since she had fifteen bullets in the Glock. Her first target went down after three shots, all of which Nervy thought hit him in the torso. Realizing they were under attack, the man behind him reversed course, heading back toward the trucks at the house to find cover. Nervy hadn't attracted any gunfire herself and made it to the nearest truck. She climbed in and turned the key, with a resulting engine roar that satisfied her. Looking over her shoulder for Candy, she saw that her slower companion was still twenty feet from the truck and was being intercepted by the man who had fled from Nervy's direct assault. He had snuck around the trucks to avoid Nervy but had now run out into the open space between the house and barn to grab Candy before she escaped. Nervy dropped the transmission into reverse, pushed the accelerator aggressively, and cranked the steering wheel. The truck executed a perfect backward arc, intersecting the space between Candy and her pursuer. Nervy waited for Candy to get in, which gave the assailant time to grab for the door handle on Nervy's door. She raised her gun to the window and pointed the muzzle at the face she suddenly recognized as the officer belonging to the sedan. Wishing to avoid the deafening consequences of firing her weapon inside the truck's closed cab, she hesitated and nodded her head toward the barn, offering him the option of avoiding the bullet there and then and trying to outrun her instead. He let go of the door and sprinted for the barn, which was now in flames. By this point Candy was in the truck, and Nervy heard the door close solidly on the passenger's side.

"Hold on," she commanded above the engine roar. She redirected the truck and accelerated on a course behind the fleeing man. She overtook him six feet before he reached the barn. The human speed bump caused an expectable double bounce in the truck as first the front and then the rear driver's side wheels passed over him. "Five down!" Nervy shouted victoriously. With no more targets to pursue, she steered the truck toward the compound's entrance for her second pass tonight, this time from the inside out. No one was manning the gate as she blew through it, knocking it free of its hinges. This time there was no spotlight or sniper to deal with and the flames of the barn could be enjoyed by Nervy in her rearview mirror for the first mile of their escape.

CHAPTER 48

Nervy drove straight to Woodrow's farm, where she directed
Candy to get out of the stolen truck and follow her in
Woodrow's truck as she ditched the stolen vehicle. They drove
for ten miles, using four different back roads, before Nervy
came to a wooded area and ran her vehicle into the grader ditch.
After wiping her fingerprints off the ignition key, the steering wheel, the gearshift and the door handle, she abandoned
it. Nervy told Candy to scoot over and climbed in behind the
steering wheel in Woodrow's truck herself. On the drive home
Nervy weighed the likelihood of a retaliatory attack from Fatty
tonight. On one hand he was now unexpectedly short-staffed
and wouldn't be able to attack with the manpower and ferocity
he preferred. On the other hand, he might feel forced to act
tonight because of the escape of two witnesses who could send
him to life in prison at a minimum and, since it was Missouri,
maybe even put a needle in his arm.

"I hope the exciting part of our night is over, but Fatty may
not be ready to turn in yet, so don't get your hopes up," Nervy
said, realizing that was the only thing that had been said on
the drive home.

Arriving back at Woodrow's, they got out of the truck and went upstairs, where Nervy told Candy to get dressed in some of her clothes quickly because they needed to dispose of the men's clothing she had borrowed. Candy obliged hurriedly, after which Nervy took the stolen clothes and shoes outside, where she threw them in the trash barrel, poured lighter fluid on them, and set them ablaze. Back in the house, Nervy took off her shoes and washed the soles clean of the soil from the compound.

Sitting down with Candy, Nervy coached her on how to tell the police that she had been kidnapped and kept at Fatty's compound, and that she had been taken in a pickup from the compound by two men tonight who were supposed to kill her, but as they were taking her to her execution, one of them tried to save her, and the men got into a fight and nearly crashed the truck. She had been pushed out of the truck and left behind as it took off down the road into the darkness. She ran into the nearby field and hid long enough to realize the men were not coming back for her and then walked to the nearest house, which happened to be Woodrow's, to ask for help. Nervy had her recite the story a couple of times. Leaving her to practice her story for another moment or two, Nervy went back outside to the trash barrel and stirred the ashes. She reapplied lighter fluid to the largest of the unburned parts and reignited them. With the fire burning satisfactorily again, she went back into the house and called the sheriff's office to report that Candy Adair had walked up to the house tonight, naked, fearing for her life, and seeking protection. She also told them that when she went to the door, she had glanced outside and noticed that her 4Runner SUV had been stolen.

The sheriff's dispatcher she spoke to said that all her deputies were responding to reports of gunfire and a major fire at a salvage yard, but she would make sure an officer would come to assist them as soon as she could divert one from the other disturbance. Nervy hung up the phone and was heading back upstairs to replace the three rounds fired from her Glock when she heard the distant sound of an approaching truck whose engine was being pushed to its limit. She and Candy looked at each other, both knowing that the sound was not law enforcement coming to their rescue.

Rather than being trapped in the house, Nervy suggested that they hide outside. Heading out the back door, Nervy grabbed the .22 rifle as Candy followed close behind. Running for cover behind the chicken coop, the women realized the truck was turning into Woodrow's drive as its headlights swept a beam of light across the yard. Once behind the coop and turning to evaluate their situation, Nervy could tell the truck was on a straight path toward them.

"Come on!" Nervy screamed as she reached back and grabbed the hand of her trailing companion. Nervy's tugging nearly pulled Candy off balance. The mismatched pair awkwardly fled deeper into the field until Nervy suddenly threw herself at the ground, pulling Candy down in a heap beside her in the shadow the coop made in the headlights. Hearing the truck's door shut, Nervy rolled onto her stomach and pointed the rifle in the direction of the silhouetted building.

Fatty's voice called, "Nervy, I know you're out there. Come over here and face me now or I'll turn the dogs loose." He never presented himself as a target for her.

She analyzed her choices. If she revealed herself to him, he would kill her and then find Candy and kill her too. If he really had dogs and turned them loose, then they would be silhouetted in the headlights as they searched for her and she would take them out but thereby reveal her location to Fatty. Still silently pointing her rifle toward the light, she let him make any decisions he wanted to. After a moment's quiet, she heard Woodrow holler her name as the back porch door slammed shut. She realized that all the uproar had awakened

Woodrow and he had just unwittingly stepped into the midst of an impending gunfight. Nervy jumped up, bolting toward the old man's voice, heedless of the danger it represented for her. She was not going to leave Woodrow unprotected.

"Go back to bed, old man, or you'll get yourself killed," Fatty commanded.

"*Nervy! Nervy girl!* Are you okay?" Woodrow's voice called louder, completely ignoring the threats.

"Did you hear me?"

"Number Three, get 'em!" Woodrow gruffly ordered.

By now Nervy was rounding the chicken coop on her way into the yard to save Woodrow. She made it to the yard just in time to see the blur of forty pounds of "the best and bravest bitch" in north Missouri launch herself onto three hundred pounds of heedless evil. Fatty was knocked to the ground, and Number Three began savaging his face and neck relentlessly. Screaming from the ground, Fatty was being eaten alive bite by vicious bite and could do nothing to protect himself, despite his frantic flailing and rolling about. Woodrow allowed his dog to continue until he saw Nervy walking toward him unharmed.

"Three . . . heel!" Woodrow barked.

Number Three backed away from Fatty and obediently laid down at Woodrow's feet, still staring warily at the screaming fat man writhing in a pool of his own gathering blood.

Nervy walked over to witness Fatty's literal downfall as Candy more slowly made it back to the yard and joined them.

"Are you two okay?" Woodrow asked.

"Pretty dandy for the moment," Nervy replied, still staring at Fatty.

Candy just stared at the old man for a moment and shrugged passively.

"Seems your meetin' didn't go too well tonight."

"Could have been a lot worse."

"Where's your truck?" he asked her.

"Somebody stole it. I noticed it was gone when Candy showed up at the door. I told the sheriff's office about it when I called them about Candy," she said, practicing her alibi. In the distance, the faint sound of a siren was becoming audible.

"Well, it would be murder to put him out of his misery, now wouldn't it?" Nervy mused, more to herself than Candy or Woodrow.

The siren grew louder in the night air, and the glimmer of approaching emergency flashers was increasingly noticeable. Nervy wiped the .22 rifle free of her fingerprints with the tail of her shirt and walked it back to the kitchen, where she replaced it behind the door. Walking through the back porch on her way outside to await the arrival of the sheriff's deputy, she bent over and pushed the Glock deep into the bag of dog food she had bought at Walmart.

CHAPTER 49

The living room was fully illuminated by bright midmorning April sunshine. Nervy opened her eyes and couldn't register where she was or what time it was. She gradually remembered she had moved to the first floor for Woodrow, but that didn't answer her question about why she had slept so late. As she realized that Griff hadn't awakened her for his morning business, a wave of overwhelming sorrow claimed her for several minutes, and she didn't even try to get out of bed.

"You okay in there?" Woodrow called from the kitchen.

"Okay, nothing great," she responded. "How long have you been up?"

"Same time as usual. Chores got to be done."

"You make any breakfast?" Nervy asked.

"Nope, never learned how. Just waiting for you," he explained unapologetically. Nervy finally smiled through her tears as she realized that another day was coaxing her out of bed with responsibilities and relationships requiring her specific touch.

"Well, did you at least feed Three?" she asked, pretending to be pushy with the old man.

"I couldn't find any scraps, and I didn't see your dog anywhere."

"I know," she lied. "I couldn't find him anywhere last night after all the excitement."

The prior night filled Nervy's mind as she fed Three, made breakfast, and got it to the table. She intermittently cried as thoughts of Griff and his sacrificial courage wandered in and out of her memory. She turned her focus to the loving burial she would give him later today.

"You reckon that fat Smith boy is gonna make it?" Woodrow questioned, bringing her back to the kitchen.

"Evil don't die easy," Nervy muttered, chewing her bacon.

When breakfast was over and the dishes washed and put away, it was almost 10:30. Nervy took her cell phone out of the charger and turned it on. There was a text waiting for her from Raleigh asking if she was all right. Nervy dialed the lawyer's number and sat back down at the kitchen table, where Woodrow was still sipping the rest of his breakfast coffee and thumbing through a farm journal. The secretary answered and put her straight through to the concerned attorney.

"What happened last night?" Raleigh asked anxiously.

"Oddly enough, Candy Adair showed up here saying she'd been kidnapped and had gotten free from her captors, so I called the sheriff's office, and before they got here Fatty Smith came looking for her. Woodrow's dog attacked and nearly killed him before Woodrow got him called off. Last I saw of any of them, Candy was in the front seat of the deputy's car, and what was left of Fatty was in the back seat," she reported. "Did you hear anything else?"

"I heard the Adair woman had been found alive but needed to be hospitalized because of all that she'd been through. I heard that Fatty had been arrested after his compound got raided last night and several of his gang were killed. It sounds like there was some sort of battle with rivals before law enforcement arrived."

"That fits," she said. "Evidently he had Candy kidnapped and imprisoned out there and she got released or escaped, and that's why he wound up at our place looking for her."

"Were you involved in the compound attack?" Raleigh asked her directly.

"Why would you even think that I was involved?" she challenged. "My name wasn't mentioned, was it?"

"I'd be a fool not to wonder if you were involved when anything remotely like this happens, especially out around Greenbriar. Remember I know a little bit about you," he teased.

"Is anybody implicating me that you've heard about?"

"No, not that I've heard. I don't think the sheriff or the highway patrol are too interested in seeking justice for Fatty. Whoever hit his place probably doesn't matter much to them. I figure they look at it as the enemy of their enemy is their friend, or at least was their friend last night," he reasoned.

"Well they turned out to be my friend too!" she joined in. "You know it was a really crazy night. By the time Candy showed up, my SUV had been stolen and my dog ran off. Haven't seen either one of them yet."

"Be careful, Nervy," Raleigh concluded their conversation, "especially with your alibi about where you were last night."

After the conversation with Raleigh, Nervy began emotionally preparing herself to go bury Griff.

"I got a couple of chores to attend to," she announced to Woodrow. "I'm going to need the truck and a shovel. Where can I find one?"

"Leftover business from last night?"

"Shovel!" she demanded, cutting off any inquiry.

"Toolshed, right inside the door to the left, leaning against the wall. Need help?"

"No, it's my problem to take care of."

"Just because it's your problem, doesn't mean you can't take somebody else's help," he challenged. "You been helping me with my problems," he reminded her, never looking up from his reading. Nervy was touched by his comment and for a moment watched the old man just sitting there reading his magazine.

"Okay, you up for a dog funeral?" she invited.

"Gonna require me to wear a tie or anything?" he asked, finally looking up.

Nervy got the shovel and put it in the truck while Woodrow got his jacket on and met her at the truck. She got him a step stool to use to get in the pickup.

"Mighty handy!" he complimented her. Nervy motioned to Number Three to get in the back. There was no conversation on the way to her garage. Arriving there, Nervy parked in front of the shattered garage doors. She got out of the truck first and set the step stool outside Woodrow's door. Once Woodrow was on the ground, Nervy got the shovel out of the back, and Three jumped out to join them. Together the trio walked to where Nervy had placed Griff's body last night. Nervy stood motionless and took in the sight of Griff's stillness while Woodrow bent down and petted the terrier's head with regard for things that he assumed had happened last night but would never be told. Number Three sniffed the terrier's body thoroughly, stepped back, and laid down facing it.

Rising, Woodrow said, "Hand me the shovel. I'll start the digging till I give out and then you can finish the rest." Nervy gave him the shovel and stooped down to pick up Griff's body.

"Follow me," she whispered with emotion stifling her voice, and began walking back to the willow tree.

Woodrow dug for about ten minutes and handed the shovel to Nervy, who, with another five minutes of digging, completed what she felt was an adequate grave for Griff. She laid his body carefully in the grave and immediately began placing shovelfuls of dirt on top of him. Woodrow and Three stood and respectfully watched Nervy complete the ending of a relationship that had supported her through the roughest chapter of her life. Finishing the task, Nervy stood fully upright and leaned against the shovel. She looked at Woodrow and asked if he could say a few words or a prayer to honor the dog and the moment. He remained quiet as he stared at the dirt and took a deep breath; he then shifted his gaze to his dog and then to Nervy.

Woodrow finally lifted his face toward the sky and calmly said in a conversational tone of voice, "God, me and Nervy want to say thank you for the dogs and the people we love. Thank you for the ones that are still here with us, and thank you for the ones that have gone on. Please keep taking care of us and all of them. Amen." Completing the prayer, he continued staring at the sky, as though hoping to see someone in particular, but after a moment he lowered his head and reached for the shovel. Nervy offered it to him, and he walked back toward the truck by himself, softly tapping the tip of the shovel into the ground with each step that he took. Nervy walked by herself into the garage and found the chain Cooker had used to secure his attack dog. She examined the chain and satisfied herself that it was an exact match to the chain that the police had given her when they returned Walter's effects. She gathered up the chain and unhooked it from its anchor. Walking toward the truck with the chain, she noticed that Woodrow had stopped and was staring at the dead pit bull.

"What do you want to do with him?" he hollered at Nervy.

"Well I'm not going to waste any energy burying him, that's for sure."

"I say we feed him to the hogs or he's gonna make quite a stink here," Woodrow suggested.

"I think it's going to take both of us to get him in the back of the truck," she observed. "Wait a minute for me to throw this chain into the truck and I'll come back and help." Together, they eventually got the big dog's remains in the truck and headed for home. After dropping Woodrow and Number Three off at the house, Nervy drove to the barn lot and then backed the truck up until the tailgate was flush with the fence of the hog lot. She got out and climbed into the bed of the pickup, where she struggled until she had lifted Smack's carcass up to the top board of the fence, where she rested it precariously as the hogs gathered below, squealing and watching eagerly. With a final triumphant shove, Nervy pushed the mortal remains of the attack dog over the fence to his new level on the food chain.

CHAPTER 50

After lunch Nervy washed up a bit from the morning's endeavors and decided to go see how Candy was doing. She checked with Woodrow to see if he wanted to go into town with her; he reported that he would rather stay home and relax for the rest of the day but wished her well on her trip into town. The afternoon drive, combined with her review of the previous night's events, provided Nervy a sense of freedom. It was as though a weight had been lifted off her shoulders. Her battles with Cooker and Fatty were concluded and she had secured a decisive victory.

After arriving at the hospital, Nervy walked into the lobby and asked for Ms. Adair's room number. She then took the elevator to the now-too-familiar fourth floor and walked to room 12. Looking in the door, Nervy could see Candy sitting in the chair beside her bed, staring at the TV overhead. Nervy remained standing in the door in plain sight of Candy and waited to see if she could get the young woman's attention. Eventually Candy noticed her and made unblinking eye contact for a solid thirty seconds.

"Come in," she offered passively.

Nervy walked in and sat on the corner of Candy's bed. Receiving no further eye contact or verbal acknowledgment, Nervy finally asked, "How are you today?"

"However a person is supposed to be after a night like that."

"Did you get questioned much?" Nervy asked.

"I stuck to the script. You don't have to worry. You know, I'd prefer not seeing you anymore. It's not like I'm not appreciative for last night, but I don't think that makes up for you getting my family killed," she accused.

Nervy felt attacked but withheld a counterattack of the magnitude she felt like unleashing.

"Cooker killed your family and tried to kill you. He killed my husband and tried to kill me. Are you blaming yourself for what happened to my husband as much as you're blaming me for what happened to your family?" She paused and then continued. "Cooker did the killing, not me and not you. I don't know if you wanted my husband dead or not, but I can tell you I never wanted your family dead. If this whole deal is going to become a blame game for you, then remember it was you that got Cooker involved in this whole thing in the first place. He was your man."

"Your man killed my sister!" Candy shot back.

"Your sister tried to kill herself, and that was the first step in her fiasco down at the university hospital. Blaming and suing Walter was a bullshit scheme that Lanny cooked up to make money by exploiting your family's pain. Your parents took his high-dollar bait so they could blame their grief on someone besides their own depressed daughter. I never believed the money was your family's motivation—it was just the lubrication that made it easier for them to attack somebody else because they were hurting." Nervy rested her case and sat in the room quietly as Candy continued to avoid eye contact and remained silent.

"The war can be over; it's your choice. You and I are not the villains or the heroes—we're the survivors, we made it through." Nervy stood and walked to the door, where she turned and faced Candy. "If you ever decide you want to talk, give me a call."

After leaving the hospital, Nervy spent the rest of the afternoon cruising through the local car dealerships looking for Toyota SUVs. She had not heard any report yet from the authorities about her "stolen" SUV, but she knew it was just a matter of time till she did. Then she would eventually get an insurance check toward another Toyota. After seeing what was currently available on the local lots, she headed back to the farm and started supper for Woodrow and herself. Her phone rang from the charger just as she was setting the meal on the table. The caller ID indicated it was Raleigh again. Nervy answered. "Man, don't you have anything better to do than call me?"

"Shut up and listen. Fatty is dead!" he proclaimed breathlessly. "Lanny shot him dead. It happened this morning after we spoke."

"What? How—" Nervy began questioning before trusting the good news.

"The story goes like this," he narrated. "After arresting Fatty last night, the deputy took him to the hospital ER for treatment of his dog-mauling injuries. They sewed his face and neck up and released him back to the custody of the sheriff's deputies within three hours. They then took him to the lockup. Judge Tucker showed up extra early for court this morning, and by 9:00 he had already allowed the prosecutor to file charges against Fatty for drug manufacture and distribution and witness tampering. The judge then set a cash-only bond for Fatty at half a million dollars. The guard at the jail is saying that Fatty was completely surprised when Lanny Peltor showed up at the jail at 11:00 with the cash in hand and bailed him out. It wasn't like anybody was surprised that Lanny was going to represent Fatty, because he had for years, but nobody has any idea how Lanny wound up there before lunch, since Fatty hadn't made a single phone call. Now comes the best part. The story Lanny told the detectives was that he was driving Fatty to his office so that they could talk in private about defense strategies when Fatty started assaulting him, trying to steal his car for some kind of getaway. Lanny just got a concealed carry permit from the sheriff last week and bought a Kimber .380 the same day. So, his story is that he feared for his life, pulled his new gun, and put four slugs into the big man. He told the cops that he kept firing because Fatty didn't quit assaulting him until the fourth shot. Lanny immediately heads for the ER and pulls up at the entrance, frantically seeking aid for his client. Fatty got pronounced dead right there in the ER driveway; they never even took him through the hospital doors."

Nervy was so stunned by Lanny's killing of Fatty that she remained silent on the phone.

"Nervy, are you still there?" Raleigh said.

"Yeah, I'm still here. Does it sound fishy to you? Would any reasonable judge set bail? I figure they would refuse bail on those kinds of charges. Legal counsel showing up with a half-million-dollar bond in their briefcase before lunch sounds prearranged between the judge and the lawyer to me. Don't get me wrong, I'm not complaining, but it all sounds to me like Fatty got set up," she reasoned calmly.

"Me too," Raleigh responded, "but it saves the county a ton of money on incarceration, prosecution, and witness protection."

"Pretty hard to see it as anything but a win for everybody involved except Fatty. Thanks for the call, but I need to sit down and digest this for myself for a while, so I'm going to hang up. Good night, Raleigh." She closed the call with the push of a button and asked herself out loud, "I wonder if Lanny showed any signs of having been assaulted?"

Nervy sat down at the kitchen table where Woodrow was already eating. Ignoring her food, she was surprised that she was feeling emotionally numb, given the implications the news had for her. She had no sorrow for Fatty but was sad that Griff wasn't there to share in the victory he had helped bring about.

Woodrow looked up from his plate across the table at Nervy. "Did I hear you say that Smith boy was killed?" he asked.

"Yeah, his lawyer shot him when Fatty tried to steal his car."

Woodrow shifted his attention back to his plate and muttered to himself, "Sounds fishy to me."

CHAPTER 51

Nervy's childhood memories of the early days of summer always included the various flowers her mother grew in their yard. The beauty of this morning awakened those memories. After cleaning up the breakfast dishes, Nervy walked out into the yard. The lilies, poppies, and redbud trees were all blooming. The day had dawned clear, and a soft breeze stirred the young leaves on the trees. It was a Monday, with things to attend to that she had been planning for weeks. She went to the living room to say goodbye to Woodrow and found him listening to the news on the radio. He nodded in response to her announced departure and continued listening to the radio. Number Three was in the living room lying on the floor at his feet, having taken to being an inside and outside dog very readily.

Heading for Clay Center, she enjoyed the drive through the farmland as she listened to the local country music station. Her mind began indulging itself in her now favorite mental recreation—planning her own farmstead. With the insurance settlement check from her malpractice case in the bank, she had begun preparations for a new life by burning the old garage to the ground and putting up new fencing all around the farm. She planned on putting her new double-wide closer to the willow tree than her childhood house had been, and she would eventually build a new garage, a small barn, and a chicken house. She enjoyed elaborating the plan in her mind and confronted herself with the selection of fruit trees and berry vines she would plant, as well as which chicken breeds she would raise.

Arriving in town, she went to the jewelry store and picked up Raleigh's gift. The jeweler proudly presented and opened the box. She found the present to be exactly what she had wanted. After sufficiently examining the gift, she had the jeweler wrap the box in gift paper and tie a robin's-egg-blue ribbon around it. Nervy left the store and headed to the river for her second chore of the morning.

She parked in the lot nearer to the jetty into the river than to the riverside footpath she had frequented with Walter. Nervy got out, opened the rear door of her new Rav4, and lifted out the length of chain she had recovered from the garage. Using both arms to clumsily carry the heavy chain, she walked clear to the end of the jetty that extended fifty feet into the river. After arriving at the end, she dumped the chain into the river. Without a moment's delay, Nervy turned and walked back to the parking lot and headed for her lunch rendezvous.

Raleigh sighted Nervy in the corner booth as he entered Ruby Tuesday's and joined her. They walked through the garden bar together and returned to the table with their salads.

"So, what's up?"

"Life is good for me," she began. "Woodrow is up to full speed and doesn't need me there to help him on the farm anymore. I traded in all the gold coins in St. Louis a while back, and I'm planning on putting my own place together over the next few months. All in all, pretty tame stuff compared to what you helped me through."

"There were times I didn't think you would ever find peace again," he admitted.

"Here, I got this for you," she said, reaching for the package.

"Wow, I didn't expect this. What's this about?"

"Unwrap it and then I'll explain," she instructed. He carefully untied the ribbon and removed the gift wrapping. Inside the box he discovered a gold Rolex. It was a thick and heavy watch and on the back was etched, *Raleigh, Loyalty, Courage, Faith.*

"It's dependable, sturdy, and very valuable—it made me think of you," she explained with tears beginning to pool in her eyes.

"Thanks . . . Thank you," he said as both of them fell quiet and stared at their plates for a full minute. "You dragged me into battles I never expected, and I don't even want to know about the wars that you hid from me," he said, lifting his eyes from his plate and looking straight into hers. "But I would do it all again in a heartbeat." He then lifted his water glass, tilted it toward her, and drank it dry. A quiet again settled across the table. It was a crossroads in the conversation, with paths that led in many directions. Neither Nervy nor Raleigh was ready to acknowledge the crossroads, at least not today. He picked up the check, and Nervy thanked him for the meal and "everything." They promised each other another lunch on another day as they walked into the parking lot and each got into their car.

Leaving the restaurant, Nervy was glad that nothing in her life currently required Raleigh's help, but his assistance had created a partnership in her mind that she now valued and trusted. Her thoughts of a deeper relationship with Raleigh were both pleasant and distressing. She feared that any affection for him would result in some diminishment of her continuing love for Walter. Nervy drove past the house and then the office, the principal places she and Walter had spent the majority of their lives together. Next, she drove to the cemetery, got out of the car, and walked to his grave. Unsure of exactly what she was seeking, she found herself talking to her absent husband, bringing him up to date about her life since his death. Her inventory of retribution and victories created no sense of connection with Walter; none of it really restored the love with him that she'd lost. Turning her face to the sky, she tearfully confessed how lonely she was and how she didn't want to let him go but didn't want to live alone. She admitted she didn't know how to love him now and wanted to know what he wanted from her. Waiting, hoping she would receive some message from Walter . . . God . . . Bertha . . . anybody, all she heard was the gentle breeze that had been blowing under a sky that was empty and endlessly, beautifully blue. Turning her attention back to the cemetery, she touched Walter's granite marker and felt how hard and cold and motionless it was. Nothing was offering her any connection with Walter.

Back at the river for a second time that day, Nervy got out of the car still seeking a visceral attachment to Walter. The path was empty, and Nervy found that she had to intentionally slow her gait to keep from running frantically in her search. Intending to mindfully focus on the details of the riverside surroundings, she examined the trees, noting their bark, their limbs, their leaves, whatever . . . anything to connect her to Walter.

Nervy stayed on the asphalt path because the surrounding ground was soft and moist. Puddles left from recent rains were scattered among the giant trees. Just ahead, the pathway itself was submerged beneath a pool of rainwater that stretched across its entire width for four or five feet. At the edge of the pool, Nervy paused. Leaning forward and gazing into the pool, she was unable to gauge its depth because of her own intervening reflection. Focusing on the woman looking back at her, she smiled and received a smile back in return. She couldn't remember ever envisioning herself with a smile and found the woman she was looking at to be welcoming and reassuring.

She reached down, slipped off both shoes, and stood experiencing the path as she never had before—cool, rough, unyielding against her tender feet. Daring herself forward, she slowly immersed one newly bared foot into the cool, wet pool, feeling for the unseen path while keeping her eyes on the spot where the path reemerged only a couple of mysterious steps away.

EPILOGUE

Nervy's trip today required her to pass through Tipton Junction. Like so many rural communities, Tipton Junction was now more a waypoint than an actual town. The town that had once prospered here was hinted at by a few remaining structures. Entering from the east, she passed the MFA that sold farm necessities like feed, grain, seed, and fertilizer and the Casey's convenience store–gas station, which were the only places of business for ten miles. Continuing into town, she passed the abandoned two-story brick schoolhouse that had been the pride of the small farming town seventy years earlier but was an eyesore with numerous broken windows now. In contrast to the schoolhouse, a freshly painted white Methodist church sat in the midst of a well-manicured churchyard across the street. The church's prized antique stained-glass windows were protected by overlying Plexiglas sheets, which the Missouri weather was making cloudier season by season. The church's spire was almost as high as the very highest structure in town two blocks away: the water tower adorned with the town's name in fading paint. On her way out the west side of town, she passed the large cemetery, whose interred population of former residents outnumbered the town's living residents by a greater than two-to-one ratio.

Her destination was a cattle farm two miles past Tipton Junction on a graveled county road. She had only been to this farm one time before—on her tenth wedding anniversary with Walter, when he had agreed that she could get a puppy. Despite the intervening years, she was remembering many of the landmarks from her prior trip as she neared the farm. Finally recognizing the Ferguson place, she pulled into the drive. Mrs. Ferguson had been watching for her arrival and came from the back porch to meet her at the car. The two women greeted each other warmly and walked across the yard toward the house. Nervy complimented Mrs. Ferguson on the appearance of her yard and the garden that was quite impressive. Mrs. Ferguson in turn asked how Nervy's new place was coming along, since Nervy had mentioned it to her in last week's phone call arranging today's appointment. She shared descriptions of her new yard, garden, and fruit trees as they neared the house.

"I think that today is going to put the cherry on the cupcake," Nervy said, revealing her excitement.

Entering the back porch, they were met by an exuberant mother Jack Russell terrier, who, seeking the possibility of some petting, leapt over the two-foot barrier which divided the porch in half. On the other side of the barrier were six wiggly, wrestling Jack Russell pups. Realizing that there were people on the porch paying attention to them, they all rushed to the barrier and made feeble attempts to climb over each other and scale the obstruction to get to the human audience. Mrs. Ferguson asked Nervy if any particular puppy stood out as she looked them over. Telling her she didn't see a particular favorite yet, Nervy asked if she had a dog toy handy. The terrier breeder searched her porch and found a short piece of tug-of-war rope and offered it. Nervy turned back to the pen of puppies and stooped over and waved the short rope back and forth twelve inches above the fascinated pups' heads. When she thought they were sufficiently fired up, she threw the toy to the far corner of their pen. One puppy was clearly the first to get to the toy and claim it. The victory was short-lived, though, as the other pups converged and a fracas broke out to determine the ultimate ownership of the toy. Within fifteen seconds of chaotic canine sibling rivalry, a clear winner emerged. She began racing clumsy laps around the pen, exhibiting her prowess at evading or shaking off all her siblings to maintain ascendant possession of the toy. Nervy stood up, still watching the victorious pup, and told Mrs. Ferguson, "I think I've made my pick." Then she bent back down and picked up her new puppy for the first time as it still ferociously held its trophy in its mouth. Nervy raised the pup higher and looked at her face-to-face. The youngster growled an assertive self-introduction to her new owner, who smiled at the pup and spontaneously growled back that she was excited to get to know her.

ABOUT THE AUTHOR

For over a quarter century, J. Calvin Harwood has been a practicing psychiatrist in a small midwestern town. This is his first novel.